STICKY SWEET

Connie Shelton

STICKY SWEET

Samantha Sweet Mysteries, Book 12

Connie Shelton

Secret Staircase Books

Sticky Sweet
Published by Secret Staircase Books, an imprint of
Columbine Publishing Group, LLC
PO Box 416, Angel Fire, NM 87710

Book layout and design by Secret Staircase Books
Cover images © Beata Kraus and Irina Onufrieva

First trade paperback edition: June, 2018
First e-book edition: June, 2018

* * *

Publisher's Cataloging-in-Publication Data

Shelton, Connie
Sticky Sweet / by Connie Shelton.
p. cm.
ISBN 978-1945422478 (paperback)
ISBN 978-1945422485 (e-book)

1. Samantha Sweet (Fictitious character)--Fiction. 2. Taos, New
Mexico—Fiction. 3. Paranormal artifacts—Fiction. 4. Bakery—Fiction. 5.
Women sleuths—Fiction. 6. Chocolate making—Fiction. I. Title

Samantha Sweet Mystery Series : Book 12.
Shelton, Connie, Samantha Sweet mysteries.

BISAC : FICTION / Mystery & Detective.

813/.54

As always, I want to extend a big thanks to everyone who helped shape this book into its final version. Dan Shelton, my husband and helpmate for twenty-eight years, is always there for me. And thank you Stephanie, my lovely daughter and business partner, for giving my business and writing career a burst of fresh new energy this year!

Editors Susan Slater and Shirley Shaw spot the plot and character flaws and help smooth the rough bits in the prose. And topping off the effort are my beta readers, who drop everything in their own lives to read and find the typos that inevitably sneak past me. Thank you for your help with this book: Christine Johnson, Debbie Wilson, Judi Shaw and Susan Gross.
You ladies are the best!

Chapter 1

Samantha Sweet studied the sketch her assistant had made for the cake design on the table in front of her. A "Gone Fishing" cake in January? Okay, maybe ice fishing—intrepid people, unintimidated by freezing temperatures, did it over on Eagle Nest Lake the other side of the mountain. But this seemed like a summer theme. The design had blue water, gentle lily pads, cattails, and river stones; the centerpiece on top was a full-color rainbow trout. The fish could be made from sugar paste, the colors airbrushed, and the effect would be fun. Still ... maybe she should clarify before starting the work.

Normally, Sam loved January. The month-long break between the Christmas rush and an onslaught of Valentine orders gave the bakery staff a chance to breathe before heading into the spring holidays and the wedding season. This year was a little different. She'd hired three new chocolatiers and four more assembly helpers to ease the load at her chocolate factory in the old Victorian house on the north end of town. Meanwhile, Becky Harper, her chief cake decorator at Sweet's Sweets, was taking a week's vacation, so Sam now worked alongside Julio the baker to turn out the pastry shop's regular fare and the dozen or so decorated cakes that had been custom ordered this week.

"Starting to snow again," Jennifer Baca said as she pushed past the curtain to the front showroom, heading toward the rack of cookies Julio had pulled from the oven fifteen minutes earlier.

"Hey, Jen," Sam said, waving her toward the worktable. "Let me be sure I understand this design. The customer wants this to look like summer?"

"Yep, that's what she said. It's her husband's birthday and he's in a slump because he hasn't been fishing in months. She thought it would cheer him up to see his favorite little fishing hole. The fish photo is of a trophy trout he got a few years ago. She says it's his pride and joy. She wants the edible sugar fish on the cake to look exactly like it. If it's different in any way, he'll know."

Seriously? Any old fish doesn't look just like the others?

Jen laughed as Sam shook her head.

"Okay … whatever." Sam set to work tinting fondant in two batches—lily pad green and summer-pond blue.

Jen picked up the tray of cranberry macadamia nut cookies and headed back to the showroom.

"Really," Sam muttered. "The guy will know whether the fish I make looks just like his real one …"

Julio, the quiet baker who could turn out cakes, cookies, and tarts all day without a word, spoke up. "Yeah, he'll know. My dad's like that. He would tell the story of this one old catfish he tried for years to catch from the stock tank where he grew up. He said he had caught the wily old fish three times but it always got away."

"Sounds like a family legend."

He nodded as he pushed his red bandanna a bit higher on his sweaty forehead. "It became one."

"So, did he ever catch the catfish?"

"Eventually, yeah. My mother cooked it up and made fish tacos, but they didn't taste very good. Guess that fish just got tougher as he got older." He dumped a heap of flour into the Hobart mixer, ending the conversation.

Sam rolled fondant and quickly covered the cake, fashioned cattails and lily pads, and concentrated on setting up the little scene. An hour vanished while she shaped the ten-inch-long trout and tested her airbrush to get the right amount of spray for the delicate colors. A subtle addition of silver glitter would bring out the shine of the fish's scales. When she glanced at the clock again, she was amazed to see the afternoon was quickly slipping away.

"I'd better have Jen come take a look at this before I box it for the customer. I think the lady is coming to pick it up right before closing." Sam said it aloud before she realized Julio must have stepped out back.

Kids filled the showroom, another indicator it was late afternoon. The elementary school a block away provided her most loyal customers, the kids who'd talked their moms out of an extra fifty cents to get a cookie to eat on the way home. Jen was behind the counter, capably exchanging cookies for quarters and sending the kids on their way.

A woman in her thirties—fluffy blonde hair, dark eyes, lots of lashes, wearing a bulky fleece jacket over skin-tight jeans—pushed her way through the crowd and picked up a single, wrapped chocolate truffle from the display near the register. Sam saw her glance around the room. When the woman's dark brown eyes met Sam's, she set the candy on the counter and held out a twenty-dollar bill to Jen.

Distracted by the horde of kids, Jen quickly rung up the two-dollar item and began counting out change for the woman.

"Sorry to pay with such a large bill. It's all I have on me," the lady said as Jen handed over the last of the coins.

She gave the customer a polite smile and turned to the most impatient of the children. Sam headed toward the coffee bar. Clearly, it would be a few minutes before Jen could answer her questions about the cake, and the beverage center always needed attention for small spills or refills of the coffee, tea and cocoa supplies.

In the background, she was aware the female customer hadn't left yet. She seemed engaged in having Jen make change for the parking meters or something. Sam refilled the coffee maker with her signature blend, topped off the water container and started the machine. When she turned around, the blonde woman had a hand on the door.

"Wait a second," Jen called out. "I don't think I gave you the right change."

"Oh, you did—I'm sure you did." She started to pull the door open but two of the schoolkids pushed forward and filled the doorway.

Jen was all cool composure as she came from behind the counter. "No. It wasn't right." She approached the blonde and casually leaned a hand on the door to close it behind the last of the children.

Sam came forward. "Problem?" She, Jen and the customer were the only ones in the shop now.

"May I see the money I just handed to you?" Jen asked.

The woman jammed her hand deeper into her pocket.

Movement outside caught Sam's attention. Beau's department cruiser had pulled into the lot. Sam stepped to the door, joining her employee, blocking the customer's exit.

"I imagine the sheriff can help sort this out," she said as she opened the door and let him inside.

Beau stomped fresh snow off his boots and gave his wife a kiss on top of her head as he came in. "Something needs sorting out?" he asked.

Sam held a hand out toward Jen.

"I believe this lady just pulled a fake-change trick on me," Jen said. "She started with a twenty-dollar bill for a small item, asked me to make change several times—you know, can you break this ten with a five and some ones—but I'll bet you right now she's got thirty-seven dollars and eighty-two cents in that pocket. She conned me out of an extra twenty."

Beau turned toward the customer, staring down from his six-three height.

She batted the heavy lashes. "Officer, really … I have no idea …" She ran delicate fingers tipped in cardinal red through her blonde curls.

He ignored the dark eyes and asked to see her identification. She rummaged in the tiny purse hanging from a thin strap across her body and came up with a driver's license from a slender wallet that also contained a couple of credit cards.

"Missy Malone. You live in Albuquerque?"

"My husband and I have a home here in Taos, as well."

"May I see the money in your coat pocket?" he asked.

"Well, if there's any discrepancy …" Missy couldn't quite meet anyone's eye as she reached into the pocket of the fleece jacket and came out with a wad of bills.

"Set the money on the table here," Beau said, indicating one of the bakery's bistro tables.

When Missy laid out the money, including a straggle of coins, it was exactly as Jen had said—thirty-seven dollars and eighty-two cents.

"Interesting, since you said a twenty dollar bill was all you had with you," Jen observed.

"Do you want to press charges?" Beau asked Sam.

Missy became twitchy at the suggestion. "Look, I'm really sorry. I miscounted and didn't mean any harm. Here's the twenty dollars." She snatched two tens off the table and handed them to Jen. "Can I just have my license back and we call it even?"

The radio mike on Beau's shoulder crackled and his dispatcher's voice came through. He looked at Sam and raised his eyebrows.

Missy's eyes reddened and her lower lip trembled. "I'm so sorry."

"Beau, we've got a 10-50-F," came over the radio.

"Sam, I need to—"

"It's okay," Sam said. "Looks like we're not out any money."

Beau handed the customer's license back and she scurried out the door and got into a red Mercedes convertible parked in front of the dog grooming salon next door. Beau leaped into his SUV cruiser and, with lights and siren blazing, roared out of the parking lot.

Chapter 2

Sam watched as the red convertible pulled out of the parking lot and turned the opposite way from where Beau had gone. The snow had begun to stick; both vehicles left tracks, and Sam briefly wondered how far Missy Malone had to drive and whether the roads would be slick. Beau's radio call involved a traffic accident with fatality—she knew from the dispatcher's code—perhaps due to the worsening weather?

But she had no time to ponder the question. The customer would arrive within the hour to pick up the fisherman's cake, which needed a bit more work. She rushed back to the kitchen. At some point while she was airbrushing the final details onto the sugar paste fish, her cell phone rang, but she ignored it. If it was important enough, the person would either leave a message or call back later.

She set the fish in place, its gracefully arched body complementing the smooth fondant and straight lines of the sugar cattails that jutted out of the water on wooden dowel stems. Overall, she was pleased with the finished piece. She placed the cake in a box and carried it out front at the same moment Mrs. Martinez walked in the door.

"Oh, Juan is going to love this!" she exclaimed when Sam lifted the lid.

Her phone rang again and she excused herself, leaving Jen to ring up the sale. The number on her caller ID looked vaguely familiar.

"Sam?" came a weak female voice. "It's Sadie. Sadie Holmes."

The friend who, about a year ago, had taken over Sam's Department of Agriculture job of breaking into houses. *Friend* might be too strong a word—they'd met a few times at Chamber of Commerce functions, and Sadie was a semi-regular customer at the bakery. She'd been there the day Sam gave notice, the day her supervisor had said she couldn't quit until she found a replacement. The rest was a matter of a ten-minute conversation and Sam giving Delbert Crow's phone number to Sadie.

"Hi, Sadie. What's up?"

"I need a favor—desperately."

Sam had a feeling she knew what was coming.

"I broke two vertebrae last week and I'm in the rehab center in Santa Fe. I thought the timing was all right, since I'm between house jobs right now. But then Delbert called this morning with an urgent one."

"Sadie, I ... gosh. My schedule is absolutely crazy right

now." Not as crazy as a month ago, but she didn't say so.

"It's just … right at the moment I only need an assessment of the situation. You, better than anyone else, know what's involved. If you could just find the time to run by the place, look it over, let me know if a simple cleaning will do, or if it's going to require three roll-offs to clear it."

Sam knew only too well. She'd seen all ends of the spectrum, including a dead woman at one place and a bloody trench coat at another.

"I was told the key is under a flowerpot at the front door. The house is in a nice neighborhood and has been empty for a couple months. Most likely, it'll be clear of possessions and I can just hire the Merry Maids or someone to go in and clean. Please, Sam? Take fifteen minutes to run by there, then give me a call and let me know?"

Come on, Sam. The woman is in the hospital and it's only a quick favor. "How soon do you need to know?" She'd promised her daughter she would help her shop for a new pair of snow boots, and they'd planned to meet at the ski shop in—yikes—fifteen minutes' time.

Sadie went into an explanation about Delbert's impatience, which was old news to Sam. She quickly flipped through her calendar and gave up finding a few clear hours. Kelly's boots could wait.

"I'll head over there right now," she told Sadie. "Give me the address."

She jotted it down, happy to realize the street was very near her old house and only about ten minutes from the bakery. A quick call to Kelly, who assured her mom she could manage the boots on her own, and Sam was on her way.

The sun had set, turning the cloud-whitened sky a

dim gray, but at least the snow had stopped falling. Sam's delivery van didn't have all-wheel drive, but the going was easy enough through the mushy streets. She made her way to the address Sadie had given her, remembering all too clearly what a pain it was to respond to Delbert Crow's calls with the sort of urgency he wanted. She could only guess this particular house was getting nibbles from buyers and he wanted to maximize the asking price.

She pulled into the driveway of a neat, territorial style home on Wicket Lane, brown stucco with white trim, bare cottonwood trees towering in the back yard, arbor vitae that could use a trim flanking the front porch. A street light across from the place provided ample light outdoors but the electricity would almost certainly be turned off inside. Sam grabbed the flashlight she kept in the glovebox and stepped out.

"If you're delivering something, no one's home over there." The female voice came from the next driveway to the south.

In the gloom, Sam made out the form of a woman—solid but athletic looking.

"It's okay. I'm just here to look over the house for a friend," she called out, aiming her flashlight toward the porch and spotting the flowerpot Sadie had mentioned.

Too late. The woman had stepped over the foot-high stucco wall separating the two properties and was walking toward her. Sam decided she might be able to get some helpful information for Sadie. Sam introduced herself with the quick explanation she always gave when a neighbor confronted her at one of her break-in properties—the fact the USDA had taken over the property and she was merely here to keep it in good order until it was sold.

"Dolores Zuckerman," the woman said. "I'm not the neighbor, actually. My father is. Arnold Zuckerman."

"Um, so you don't know how long ago this family moved out?" Sam asked.

"Someone was here the last time I came by, right before Christmas. I'm an accountant in Santa Fe. The end of year is the second most insane time for me, next to tax season. Still, I try to get by here every few weeks to check on Dad. Trying to get him to agree to move into assisted living is like talking to a brick wall. He won't hear of it. Won't even let me take over handling his finances. He's eighty-seven— you know how they get at that age."

Up close, Sam realized Dolores Zuckerman was older than the first impression conveyed. She had to be in her sixties, despite the unnaturally dark hair, slim jeans and fitted down jacket.

"My parents live in Texas," Sam told her. "Luckily, they still have each other to drive crazy. But, yeah, I suppose I know what you're saying."

"Oh, Dad's not alone," Dolores said with an edge to her voice. "He always loved to show off a good-looking woman on his arm. It's just weird when they start to be a lot younger than him, you know?"

As much as her mother drove her nuts, Sam felt thankful she truly didn't know what Dolores faced with her father. She glanced at the lit windows of the Zuckerman house, swearing the living room curtain moved a little.

"Well, I guess I'd better …" Sam waved the flashlight beam toward the empty house.

"Yeah, me too. I still have to drive back to Santa Fe." Dolores turned back to the other property and got into a blue minivan.

Sam wished her luck and warned about the road conditions. The minivan backed out and headed toward Kit Carson Road. Sam followed her flashlight beam to the porch where massive Mexican pots sat on each side of the blue-painted front door. She had to set the light down and use both hands to push one aside. Of course, her first guess was the wrong one so she scooted it back and moved the other. There was the key, just as Sadie had promised.

The moment of truth would come when the door swung open. Would she find just an empty house, or would it entail a massive clean-up job?

Chapter 3

The ease with which the key turned in the front-door lock told Sam it hadn't been many weeks since the owners' departure. She'd seen doorknobs so corroded they wouldn't turn, even with the help of her large pipe wrench; she'd worked long stretches with lock picks on a number of occasions. Very seldom was she provided with a key and a smoothly working mechanism. She smiled when the knob turned and the door opened with nary a squeak.

She located a bank of light switches beside the door, but flipping them confirmed her suspicion that the power had been cut off. The house felt cold and tomb-like inside.

"Okay, I'm only here for a quick checkout," she murmured to herself. Her voice echoed off the travertine flooring in the foyer.

The flashlight revealed a spacious living-dining L to her left, a long hallway with multiple doorways to the right. Ahead, a step down led to a den where a whitewashed kiva fireplace sat like a hunched-over old ghost in the corner. No furniture—that was the good news—although a scattering of packing boxes remained, along with dust-balls the size of prairie dogs.

She followed her beam down the single step, noticing dusty but beautiful, intricate parquet flooring. A granite-topped bar separated the den from a massive kitchen fitted out to please the pickiest chef. Sam tamped down a faint twinge of envy. She'd always either made do with whatever came with the places she lived or she'd outfitted her work kitchens in the most economical way. *However*, she thought as she looked at the gleaming appliances, *with Book It Travel and the influx of business Mr. Bookman brought, I could afford to upgrade a bit.*

She put aside visions of a fancy kitchen remodel and quickly moved through the rooms. Ten minutes later, she'd made a list of necessary tasks for the house, relocked the front door, and was on her way west on Kit Carson Road. Now that the slush was turning to ice, traffic crept along north of the plaza. Sam bit back her impatience and stayed with the pace until she turned off the road and saw the golden lights of their ranch house.

Nellie and Ranger greeted her at the front door, their eager breaths making clouds in the air. Already, the temperature had dropped into the teens and was forecast to go sub-zero by morning. She ruffled their fur and accepted doggie kisses on her gloved hands.

Beau held the door open while Sam and the dogs tumbled inside. The scent of green chile stew filled the air.

"Hey," he said after bestowing a warming kiss. "Getting

cold out, huh."

She peeled off her sheepskin coat, muffler, and gloves and touched a chilly hand to his neck. He tucked the hand against his flannel shirt and did the same with her other one.

"Let's get some of that nice, hot stew in us," he said. "I put the tortillas in the oven awhile ago, so everything's ready."

She noticed he'd already set out flatware and napkins on the dining table. They went into the kitchen, where the crockpot steamed with the scent of chile, tomatoes, meat, and hearty broth. Bowls sat beside it, and Beau dipped stew into them while Sam brought the tortilla warmer from the oven.

"Roads are icing up already," she said. "Was that the cause of the accident you got called out to?"

"No," he said, carrying the two bowls to the table. "Everything was just slushy at that point. We're still investigating, and I had the victim's body sent to the OMI for tox screening. According to the other driver, the guy was weaving all over the road. Said the white Mitsubishi grazed the side of his SUV then went off the road. It happened in the canyon south of town, and the car rolled. Driver wasn't wearing a seatbelt, so he got thrown around."

"What a tragedy. Was it anyone we know?"

He shook his head. "The fatality was a Percy Lukinger. New Mexico driver's license, but it was only issued six months ago. Taos address. I've got Rico trying to track down next of kin. The other driver was Brian Reese. His dad is Clint Reese. I've known the family since Brian was a toddler. The kid's only twenty-two, but he's always been a responsible guy. He's worked at the lumber yard since he was in high school."

"Was he hurt?" Sam dipped a spoon into the steaming stew and found it had cooled enough to take a bite.

"Not a scratch, luckily. The damage to his Bronco is consistent with what he told me. He followed all the rules—steered to the right to avoid oncoming traffic, slowed his SUV gradually and got it off the roadway, came to a stop and called for help when he saw the other car had crashed. We won't know for sure until the blood tests come back, but it sure looks to me like another of our famed drunk-driving cases. I'm just thankful the innocent party wasn't hurt."

Beau had managed to put away his bowl of stew, and he headed toward the kitchen for more. When he came back, he changed the subject.

"So, how was your afternoon? I called the bakery after I left the accident scene, in case you needed me to pick up something at the market on the way home. Jen said you left a little early because of a call from Delbert Crow?"

"Well, not directly from him." Sam went into the reason she'd stopped to check out the abandoned house on her way home. "It's not far from Kelly's—well, my old place. Couple blocks north of there and a little way east. It's amazing the difference in the neighborhoods. My little two-bedroom could fit twice inside this other place. Bigger lots, old cottonwoods all around. Double the size of mine, and more than double the price, I'm sure. I met the neighbor—actually, his daughter—and the bit I could tell about his house is that it's even larger. I made a list of what the job will entail for Sadie, but I'm kind of toying with the idea of doing the work for her."

"Sam …"

"I know. I do not need another item on my to-do list, but I feel for Sadie. Now she's got medical bills and will be faced with paying a maid service to do the cleanup. Those break-in jobs don't pay a whole lot. Anyway, it would just be one of those little pay-it-forward things I could do for a friend."

"Well, you know how much you can handle. The chocolate factory's running pretty efficiently on its own, right? But what about the bakery, with Becky on vacation?"

She debated taking a second tortilla but pushed the basket aside. "I'll think about the job before I commit."

Beau cleared the dishes and began to load the dishwasher while Sam went upstairs to switch her bakery clothes for a lightweight pair of sweats and comfy sweater. As she brushed her short hair, she caught sight of her jewelry box sitting on the bathroom vanity. She *could* always call upon a little supernatural help and get Sadie's cleaning job out of the way quickly …

The carved wooden box was attractive in its own homely way. Sitting there, the wood was dark brown and unevenly carved—not the work of a skilled craftsman and definitely not the modern product of laser-sharp machinery. Sam reached out and picked it up, running her hand over the lumpy surface. Almost immediately, the wood's inner life began to rise and the surface became golden colored and warmed to her touch. Where the carved pattern formed X shapes, the red, green and blue stones mounted in the crevices glowed.

Sam knew the longer she held it, the brighter the stones would sparkle and the wood would warm until it was nearly too hot to hang onto. It would also energize her body— in the past, she'd used its power to work all night at the bakery and to accomplish amazing tasks at her break-in houses. She set the box down quickly.

Not tonight. She wanted a cozy evening at home

and a normal bedtime where she would snuggle with her husband under thick comforters while the temperature dropped outside.

Downstairs, Beau had stretched out in his recliner with a hunting magazine in hand. A steaming mug sat on the end table.

Beau caught her glance. "Water's hot but I wasn't sure if you'd want tea or cocoa." He started to get up but she waved him back to the chair.

"I'll get it—you relax." She walked into the kitchen to the chime of a message coming on her phone. Sadie Holmes. She dialed while she reached for a packet of cocoa mix.

"Sam, I don't mean to be a pest," Sadie began. "It's just these calls from Delbert—"

"Not a problem. I was going to touch base anyway and let you know that I stopped by the place. The good news is the owners actually moved their things out. The bad news is it's a fairly big house—I'd say close to three thousand square feet. Four bedrooms, three baths, den, living room, dining, and a huge kitchen."

A tiny groan came from Sadie's end of the line.

"Look, why don't you let me handle this one?" Sam asked. "There's no way you need to be doing that much work, even if you could be up and about in time. And hiring a maid service really isn't practical. There's no electricity in the place. Maids aren't going to have a portable generator—which I do—and, well, it'll just be a lot simpler."

"Sam, I can't ask—"

"You didn't ask. I offered. Now just lie back on your big pile of pillows and concentrate on getting well."

A sigh. "Sam, I can't thank you enough for this. You

know how Delbert can be … I've really been feeling the pressure."

"Well, now you can let go of the worry. When does he want the job completed?"

"In typical Delbert fashion, he *says* it needs to be finished this weekend. Apparently the foreclosure has gone through and they want to get a For Sale sign up in the yard by Monday."

Sam gulped and sloshed the water she'd been pouring into her mug. Cocoa powder wafted onto the countertop. The arbitrary deadline gave her only a few days.

"I know," Sadie said. "It's crazy and I wouldn't blame you if you change your mind."

"Don't you worry about anything. I've got this. Get your rest and we'll talk later. I'll call you when I'm finished."

She clicked off the call, cleaned up the cocoa spillage, and wondered when she was going to fit a two-day cleanup job into an already hectic schedule.

Chapter 4

Sam knew the answer before she'd even crawled into bed, but she spent a fitful night trying to work out alternatives. Magic couldn't always be her go-to answer in a jam. But then, why not? She'd been given the box to help others. This was absolutely a case of helping someone.

Somewhere around three a.m. Beau rolled over and draped his arm over her, pulling her close and making gentle shushing sounds, his way of getting her to settle down so they both could get some sleep. She let her body relax.

When Beau got up at five to begin his day, Sam sat up and rubbed her eyes.

"Can you help me with a little project before you leave?" she asked.

Bundled into heavy sweatpants, flannel shirts and their warmest coats and gloves, they went outside. Ribbons of mist trailed across the face of the distant hills, barely visible in the early pre-dawn gray light. The thermometer on the front porch showed ten below zero. Sam watched her breath form tiny ice crystals.

She started her pickup truck and backed it to the barn door. Together, she and Beau lifted the portable generator into the back, and he strapped it down tight with a couple of tie-downs. Sam set a vacuum cleaner in the back seat.

"You really going to clean an empty house when it's this cold?" He'd already headed toward the horse trough with an axe in hand to break through the layer of ice on top.

Sam stomped her feet to warm them, wondering about the wisdom of her act of kindness. "Let me go see what the forecast is. I may put this off a day or so."

She couldn't put it off very long, she knew. On the other hand, Delbert Crow could hardly fire her, and the real estate agent wouldn't likely be showing houses anytime soon either. However, it didn't mean Delbert couldn't make Sadie's life stressful in the meantime.

She switched on the television in the living room and hurried to the kitchen to start the coffee machine. Normally, Beau fended well for himself in the mornings, letting her sleep a bit longer, but since she was already up she knew some eggs and toast would fortify both of them. By the time Beau came in after feeding the horses, she had breakfast ready.

The weather forecast didn't sound very cooperative. High for the day was to be a balmy twenty above zero. At least the clouds had moved out, leaving a classic New

Mexico blue sky above the frigid air.

"Promise me you won't spend all day in that empty house if it has no heat," Beau said as he headed for his cruiser. "You won't do anyone any favors if you get sick."

Sam made the promise with confidence. She had no intention of spending all day there. After he drove away, she gathered her collection of brooms and mops, plus the crate of cleaning supplies and rags. Since she'd quit the USDA job more than a year ago her materials had become scattered between home and bakery, but she managed to round up enough of the basics. The last item she picked up was the carved box.

Once everything was stashed in the truck, her first stop after leaving home was to go by the Victorian house she'd leased and converted to her chocolate factory last fall. Sweet's Traditional Handmade Chocolates might be a lengthy greeting when answering the phone, but the name perfectly described their product. Their primary client, Stan Bookman, owner of Book It Travel, had been bowled over by Sam's attention to detail and the handmade quality of the first box of chocolates he'd bought for his wife. He had immediately ordered Sam's candy creations as the only chocolate served aboard his company's charter jet flights, which catered to the ultra rich, then he'd gone on to include them at the upscale hotel and resort properties where their glamorous guests stayed.

Now, he was talking about selling to cruise lines and entire hotel chains—Sam had to admit the scope of it frightened her a little, but she would decide how to handle it when the time came. She was realistic enough to know her contract with Bookman went on a year-by-year basis and somewhere during his world travels the man might find another treat to usurp hers. She might believe in certain kinds of magic, but Sam prided herself in keeping a level head and being a realist.

She pulled into the employee parking area they'd created behind the old house, pleased to see nine cars. Despite the cold, everyone had showed up for work. She walked under the portico and entered at the kitchen side of the building.

"Hey, Sam." Benjie Lucero stood at the huge stainless steel worktable, rolling truffle mixture between his palms.

Sam admired the way he worked quickly but paid attention and made certain each delectable bite of candy was uniform in size and shape. Beside him, two other chocolatiers worked, one tempering chocolate in a massive bowl and the other girl filling inch-square molds with dark, molten chocolate. At the stove, their newest employee stirred a new batch in a glass bowl over a copper pot of hot water.

"Everything going okay here?" Sam asked, her eyes taking in the works-in-progress, her instinct noting that the work areas were filled but tidy.

Benjie nodded, barely taking his eyes off the truffle ball in his hands. "Just fine. You might want to take a look at the furnace ... or maybe it's the propane supply? The place was pretty chilly when we got here this morning. It's warm in here now, but that's 'cause we've had the stove going for an hour or so."

Sam stepped into the first assembly room, where three workers, supervised by her first hire, Lisa Gurule, were inserting the finished chocolates into boxes. She noticed they all wore their coats and scarves.

"Benjie mentioned the heat might not be working right," Sam said. "You guys all look a little chilly."

Lisa nodded. "Yeah. There's warm water running through the radiators, but it doesn't seem to be having an effect."

"I'll go check it right now." She placed a hand on one of the old-fashioned metal registers. Lisa was right—it only felt lukewarm. Great.

She knew next to nothing about the old boiler in the basement, only that a propane-fired burner heated water in the reservoir and a pump sent it circulating throughout the house via pipes and the metal radiators in each room. There were thermostats in four zones—two upstairs and two downstairs. Beyond that, she wasn't sure what to check. She stared at the boiler for a few minutes but could see nothing amiss.

The upstairs thermostats for Sam's private office and three other rooms were set at sixty—conserving fuel since no one was actually working up there today. The downstairs units were both set at seventy, which should have provided a comfortable temperature. She had the unsettling thought that perhaps the old house had little or no insulation. All their heat could be seeping out the walls. But an inspection before she signed the lease hadn't revealed any problems along those lines. She re-zipped her jacket and went outside to take a look at the five-hundred-gallon propane tank out back. It showed fifty-percent full. So, now what?

Back indoors, she pulled out her phone and called the gas company. Could the gauge on the tank be broken? When was the last time they filled the tank?

The woman at the other end gave a patient sigh. "It's the extreme cold," she said. "Your tank just can't deliver enough pressure. It should get better once the temperature outside warms above zero."

Sam got the feeling the lady had repeated those words

a few hundred times already this morning. She thanked her, gathered her employees, and reassured them.

"If you can, keep working with your coats on. I promise the situation will get better. If it's too much to handle or if you feel that you'll get sick from being chilled, by all means, go on home. I'd rather have you miss part of a day now than to be working around the candy if you're sick. We can't have that."

One of the newer girls said she felt she'd better go home. Everyone else said they would be all right and would stay.

Semi-crisis, semi-averted, Sam thought as she went out to her truck. At least the building had some heat, and as the outdoor temperature rose the heating system would become more efficient. She debated whether to push on with the cleaning job today or hope for better conditions tomorrow.

What am I thinking? That house wouldn't warm up on its own until it was seventy degrees outside, and that wouldn't happen until May or June. *Get moving and just get it done, Samantha.* As her mother would have said.

The wooden box sat on the passenger seat beside her. Sam slipped her gloves off and picked it up. The cold surface began to warm immediately. As soon as her hands were toasty warm, she set the box in her lap, put her gloves back on, and started the truck.

Fifteen minutes later, she was making her way down Wicket Lane. The neighbor's minivan was gone, but a dark blue Ford pickup truck sat in the driveway. It was a super deluxe model, complete with every chrome accessory a person could tack onto the thing. Spotlessly clean, obviously it had not been driven on the local roads in the past couple of days. The garage door was in the process of sliding down and Sam caught a glimpse of another vehicle parked inside.

She maneuvered her truck, backing into the driveway of the property she'd visited the evening before. Warmed and energized from handling the box, she stashed it under the seat. The little temperature indicator on her mirror showed the outside temp at ten degrees above zero, a twenty degree change from this morning when she'd been outside with Beau. Things were looking up.

Chapter 5

Sam went to the warmest room first, where a large block of sunshine lay across the dining room floor. Packing boxes, left behind, served as trash receptacles as she started with broom and dustpan to gather dust bunnies, tidbits, and scraps from the expensive travertine floors. A camera would have caught a woman frantically sweeping at breakneck pace, but to Sam it felt like a leisurely activity. The Zen of sweeping, or some such thing.

She covered the kitchen, dining, and living rooms, filling two boxes with the collected detritus. Fifteen minutes had passed.

Beyond the kitchen, a small bedroom and bathroom she'd not noticed before must have been maid's quarters. A twin-sized bed with bare mattress, an upright chest of drawers, and a small closet with wire hangers on the rail were the only items in the room. Apparently, the family had not felt a need to take the cheap furniture with them.

A quick check of the closet shelf and the dresser drawers showed nothing at all. Thank goodness. Too often, it was the hidden crannies in a house that revealed deadly secrets and dragged both Sam and the sheriff's department into a whole new mess.

Sheriff's department—Sam caught herself thinking about what Beau had told her last night about that traffic fatality. Was it truly a cut-and-dried case of drunk driving? Somehow she had a feeling Beau had other suspicions. A careful investigator, he would never draw a conclusion until he had all the facts. But he had good instincts and Sam had learned to read his moods—the things he said and the things he left unsaid. He'd been preoccupied this morning during breakfast, and she knew he was thinking about the accident.

Pondering all this, she finished the floors in the maid's area and had already worked her way back to the den. A third box of sweepings was already filled and she carried them out to her truck. Inside, the bedrooms were carpeted, requiring the vacuum cleaner. She took it from the back seat, then lowered the tailgate to reach the generator. With a press of the starter, it roared to life.

She plugged in her fifty-foot extension cord and uncoiled it through the open front door. She'd vacuumed half the first bedroom when a shadow crossed the threshold.

"Ma'am!" A surprisingly deep voice came from the diminutive, white-haired man who stood with both hands on the doorframe.

Sam tapped the Hoover's power switch and the

machine whined to a stop.

"Hi. Sorry, I didn't see you there."

"That's a horrible racket you're making out there," he said. "I was spreading seed for the ravens and they all took off when that thing started up."

Sam realized he was talking about the generator.

"Yeah, sorry. There's no power in the house and I have to vacuum the carpeted areas. Shouldn't take more than another half-hour or so."

"Well, my wife likes to sleep late and I imagine I'll catch hell for this."

"It's not your fault. And, like I said, I won't be here much longer."

"Can't let you do it." The man turned and headed for the front door.

By the time Sam caught up with him, he'd hit the kill switch on the generator. Silence echoed through the neighborhood. He yanked the extension cord from its outlet.

"You can borrow some electricity from my house," he said, stomping across the dividing space between the two houses and jamming the cord's plug into an outlet on the side of his garage.

Sam trotted after him, about to protest, but what the heck. He was offering free, quiet power for her to finish her work. As long as the cord was long enough to stretch to the farthest of the bedrooms, it was an arrangement made in heaven.

"Um, thanks," she said when he stood and faced her again. "I'd be happy to pay for the power."

"Sure you will. Ten bucks an hour."

Okay, that was quite a bit more than she could possibly use, but well worth keeping the peace. She indicated she would get her wallet from the truck.

"Pay me when you're done. Don't know how long it'll take," he said. "Anything's better than that infernal machine running."

"Well, thank you so much. You must be Mr. Zuckerman?"

"That's right. Arnold Zuckerman. Do I know you? Maybe from my jewelry store—although that was awhile back."

Sam remembered a Zuckerman Fine Jewelry in Taos. It had changed hands and was renamed sometime in the early '90s. She smiled and extended her hand. "Actually, I met your daughter here last night when I came by to check the status of this house. I'm cleaning it up for sale through the USDA."

"Humph, Dolores. Yeah, she was here all right."

Something told Sam not to mention the daughter's comments about her father's competence. From what she could see, the old man could handle himself pretty well.

"Damn youngsters think just because a guy's almost ninety he can't do a damn thing for himself. My wife fusses over me, my daughter nags me. I like my life and I'm just fine, thank you very much."

"I can see that," Sam said, although the man was shivering in his flannel shirt and khaki trousers. "I'll just head back to my work so you can get in out of the cold. I'll bring you some money when I'm done."

"Eh, don't worry about it. I did pretty good for myself. A few bucks' worth of electricity won't send me to the poorhouse." He waved back at her as he headed toward his own front door.

Sam turned back to her work, intent now on finishing with the vacuum cleaner quickly so the man wouldn't think she was taking advantage. Creating smooth, clean swathes across the carpet relaxed Sam, as she felt her energy returning to normal levels. She'd made good progress and it wasn't quite noon yet. A mop applied to the wood and tile floors, a diligent swipe over the bathroom surfaces, and the place would be in decent shape.

Back at the truck, she exchanged the Hoover for her mop and bucket after unplugging the extension cord from Zuckerman's place. She made a little show of rewinding the cord and putting it away, in case he was spying from behind the curtains. She glanced over, but saw no movement at the other house.

Sadie Holmes and Delbert Crow would both be pleased when Sam reported she'd finished the cleanup job in a day, *and* she would still have the afternoon to catch up on her own work at the bakery. She carried the mop bucket into the utility room, hefted it to the spacious sink, and turned the tap. As she'd feared … no water.

Evidently, the city had turned that particular utility off. Oh well, she thought. She could bring two or three five-gallon buckets from home tomorrow and finish the job quickly enough. She peeked at the screen on her phone and saw it was almost noon. Her stomach growled.

"Guess I worked harder than I thought," she said to the empty house as she locked the door.

Before she could put her truck in gear, the phone vibrated on the seat beside her and Beau's name showed.

"Hey, darlin' what's up?" he said.

"Reached a stopping place on the cleaning job and I'm ready for food and checking in at the bakery—in that order."

"Lunch at Maria's? I can be there in fifteen minutes."

"Hmm … yeah, that sounds great." Only the very best

posole in town. Who could resist?

Sam was no more than six minutes away, so she said she would grab a table and place their orders. One thing about dining with a law enforcement man, she'd learned he often got called away mid-meal. It never hurt to have food on the table when he arrived.

Beau walked in the door of the tiny eatery two blocks off the main drag, Paseo Pueblo del Sur, right on time. Sam had watched him get out of his cruiser and set his felt Stetson on his head before adjusting the heavy belt of lawman gear—radio, cuffs, baton, sidearm and more. Her heart picked up its pace and she remembered exactly how lucky she felt to have this man in her life.

"Hey, you," he said as he gave her a kiss. "I'm glad this worked out, us meeting for a quick bite. Afraid I'll have to dash off soon."

"Me too. I haven't touched base with Jen all morning, so who knows what awaits me there." She picked up her spoon and stirred her steaming bowl. The hearty combination of pork, hominy, and red chile sent up a heavenly scent. "So, how was your morning?"

He finished chewing the bite he'd taken. "Well, my accident case from yesterday seems to have turned a little more complicated. Got a call from the OMI's office in Albuquerque, and the chief medical investigator wants me to drive down there to go over the autopsy results. Says he'll be done in the morning."

"What do you think it means?" Sam glanced around the room to be sure no one else was paying attention to their conversation.

"Usually, the only time law enforcement is asked to take a look is if there's something suspicious in their findings."

Sam paused in the midst of ripping a tortilla in half. "Suspicious—so it's not a case of drunk driving?"

Beau held her gaze. "I don't know, but that's my guess."

Chapter 6

Sam parked in the alley behind Sweet's Sweets. The shady areas still contained frozen slush, but everywhere the sunshine touched was drying nicely. Julio's Harley sat in one of the frozen areas, and Sam wondered how the man tolerated the cold and the iffy roads through the winter months. She walked into the kitchen to find him pouring brownie batter into a large pan.

"How's it going?" she asked.

Julio, famous for being a man of few words, merely tilted his head toward the curtain that divided the kitchen from the showroom. Sam hadn't noticed the cacophony of voices, but she heard them now.

"Oh, gosh. Poor Jen."

She quickly switched her outdoor coat for her white

bakery jacket. The customer area was jammed and Jen looked more than a little frazzled.

"Who's next?" Sam asked, stepping behind the counter beside her employee.

"If you could talk with the lady in the orange jacket over there," Jen said. "She wants to order a birthday cake and I haven't had a spare second to get the details."

"What about here?" Customers were lined up three deep at the counter.

"We have a little system going," Jen whispered to Sam. "I'm giving everyone two free cookies to thank them for their patience. It seems to be working."

Sam gave Jen's arm a squeeze. "Thanks. I'm so sorry I didn't come earlier."

Jen had slid open the glass door and was placing cheesecake slices into a bakery box for a man in a business suit. "You know how it goes. It can be dead quiet for an hour then the room fills up in five minutes. Sort of bakery-radar, or something."

Sam picked up the order pad and hurried over to the bistro table and the woman who was browsing through a photo album of cake design ideas.

"Thank you for waiting," Sam said. "May I refill your coffee?"

"No, I'd just like to get the cake ordered so I can get back to work."

Sam mentally tagged a discount onto the order because of the delay. She recognized the woman as a clerk at Walmart, a chatty type who could spread nice recommendations or nasty gossip. She put on her brightest smile and asked whether the lady had found an appealing design. Luckily, as far as time was concerned, the customer was happy with a doll cake. The birthday was her young daughter's fifth, a great age for something inspired by the Disney princesses. Sam noted her preferred colors.

The customer relaxed. By the time she left, they were on a first-name basis and Sam felt at ease about having the cake ready by the following afternoon.

Jen had made headway at the counter—the crowd was down to five people, and no one else had walked in during the past few minutes. Sam helped fill the final few requests, noted the items that were running low, and took a deep breath.

"Well, that wasn't so bad," she said. "I'll give Julio a list of what to bake before quitting time."

"Yeah, well … you'll want to look at your In basket. I took four custom orders this morning, and one of them is a wedding cake due by next weekend."

Sam's good mood slid a notch downward. A wedding cake on a few days' notice? What were people thinking?

"When does Becky get back from vacation?" she asked.

"She would come in now if she was in town," Jen said, "but I think they went—"

The bells on the front door interrupted. It took Sam a minute to place the petite woman with curly blonde hair. Missy Malone—the one who may or may not have tried to trick Jen out of an extra twenty dollars yesterday.

"Look at me—here twice in one day," Missy said, eyeing Sam but turning her attention to Jen. "The box of truffles I got this morning … well, they went over so big, my husband just raved. The man does love his sweets. So I want to get some more—" She reached into one of her voluminous coat pockets and pulled out two small boxes. "—and I brought each of you a little present."

She held out the boxes toward Jen and Sam. "A small apology for the mix-up I caused."

"Oh, how cute!" Jen exclaimed when she opened hers. She pulled out a tiny unicorn carved of jade.

Sam looked into the other box. A cupcake carved from a stone that resembled ivory, decorated with pink and red coral, sat on a bed of cotton. The item may have been mass-produced, but the craftsmanship was fairly good. The two gifts surely cost more than the twenty-dollar mistake, a mix-up that hadn't actually cost the bakery any money. The gesture seemed a little over-the-top.

She started to give the boxed gift back. "It's really not necessary."

Missy stepped back and put her hands behind her back. "No, no—you keep it. I sincerely feel badly about the little scene. I got so confused there for a minute. I just—" Her eyes began to water up, and Sam lowered her hand with the small box in it.

"Okay, if you insist. I'm just glad we caught the error."

Missy gave a grateful smile and turned toward Jen, reaching to squeeze her hand. "Enjoy your little unicorn," she said.

"Thank you for the thoughtful gift," Sam said. "Sorry, you'll have to excuse me now. I've got a ton of work stacking up in the kitchen."

Missy insisted on giving Sam a hug the minute she was no longer behind the sales counter. The instant familiarity seemed a bit much, but Jen had clearly done a good job of establishing rapport with the customer. After all, that's what any business wanted.

The two younger women continued to chat as Sam made her way to her desk. As Jen said, four new orders lay on top of the basket—five, with the doll cake order Sam had brought with her. The wedding cake was the most complex. Three tiers and a lot of piping.

The other orders included three dozen cupcakes, decorated with monster themes for a kid's birthday at school. Those were due Friday. A flower bouquet atop a sheet cake—normally Sam and Becky would take the time to create a mixed bouquet with sugar paste flowers, but there was no time now. Piped roses would have to do.

The final order was for a beach and surf design. What was with people this January week—? Everyone seemed in the mood for sunny days and outdoor activities. Flowers, fishermen, beaches … Sam quickly sorted the orders by difficulty and due dates, and told Julio the sizes and flavors of cakes to bake.

While he measured ingredients for lemon-poppyseed batter for the wedding cake, Sam checked her supplies of sugar paste, fondant, and icing sugar. A quick phone order to her wholesaler included the bride-and-groom cake topper selected by the client with the last-minute wedding order. She felt a tiny spark of residual energy from the carved box, so she set to work making a surfboard of fondant for the beach cake.

By five-thirty, her energy was definitely flagging. Julio had baked most of the cakes, which were now cooling in the big walk-in fridge. He would do the three dozen cupcakes tomorrow, if Sam didn't mind; he wanted to get home before the roads became icy again. She nodded and looked at the work she had accomplished. If no new orders came in tomorrow or the next day, she could deliver the existing ones easily enough.

Yeah, and if wishes were horses …

Two alternatives presented themselves. She could handle the box again and stay at the bakery to work all night, knowing she would be physically wiped out later. Or, she could go home and get a good night's rest and start fresh in the morning. Beau's offer to pick up pizza for dinner took one item off her agenda, but didn't exactly answer the question of whether to work or go home.

She dusted powdered sugar off her hands, noticing for the first time she was dressed in jeans and flannel shirt under her bakery jacket. She'd completely forgotten about going back to the abandoned house to mop the floors. She washed her hands and picked up her phone.

"Take the pizza home," she told Beau. "I'll be along soon."

She spent an uneasy night. Pizza on top of worry was never a great combination. Thoughts kept charging through her head—finish the cleanup job first or tend to her bakery orders and let Delbert Crow have a tizzy if he wanted to. When Beau switched on the lamp at two a.m. to ask what on earth was making her so restless, she dumped the decision on him.

"Go to the bakery first," he said. "Your customers are more important than the old grump."

"Thank you. I needed to hear your common sense advice." She smiled and he rolled toward her.

"I know something else that'll make you sleep real good," he said. A gleam came into his blue eyes as he reached for the top button on her pajamas.

He was right—*so* right.

Chapter 7

Sam woke at five with a residual feeling of euphoria from their middle-of-night lovemaking. The glowing feeling lasted only until her mind switched back to the worries of the previous evening. She shoved them back, intending to join Beau in the shower, but by the time she tossed the covers aside and entered the steamy bathroom, he was already wiping moisture off the mirror and picking up his razor. He managed to plant a shaving-cream kiss on her cheek before she could duck out of his way.

"You're in a feisty mood this morning," she teased, picking up her toothbrush.

"It's an act." His words came out slightly blurred as he stretched his mouth to get the best angle for shaving his jaw. "Remember? I have to drive down to Albuquerque and attend the autopsy on our traffic fatality."

"Ugh. Sorry." She had to admit, compared to his job, she couldn't very well complain about mopping floors or being swamped with bakery orders.

While he rinsed his razor and headed for the bedroom to dress, she went through a mental list of priorities. Shower—check. Hair—check. Put on bakery clothing, gather alternate grubby clothes to change into if the day's work allowed time to go back to Sadie's break-in job. Add wooden box to the stack—just in case.

The smell of burnt toast wafted up the stairs, and she knew Beau had forgotten that the timer on the toaster oven wasn't working. She stuffed her things into a tote bag and hurried down to give him a kiss before he headed out the door.

"Be safe," she whispered in the direction of his cruiser.

The good thing about arriving at Sweet's Sweets early was there'd been no time for Jen to add to the stack of orders. Customers couldn't come in until seven so there was a blissful hour in which to whittle away at the backlog.

Sam assembled the beach scene cake, placing the surfboard and palm trees on top of freshly spread brown sugar sand. The flower bouquet sheet cake came together quickly, with piped roses and daisies and the birthday greeting in beautiful flourishing script.

Julio had just pulled cupcakes from the oven and they would need to cool completely before they could become monsters for the little monsters at the school. Sam turned to look at the wedding cake design Jen had sketched on the order form. The tiers, in three sizes, were baked. She brought them from the walk-in fridge and began the process of filling and stacking, using dowels to handle the weight as the cake grew taller.

Sometime between brown sugar beach sand and piped roses on the sheet cake, Jen had come in and the sounds of customer voices began to drift toward the kitchen. Sam, as usual, tuned them out until a familiar giggle came through. She glanced up at the wall clock over the oven and saw it was already after ten. Half a morning had passed with the slipperiness of an eel.

"Kelly? Is that you?" she called out.

"Hey Mom." Her daughter's cinnamon curls did a little bounce as Kelly peered through the curtain dividing kitchen and sales room.

Sam returned her attention to the stacked tiers, checking to be sure they sat levelly on their base.

"Hey. Not busy next door right now?"

"Not bad. Riki's brushing out a cocker spaniel, which takes a good hour or so. Two schnauzers are under the dryers, and I think the next client is bringing in a Lab around noon."

"How would you like to create some monsters?" Sam tilted her head toward the rack of cupcakes.

"Ooh, fun!" Kelly hung up her coat and washed her hands. "Can I do anything I want?"

"Within reason. They're for third graders. Aim for more cute than gory, please."

Kelly checked out the shelf with the food color paste and chose brilliant orange, lime green, black, and a new one—Day-Glo yellow. She set the bottles at one end of the large worktable and began stirring a generous amount of the orange into freshly made buttercream icing.

From the corner of her eye, Sam caught movement at the salesroom door. Jen sidled across the room and dropped some pages into the basket on Sam's desk. When she noticed Sam had seen her, she gave a sheepish little smile.

"Another wedding cake and three birthdays. The good news is you've got three weeks for the wedding cake …"

Which would put it due as they were getting into the Valentine season. Most February brides had ordered their cakes months ahead, but this one would just have to go into the queue. At least Becky would return in a couple more days. Sam lifted the top tier and placed it on the cake in front of her. One thing at a time.

"Weather's warming up," Kelly said, apparently to get Sam's attention away from the overflowing basket of orders. "It's already forty-one out there."

As if in response to the comment, Sam's phone rang down inside the pocket of her white jacket. She steadied the six-inch tier of cake, wiped her hands on the damp towel on the table, and reached for the phone. The screen showed Sadie Holmes as the caller.

"Hey, Sadie, how's your back?"

"Rehab's going slowly. I can't believe I'm not already hopping around like a kid again."

"Um, sorry to hear it. But don't worry, I've almost got your job finished. I'll leave the bakery in plenty of time before—"

"Uh, that's the thing … Delbert just called. It's an emergency."

Sam looked at the cake creation in front of her and tried to will away Sadie's last word.

"Apparently, a neighbor called and said there is water running out from under the front door of that house."

Oh, great. Super cold temps in a house with no power, forty-degrees now …

"I don't exactly know what to do. This hasn't happened to me before," Sadie said.

Sam sighed. "I'll call the water department. They'll get someone out there and shut off the water main."

"But the—"

"Cleanup. Yeah, I'll go right over there and see what needs to be done. You just take care of that injured spine, and I'll report back to you." She tried very hard not to let frustration creep into her voice. No good deed goes unpunished, she reminded herself.

She looked up the number for the water department and waited on hold while they undoubtedly handled several hundred calls identical to hers. Capping the container of white buttercream icing she'd been about to scoop into, she wheeled the wedding cake into the fridge and slipped her bakery jacket off while pacing the room with the phone to her ear.

"This is ridiculous," she finally said. "I can probably find the shutoff valve myself."

She reached for her winter coat and told Kelly to be sure Jen knew when the cupcakes were finished so she could call the customer. The whole time she was bustling about and heading for her truck, she could only picture those beautiful parquet wood floors now covered in water. Water and who knew what else—Sam had left some boxes of rubbish and a couple garbage bags with the dust and dirt she'd vacuumed the previous day. She could be starting the clean-up job all over, farther back than square one.

She steered the streets cautiously. Melting snow and, no doubt, other broken lines had turned ordinary roads into rivers of muddy water and floating litter. She dodged a quartered log of firewood that was headed toward a storm drain at the central intersection near the plaza. *There's a clog-up waiting to happen*, she thought. She crossed the intersection, creeping along in traffic as other drivers dealt with the same obstacle course. No wonder the water department wasn't answering its phones. It might take days before anyone attended her call.

A wave of tiredness threatened, the penalty for skipping breakfast this morning and spending too many hours running at a frantic pace to get everything done. She realized she should have stopped for an early lunch, but she was already into the residential area at this point. The wooden box sat on the passenger seat, within easy reach.

Sam, Sam ... not a good thing to keep going on the rush you get from the box. Your body wants nourishment.

Shut up. Deal with the emergency first, then figure it out.

She would figure out *something*. If nothing else, there was probably an old granola bar in the glovebox. She had spotted the house when her phone rang again. She recognized the number at her chocolate factory.

"Sam, it's Benjie. I'm afraid we have a little emergency."

Chapter 8

Beau cursed the fact that he'd timed his arrival in Albuquerque to the morning rush hour. Crawling along in traffic on I-25 reminded him just how much he hated cities. He was a country boy at heart and always would be. On the radio the traffic report girl, in a voice that sounded like a twelve-year-old, informed drivers of a crash in the southbound lane. Dead ahead of his current location.

He let his cruiser coast along, trying to leave adequate space from the vehicle ahead of him, but each time a car's length opened up someone would swerve to fill it. No matter that they weren't gaining any sort of advantage, they did it anyway. He wished he'd lingered over coffee before leaving Taos or, better yet, stayed home in bed with Sam an extra hour.

Once past the Big I interchange, the lanes of cars magically began to move. No sign of the reported crash, which no doubt had happened much earlier. He exited and discovered the maze of roads had been rerouted and it was no longer a straight path to the OMI's office. He berated himself for not programming the cruiser's GPS with the destination. Now he would have to wend his way along one-way streets until he found the distinctive building with its walls of glass and concrete.

The macho attitude of navigating by intuition didn't serve him at all in a city this size. He gripped the wheel and felt his teeth grind. Doubling back cost an extra ten minutes but he eventually recognized the series of turns and spotted the blue-green windows of the place he'd not visited for several years.

He found a parking space in the lot across the street and welcomed the chance to stretch his legs after the two-and-a-half-hour drive. The stretch ended quickly though, as an icy wind off the mountains stole all the warmth his heater had provided. He hurried through the lot, heading toward the automatic front doors.

Inside, the smell of coffee wafted through the lobby. He approached a reception desk and presented his credentials, admiring the elaborate tile mural which covered walls and pillars while the young woman behind the desk checked the schedule and phoned someone deep inside the building to announce his arrival.

Three minutes later, a lanky thirty-something guy with jeans, a plaid shirt, and sandy brown curls that touched the white collar of his lab coat came through the double doors at the far side of the lobby. The two were exactly the same height although the other man's narrow frame put him at twenty pounds lighter.

"Sheriff Cardwell? Good to meet you." He met Beau with a handshake and sincere gaze. "I'm Winston Reed, toxicology technician. Can I offer you some coffee?"

Beau shook his head. "I'm fine, thanks." He didn't admit that stepping into a room of stainless steel and person-sized refrigerated beds always sent his discomfort meter skyward. This was the least favorite part of his law enforcement job, but one that was becoming more crucial, nearly mandatory, these days. When solving a case nearly always relied on evidence gathered from the victim's body, every lawman became involved at some point.

He could have sent one of his deputies for this task; Rico was diligent with details and good at asking the right questions. But Rico also had a tendency to get lightheaded at the sight of a cut-open cadaver. Already this case was looking like a situation where the details would matter a lot.

Reed ushered Beau back through the double doors from which he'd emerged and down a long corridor.

"I believe the preliminary incisions are done, organs removed and weighed, initial notes recorded," he said as they walked.

"It was a traffic fatality, so there's probably not much doubt about the cause of death," Beau mentioned. "Mainly, we're curious as to whether the victim was under the influence. A witness said he was weaving quite a lot before his vehicle went off the roadway and rolled."

"That would be my department. We'll pop in and pick up the blood and tissue samples and I'll get them into the lab." Reed pushed a heavy stainless steel swinging door, which whooshed against the shiny tile flooring. "While I start the testing process, you can speak with Doctor Plante, the pathologist on this case."

The temperature in the room was chilly, making Beau glad he hadn't removed his jacket in the warm lobby. A shrouded body lay on a stainless steel table, the white sheet sticking up in points over the toes. Beau glanced away. A man in green scrubs and white lab coat stood beside a desk, leafing through photographs.

"Winston, your samples," he said to the younger man, handing over a tray containing a dozen or more vials with gory contents and neat white labels.

He turned toward Beau. "Sheriff—hi, I'm Ralph Plante."

Beau shook the man's hand, resisting the urge to look down and assess its cleanliness. C'mon, he told himself, they wear gloves during the whole procedure.

"So, Winston says it'll be a little while before we know if our vic was under the influence?"

"Yeah, some of the tests take a day or so for results to show up. Do you plan to stay in Albuquerque and wait for them?"

"Hadn't planned on it. Mainly, I just have to cross the T's, make sure my accident report covers the same basics as the autopsy."

Doctor Plante paused a moment. "I need you to see something. You want to look at the body or do you prefer the photos?"

"Can I see what I need to in the pictures?"

Plante smiled. "Sure. Either way, I can tell you what it is you're seeing." He held up a small sheaf of eight-by-ten color photos and fanned them like a hand of cards. "These two probably show the injury best."

Beau recognized Percy Lukinger's head, both by the color of his hair and by the large bloody gash at the temple.

"Yeah, we saw that. He wasn't wearing his seatbelt. It was pretty obvious he'd been tossed around inside the car."

"But this wasn't the cause of death," Plante said.

"So ... what, then? Internal injuries?"

"It's easier to tell on the body, but this head injury happened some time before the accident. Clotting around the wound indicates this happened at least thirty to sixty minutes before the other injuries."

"Our victim got a head wound—somehow—and then went on to drive down the highway. It sure could explain the erratic driving."

Plante nodded at Beau's assessment. "I'm not prepared to state the cause of death yet," he said. "Each of the physical injuries, taken on its own, isn't serious enough to cause death—including this one on the temple. I want Winston's tox report before I make a determination."

Beau nodded. Thoughts buzzed him like dive bombers. A fairly hard bash to the head, a rollover traffic accident, not to mention how much booze or drugs the man might have in his system—any or all of it might have contributed.

"I appreciate that," he told the doctor.

"I'm definitely not prepared to concede it was an accident," Plante said. "And because of that, I've made you a folder of my findings."

He picked up a manila folder and handed it to Beau. A quick glance showed the collection of photographs, a set of fingerprints, and an autopsy report clearly labeled 'Preliminary.' A large plastic bag contained bloodied clothing, a ring, and gold neck chain.

"Those sad rags are what we cut off him. I assume your department already collected his wallet, and any other personal effects?"

"We did. My deputy has been looking for the next of kin."

The doctor nodded. "I can email you digital files of any of this, along with my final report."

Beau thanked him and retraced his steps out to his cruiser. Mid-morning and his quest for answers had only dealt him more questions.

Chapter 9

Sam watched as water flowed from beneath the garage door and sheeted down the driveway while she tried to register Benjie's word 'emergency.'

"What type of emergency?" She envisioned the hardwood floors at the old Victorian flooded in water, but surely he would have reported that sort of situation well before ten-thirty in the morning.

"FedEx called to say the truck with our order went off the bridge down near Pilar. Boxes went into the river and … well, we won't be getting that shipment at all."

Sam tried to recall what was in the shipment that would classify this as an emergency.

"It's the cocoa powder—the Brazilian Select. We are totally out, and Mr. Bookman's order is due day after tomorrow."

Yikes. She took a deep breath, dimly aware of the old man watching her from the house next door. She gave a pointed stare and watched him duck behind the curtain.

"Okay," she said to Benjie. Deep breath. "Get on the phone with Tanner Wholesale and tell them to do whatever it takes to get a duplicate shipment to us overnight. Better yet, if they'll put it on a plane that will arrive tonight, I'll run to wherever it takes to pick it up. You'll find their contact info on my desk upstairs. Stress the absolute importance of it and get a promise before you let them off the line. Okay?"

"Got it."

Benjie was such a mild-mannered sweetheart, Sam felt the need to reiterate that it was all right in this instance to throw a little urgency into his words.

"Once you've got their commitment, call the employees together and inform them everyone will be pulling double shifts for the next day or two. If anyone from Book It Travel calls to ask about the order, do not tell them about this. Just tell them I'm out of the office and will get back to them soon."

"Got it."

The water from the driveway continued to flow, racing down the gutter and forming a small lake at the intersection down the hill. Sam felt her blood pressure rise. Too bad she hadn't thought to carry Wellies in her truck. She stepped out, making a leap for the sidewalk beyond the river in the gutter.

Scouting the front of the property, she spotted the town's metal cover over the water meter. It required a special tool to lift it. Second choice would be if there was a master shut-off valve somewhere along the line. As she remembered the layout of the house, the hot water heater was in the garage, with a small bathroom the other side of the wall. Logic said that would be the point where the line entered the dwelling so she visualized a straight path from point A to point B.

The house key was under the flowerpot where she'd replaced it, so she grabbed it and dashed in. The travertine entry was dry, but the parquet in the den already had nearly an inch of water. The culprit was a stream coming from the kitchen. Great. Multiple breaks in the house pipes, no doubt. No time to analyze it at this moment—Sam dashed for the connecting door to the garage.

Within five minutes she'd located a valve and muscled it closed. The flow eased and then stopped. Now the real work would begin.

The doorbell chimed about two seconds before her phone began to ring. With a backward glance at the wet garage floor, she pulled the phone from her pocket and headed for the front door.

"Sam, I think I have some good news on the cocoa," Benjie said. "Tanner Wholesale located about half of what we need in Albuquerque. They can have it delivered by noon tomorrow."

"Better yet, Beau's there today. If he hasn't left yet, I'll have him pick it up. Give me the address."

"I'll need to call them back. The rest of the order will be shipped today, overnight. Surely FedEx can't lose two trucks in two days, right?"

"Perfect. Get me that address right away. I'm getting hold of Beau now."

With one thumb, she ended Benjie's call and hit the quick-dial for Beau's cell while she reached with the other hand for the door. Arnold Zuckerman stood on the porch, tapping his toe.

"Hey, Sam," Beau answered.

She held up an index finger to Mr. Zuckerman in a 'wait' gesture. "Have you left Albuquerque yet?"

"Just leaving the OMI's office. Thought I'd grab a burger then I'm on the road. Why?"

She explained and told him she would call right back as soon as Benjie gave her the address.

Zuckerman sputtered. "What the hell? You're here talking on the damn phone all morning while the neighborhood floods?"

Sam put on a smile and pointed at the driveway. "I've shut the water off. The last of the flood is on its way past your house right now, and it should be dry very soon."

"Well, it had better be. My wife's on her way and it's a good thing she won't see this mess." A gleam came into his eye. "I got romantic plans for later, don't want her upset over anything."

Seriously? A mid-afternoon tryst with an eighty-seven-year-old man? Well, his daughter had said the new wife was younger, and men these days had their magic blue pills and whatever other assistance. Sam suppressed the urge to chuckle.

The old man started back on the subject of the broken water pipes when her phone rang again. The chocolate factory number showed on the screen, so she wished Zuckerman well and closed the door in his face. She still had a lost shipment to deal with and a few hundred gallons of water to get off that parquet flooring before it seeped through the sealant and ruined it forever.

She put a smile in her voice as she answered the phone.

Chapter 10

Beau pulled away from the warehouse on Academy Parkway where Sam had sent him to get a package. One box turned out to be five and the stock clerk, who exuded a faint scent of pot, seemed a little edgy as he helped load them into the back of the Taos County Sheriff's Department cruiser. On his own turf, Beau would have asked a few questions, ferreted out some answers. But he was several counties away and wanted to get home in time to stop by the station and see how the day had gone for his deputies.

He steered into the drive-thru lane at a corner McDonald's, having nearly forgotten he'd planned to eat something before driving home. He dropped the folder of autopsy photos to the floor to make room on the passenger seat for the little box of chicken nuggets he would munch while he drove.

Once on I-25, the conversation with Doctor Plante ran through his head again. He tried to imagine circumstances where Percy Lukinger would have sustained a bleeding head injury and then felt the need to go driving out of town—southbound, away from Taos and available medical care—on snowy roads. He lived in Taos. Even if the injury happened away from home, he should have been headed north. A person would normally go to a doctor or hospital, or simply go home and try to care for the wound himself. It didn't make sense.

Maybe he had a friend—girlfriend?—who lived south of town and he'd hoped to make it to her place. Maybe Lukinger hadn't realized the extent of his injury—one of those bravado types who assert that they're just fine, thanks. Maybe he was disoriented and didn't realize he was getting farther from help?

Beau popped the last chicken nugget into his mouth. He could 'maybe' the situation all day and not know the answer. This wasn't going away, and what he needed were facts, not speculation. He asked his hands-free phone to call Rico.

"Hey," he said when the deputy picked up, "any luck finding next-of-kin for our traffic fatality, Percy Lukinger?"

"Nothing yet, boss. I went to the address on his license. No one home. A neighbor told me it's a rental and said he doesn't know the man, but there's a wife or girlfriend in the picture. The man wasn't too sure. Just said a woman comes and goes, but she doesn't always stay the night. Said they don't seem to have any kids or pets. Lukinger himself would sometimes be away for days at a time, and the neighbor thought maybe he was a traveling salesman or something like that. With the internet and all, is there still such a thing as a traveling salesman?"

"Probably. Surely there's still something that can't be bought online. I don't know what it would be." Beau set down his paper cup of Coke. "For a guy who claims not to know his neighbors, your interview netted a lot of info."

"Yeah, the man said he's recently retired and his wife still works. I got the feeling he hovers around the windows all day, checking out neighborhood comings and goings. I went back to the Lukinger place and walked around back. Everything he said about kids and pets seemed to check out. Maybe the couple both work at jobs that take them on the road a lot, so the guy next door only catches glimpses when they both happen to be there."

Could be that Lukinger's job was the reason he felt pressed to get in his car and drive when he really wasn't in condition to do it.

"If there's nothing urgent on my desk, I'll go on home when I get back to town," Beau said. "I've got a folder full of stuff we'll go over in the morning, but you can let me know if anything new comes in."

It was nearly dark when he pulled up the long gravel drive at home. January days were still way too short. Lights gleamed at the living room and kitchen windows, but Ranger and Nellie didn't greet him. Sam must have let the dogs inside.

She apologized immediately because dinner would be a chicken and pasta casserole from the freezer.

"Long day, huh?" He took her in his arms and felt the knots in her shoulder muscles.

"Broken water pipes, nasty mess to clean up, grumpy old man, missing shipment of cocoa and a deadline order. That pretty well sums up my day, so tell me about yours."

"Didn't love the drive to Albuquerque, but it went okay. OMI threw a new wrinkle in my traffic fatality case. Rico hasn't reached next of kin yet. You know—just standard law enforcement stuff." He planted a kiss on top of her head. "I did stop by and dropped off your cocoa shipment at the chocolate factory on my way."

"Did I ever happen to mention how fantastically lucky I was to meet you?" Sam glanced at the oven timer. "Can you watch that for me? I'm going to take a super hot, super quick shower, and I'll want a glass of wine when I get back."

He gave a thumbs-up as she dashed from the kitchen. Ten minutes later, the oven timer buzzed and Sam came back, dressed in thick gray sweats and a purple pullover. Her damp hair stood up in little spikes where she'd fluffed it with her fingers.

"Now," she said, taking her wine glass, "tell me what it is about this case of yours that has you so perplexed."

"Perplexed? You can tell?"

"Something about the way you hugged me. Plus, there's a little something ..." She avoided coming up with the word by reaching instead for the hot casserole pan he'd set on a mat in the middle of the kitchen table.

Beau guessed the word she might have said was 'aura.' Sam thought she kept the supernatural stuff from him, but he knew when she handled that jewelry box she sometimes saw auras around people. The way she'd explained it, depending on the color of the haze around the person, she could often sense mood or certain deeper aspects of their personalities. He wouldn't ever bring up the subject in law enforcement circles, but privately he was glad. She'd helped him solve more than one case.

"Sam, do you know a Percy Lukinger?"

She shook her head. "Don't think so. Well, not by name. Between bakery customers, bookstore friends, and people I see around town, I might."

"He's our new fatality, and we're having trouble locating his next of kin."

"You have a picture?"

"Quite a few. But you wouldn't want to look at them during dinner. He's forty years old, five foot nine, dark hair that's receding, brown eyes, sharp nose. I realize that doesn't differentiate him from more than half the other white guys in this town."

Clearly, she drew a blank from the verbal description. "I can handle looking at the photos later," she said.

"Wait—I have a copy of his driver's license. That'll work."

He left the table and went to the manila folder he'd left on the arm of the sofa. Paging past the autopsy photos, he came to the license and pulled it out. At the office, he'd enlarged it to fill most of a sheet of copy paper.

Back in the kitchen, Sam wiped her hands on a napkin and took the page from him. She studied it carefully.

"Hm. I *have* seen this man. I don't know him well, and am very sure he never introduced himself as Percy. That's a fairly distinctive name. But I'm pretty sure he's been in the bakery a few times."

"Recently?"

She let out a breath and looked toward the ceiling, remembering. "Within the past week. Monday, maybe?"

"Was he alone or with someone else?"

Her head shook slowly. "I just don't know. Jen was waiting on him and there were other people in the room, but I can't say for sure whether he was with any of them. Sorry."

Beau stood to clear their plates.

"Want me to show the picture to Jen?" she asked.

"I suppose it couldn't hurt. We have an address for the man, but there was no other contact information in his wallet. It's turning into a situation where one of the deputies has to drop by frequently, trying to catch someone home. If Jen knows anything about him—where he worked, names of relatives or friends—anything like that could be helpful."

What a puzzle. No other Lukingers were listed in the county; Percy's driver's license had only been issued a few months ago. It was as if he'd sprung up in town without a past.

Chapter 11

Two items topped Sam's agenda the next morning, and she didn't want to do either one of them. First was to line up a plumber to fix the broken pipes at the break-in house. Fairly simple task—Taos had at least a dozen plumbers. Only problem was, after the sub-zero temperatures it seemed there were a hundred-dozen water leaks around town. Every place she called she got the same answer: We're fully booked for the next week to ten days. Priority was given to homes where people actually lived. Vacant buildings just had to take a place in line.

So, now she had to call Delbert Crow and inform him. She'd avoided contact with her old supervisor for about a year now, but it wasn't fair to force Sadie to continue as go-between when the poor woman was still under medical care. Sam took a breath, dialed the phone, and resolved to hold firm with Delbert.

"It isn't as if real estate agents can't show the house," she said. "No one's going to buy and expect to immediately move in. I've got a plumber lined up for Tuesday after next, and we're waitlisted with two others. It's the best anyone could do at this point."

He grumbled about the house not being spotlessly clean for showings, reminding Sam of the irascible man's manner. He grouched about everything—why not this?

She hung up and glanced at her desk. A wedding cake and two birthdays to finish today. It would be so good to have Becky back at work tomorrow. But before Sam washed up and started the cakes, she should do as she'd promised Beau and ask Jen about the license photo of Percy Lukinger. She fished the folded page from her shoulder bag.

"Yeah … I think so," Jen said. "He has kind of a pointy nose? The picture doesn't show it very well."

"That's what Beau said. So, this man has been in here?"

"A few times. He's not really a regular."

"Beau wanted to know if he's usually with anyone. They're having a hard time locating relatives."

"Hmm … I don't remember anyone being with him. He always got one slice of cheesecake, to go, in a little box. He seemed nice, always chatted a little. Tried to be flirty, but he definitely wasn't my type. Older and, well—"

The bells above the door tinkled and Missy Malone came in on a cloud of perfume, swathed in a large fluffy coat. Wisps of her blonde hair peeked from the edges of a matching hat. Although it was surely faux fur, it wouldn't be a popular style here in eco-conscious Taos.

"Hey, Jen!" Her high voice went several notes higher.

"And Sam! It's excellent to see you again."

Sam wondered if these chirpy visits were going to become a regular thing.

Missy toddled to the sales counter on high-heeled boots, her eyes edging toward the photo Jen held, although Jen seemed unaware. She'd already started to hand the page back to Sam. Something in Missy's expression changed, ever so subtly.

Sam held the printed side of the paper toward their guest. "Do you know this man?"

"Um, don't think so. Why?"

"The sheriff is inquiring," Sam said.

Missy's dark brown eyes met Sam's. "No, sorry, I don't know him."

"Okay. He's been in the bakery a few times, so we were just curious."

Missy shook her head and turned her attention to the bakery case. "I just *had* to have one of your fantastic brownies. Must be some hormone thing—I am *really* wanting chocolate right now."

Sam left Jen to fill the order, turning her own attention to the decorating that needed to happen in the kitchen. One of the birthday cakes was a fairly standard princess cake, and Jen had talked the customer into going with non-traditional colors of bright turquoise and yellow, rather than the standard pink or lavender. The other order was for an elderly man's birthday and since the instructions said "Surprise Me!" Sam thought she had the perfect idea.

"Julio, I need eight-inch layers, vanilla cake. Tint each one very bright—red, orange, yellow, green, blue, purple."

"Okay, boss." Without a blink, he turned to the shelf containing the color paste.

She began tinting fondant in the same set of colors, forming narrow strips into the shape of a rainbow. One of her signature frostings was known as White Cloud, fluffy and somewhat shapeable. The fondant rainbow would arch above the white clouds, and the surprise would come when the cake was sliced to reveal rainbow colored layers. A small storage box on the shelf caught her eye. Ah—multicolored chocolate candies would add the perfect touch, held within a secret space she would create in the center of the cake.

While the colored layers baked, she turned back to the princess. Ruffles and flourishes were always fun, and since there was no limit to the amount of frou-frou allowed on a beautiful ball gown, Sam let her imagination take over. In under thirty minutes, the cake was glorious and safely boxed. Sam carried it to the sales room for the customer to pick up, catching a glimpse of a brown fur coat outside the front windows.

"Was Missy here all this time?" she asked Jen.

"She hung around long enough to eat two brownies, drink a cup of coffee, and … she brought me this." Jen held up a delicate gold chain with an astrological sign pendant.

"Wow, what's with all the gifts?"

Jen shrugged. "She just seems friendly and interested in lots of things. She's got great taste in jewelry. Did you notice her rings?"

Sam hadn't. "What do you guys talk about?"

"Well, right now she's thinking of going to forensics school, so she's been asking a lot about Beau's work and how a police investigation works."

Sam thought back to the morning Missy had quickly scooted out the door when Beau showed up. Would she actually be comfortable working with the law all the time? Well, whatever. Maybe it was an excuse to keep up a friendship with Jen. Sam shrugged off the subject. Work in the kitchen beckoned again.

"I've got that wedding cake to finish and deliver," Sam told Jen, pointing out the shelf where she'd set the rainbow cake for Mr. Rivers, whose daughter was to pick it up around three o'clock.

The steps of stacking the tiers and giving the wedding cake an initial rough coat of white buttercream had been done yesterday; now Sam could get to the fun parts. She reviewed the sketch Jen had made on the order form. The bride had left a small swatch of pale apricot fabric, and the notation on the cake order said, 'lighter than this, please.'

Sam took a large ball of fondant and placed one drop of yellow and two drops of orange color paste on it. Kneading quickly, she worked the color in, happy to see that her proportions had worked out perfectly. The tone was a good match for the fabric. She ran the fondant through her roller machine and came out with a circle to fit the middle tier of the cake. With the same formula for the color, she tinted a batch of sugar paste and began forming huge, full-blown roses from it. Five of them would cover the top of the smallest tier, with two or three more to tuck artistically elsewhere.

The best offset color for the pale apricot would be ivory, so she added the color to white buttercream. With fondant covering the middle tier, Sam set about piping swirls to cover the sides of the others. Soon, the top and bottom tiers were completely covered, and the result looked like a million rose petals opening to face the audience. She added a subtle sprinkle of iridescent sugar to catch the light, then piped a few decorative swags on the apricot-colored layer. Off to the fridge so everything could set up nicely, then she would add the sugar paste flowers right before taking the cake out to her bakery van for delivery.

A glance at the clock told her she still had a couple hours before she would need to leave. A day without a crisis felt a little strange, but Sam cautioned herself not to count on anything. In the other room, she heard the front door bells followed a minute later by a shriek. Oh god, what now?

The shriek turned to a giggle as Sam parted the curtain to check it out. Barbara Rivers, a longtime customer, was looking at the rainbow cake Sam had finished for her father. Jen had explained about the hidden cache of candy inside.

"It's perfect, Sam. He'll love it!"

Sam gave the customer a warm smile and a hug and watched her carry the cake box to her car. Everything Sam had produced today had turned out beautifully. Why, then, did she have a nagging sense of trouble hovering nearby?

Chapter 12

The man without a past—Beau chided himself for having the thought about Percy Lukinger. Everyone has a past; he just needed to discover this one. He sat at his desk, tapping a pencil against the case folder with the photos and notes.

The squad room was empty except for one deputy—a new transfer from Mora County—who was writing up his morning's worth of traffic citations. Everyone else had been dispatched—a home robbery, two missing dogs, and a gas station holdup. In broad daylight. In Taos. Things were changing around here, for sure.

Okay, Percy Lukinger. I'm doing my best to find your family. I will do my best to figure out what happened to you.

Beau closed the folder, taking only the license photo

with him, and grabbed his hat and coat from the rack beside his office door. He stopped by the desk of their dispatcher-secretary.

"Dixie, did you find contact information for the owner of 54 Montaño Lane?"

"Sure did, Sheriff." She handed him a pink message slip. "Name, address and phone number."

He mumbled a thanks and headed for the back door, switching off the squad room coffee maker on his way through. Never understood how the men could sit in there, smelling the thick dark odor of day-old brew, without doing it themselves, but they didn't. He slid his arms into the sleeves of the department-issue down jacket and planted his felt Stetson on his head.

Slush from two days ago had frozen in heaps around the concrete bumpers the vehicles parked against, but otherwise the employee lot had pretty well melted clear. He started his cruiser and sat there with the sun shining through the window until the heater began to produce warmish air. After coming up empty by checking the voter rolls, DMV, and county property records, visiting Lukinger's landlord seemed the only way to find out where the man worked or if he had a wife.

This accident case was taking way too much of his time. So far, he had no evidence it was anything more sinister than a guy making the very bad choice to keep driving when he shouldn't have. Finding a family member to claim the body shouldn't be this difficult; once he did so, he could close the case and be damn thankful Lukinger hadn't taken out other innocent drivers in the process.

He dialed the phone number Dixie had given him for Charles Romero, and it was answered on the second ring. Beau introduced himself and said he needed a little information on the tenant on Montaño Lane.

"I'm trying to find a way to contact someone who's related to him. Did he have a wife or girlfriend living with him?"

"Why you need to know that?"

"Can you just check the application he filled out when he rented? He hasn't been in town long, so it can't be filed that deeply away."

"I, uh, I don't keep that stuff."

"Really? So, if he damaged the house or skipped out on the rent, you don't have any way to find him?"

"Nope." The line went dead.

Okay, there's a guy who's hiding something. Beau backed out of his parking slot and hit his strobes. *Don't mess with me, you little jerk.*

Romero's address was only three blocks from the station. As traffic glided away to the sides of the road, it took Beau under a minute to screech to a halt in front of a tan little adobe box. He was out of the SUV and on the front porch ten seconds later. Pounding on the door, he shouted.

"It was a simple question, Mr. Romero. Would you like to answer it here or down at my office? I can make enough noise your neighbors will start to take an interest."

The front door opened a couple of inches, revealing a short man with a fair amount of gray in his hair.

"Thank you." Beau brought his voice to nearly a whisper, forcing Romero to open the door wider to hear him. "Now. May I see the rental application Mr. Percy Lukinger signed when he rented your property on Montaño Lane? Please."

Romero fidgeted. "Look, Sheriff, I wasn't lying. I really don't keep any forms or anything."

Not good business practice, but not strictly illegal.

"Then maybe you can just tell me how many people live in the house? Does Lukinger have a wife, kids, any family who live there?"

The shorter man shook his head. "He told me he'd be living alone. Look, he don't cause no trouble. Been there a few months and no complaints."

"Okay. Well, then I'm sorry to inform you that Mr. Lukinger was killed in a traffic accident a couple days ago. I'm just looking to reach his next of kin. Anything you know would be helpful. He had recently moved to Taos. Did he ever say where he came from?"

Another head shake. "He kept his business to himself. Brought me an envelope the first of each month. Usually it was 'hi' and 'bye' and not much more."

Rent paid in cash, almost certainly undeclared income ... which explained Romero's dodging him at first. He could make an issue of it if he had to, but he wasn't the tax man.

"He never mentioned anyone else—a lady friend, a buddy, what he liked to do on Saturdays or where he was going once he dropped off his rent money?"

"None of that."

"I'd like a key to the house," Beau said. "Maybe his possessions will give some clues."

Romero disappeared for a minute and came back with a bristling key ring. He looked at tiny labels on keys until he came to one with a 54 on it. He ran it around the metal ring until it came off.

"That's my last copy, so don't lose it," he said.

"I'll have it right back to you when we're finished." Beau met his gaze straight-on. "It can become a sticky mess, you know, if you don't happen to be reporting that cash income on your taxes."

Romero's eyes widened slightly. He got the message.

Back in his cruiser, Beau sent a little salute toward Romero's front window. No doubt the man was watching to see how long he would hang around.

Montaño Lane was only a half-dozen blocks west, so Beau headed there. The small house at number 54 proved to be nearly a carbon copy of the landlord's own home. He pulled his SUV into the driveway. No one answered his tap at the door, so he used the key.

Curtains were drawn at all the windows, making the interior dim, chilly, and cave-like. He flipped the switch nearest the door; it illuminated an overhead fixture with woefully inadequate light. Probably meant to hold three bulbs and only one remained functional. The layout was basically living-dining L, cubbyhole kitchen, one bathroom, two bedrooms. Furniture consisted of mismatched castoffs. Whether they belonged to the landlord or the tenant, they were dingy brown lumps with the personality of hedgehogs in hibernation. A scarred coffee table in front of the brown sofa was littered with a week-old newspaper, a coffee mug with dried sludge at the bottom, a paper napkin with a browned apple core, and a single white sock.

The kitchen sink held a plastic drain rack with some forks and knives in the square compartment meant for flatware. A tall trash bin near the back door was stuffed to overflowing with used paper plates and bags from fast food places. An empty gin bottle topped the precarious mess. The countertop showed no signs of meal preparation, no small appliances other than a tiny one-serving coffee machine of the type you'd find in motel rooms. Fridge had a pizza box with two dried up slices of pepperoni and a bottle of French vanilla coffee creamer. Beau pulled open the few drawers, wondering if one served as the catch-all for mail, but they contained only the most basic of kitchen tools—a single corkscrew.

He moved on to the bedrooms. One had an unmade double bed—mattress and box spring only—and a cheap nightstand. A peek in the closet assured him no one had lived in the room. The other, slightly larger bedroom also had a double bed, the nightstand to match the one from the other room, and a chest of drawers with a mirror above it.

The top drawer contained a half-dozen pairs of men's white briefs, a mound of dark socks, a leather belt, and box of condoms. The second drawer held a few T-shirts, men's size medium. A few items of women's size small clothing had been dumped into the third drawer, and the fourth was empty. Wire hangers in the closet held a navy sport coat, four long-sleeved men's shirts and two pair of jeans, black dress shoes on the floor, and a suitcase easily large enough to hold every personal item in the place.

There'd been no stashed boxes on either closet shelf— no photo albums or mementos, no Christmas decorations, tickets to events … not a trace of the collection of things most people moved around with them through their lives. Still—what about the present-day stuff? Nothing in the nightstand drawer—no paycheck stubs, no checkbook, no passport, no utility bills. Where did the guy work? How did he pay his rent?

So far, his findings tended to uphold what they'd learned. A man who could pack up at a moment's notice and a woman who spent very little time here. Toiletries in the bathroom fit the same picture. Rico had speculated maybe Lukinger was a traveling salesman, but there was no evidence of samples or product brochures.

And what about the woman? Casual dates didn't leave their clothes, toothbrushes, or makeup behind. She had to be someone Percy had cared for. But Beau had found nothing in the whole place to identify her.

All he could figure was that their victim somehow worked within the underground economy, some type of off-the-books job that paid in cash. Could be as simple as washing dishes in a little café somewhere, or as sinister as dealing drugs. Small town or not, that stuff went on everywhere.

He would give one last shot at getting the woman's name by talking to some of the neighbors. As a last resort, they could go to the media with Percy's picture and, without saying why, let it be known they were looking for relatives. It wasn't ideal. No one wanted to learn of the death of a loved one by seeing his photo on the evening news.

Beau switched off the lights he'd used along the way and was ready to close the front door behind him when his phone rang.

"Sheriff Cardwell? This is the Medical Investigator's office in Albuquerque," said a woman's voice.

Beau stepped back into the house and closed the door. "Yes, what's up?"

"Winston Reed asked me to give you a call. He just wanted to say, once you've looked over his reports, feel free to call with any questions."

"I'm not at my office right now, but thanks—I'll do that."

The woman added, "At least you found his next of kin."

Beau froze. "What?"

"Mr. Lukinger's wife. She came in early this morning, identified the body, and sent the funeral home folks to get him."

Chapter 13

Amillion questions ran through Beau's mind, but all the woman on the line could tell him was that a lady with long black hair, wearing a black coat, had identified Percy Lukinger as her husband. She left without even collecting her copies of the death certificate, but the OMI had provided the necessary one to the funeral home people who had taken the body away. It was Sanchez Mortuary in Taos, and they had left about an hour ago.

So, maybe it was just that simple, Beau thought as he locked the Lukinger house and got into his cruiser. The wife had somehow heard about the accident, probably without realizing the Sheriff's department was trying to locate her. How she had known to go to the OMI's office was still a mystery, but there were dozens of ways an ordinary citizen could find out where the state's autopsies were performed.

He would read over the reports Winston Reed had emailed, tying up the loose ends in the case, and he could get on to other things. Sam had been working overly hard the past couple weeks, and he remembered Becky was to be back at work tomorrow. Maybe he could get Sam to agree to a few days off and the two of them could go somewhere nice.

Back at his desk, Beau opened his email and discovered Reed's attached reports. The first thing the toxicologist had noted was the presence of something called benzodiazepine in Lukinger's system. A lot of the medical-speak was beyond him so he dialed the OMI's office once again.

"Yeah, Sheriff," said Reed when he came on the line.

"Hey, Winston. I'm looking at the Lukinger results and I need you to tell me if I'm reading this right. This chemical substance was actually the cause of death?"

"A contributing factor. Basically, benzodiazepines—benzos—are the classification for the brand names Valium, Xanax, or a dozen others. What I noted is, in dosage quantities they're okay. People take them in pill form for anxiety or insomnia. It slows the breathing and heart rate. Hospitals use it pre-surgery to calm patients who are nervous.

"The bad part comes when combined with alcohol or other drugs—those effects can quickly become intensified. Placed in an alcoholic beverage, it's what people call the date-rape drug. Extreme lethargy leads to unconsciousness. You sure don't want to attempt to drive in that condition. Most likely, this victim lost consciousness at the wheel of his car, went off the road and got thrown around inside the vehicle—by the time EMTs got to him he was deceased."

"So, he drugged himself for anxiety but proceeded to drive."

"Well, that's the thing. If you flip to page two you'll see some additional notes. There were no pills in his stomach, so we began looking for another way the drug got into his system. It took awhile, but we found a small injection site in his back, just beside the right shoulder blade."

Beau caught himself reaching for the spot on his own back. Right-handed, he could barely touch it with his fingertips.

"I know what you're doing," Winston said. "And you're right. It's tricky for a person to reach that location on his own body, nearly impossible to hold a syringe at the right angle and inject himself."

"So someone else injected this drug?"

"And administered it directly into the lung. It was a great enough concentration to have slowed his breathing dramatically within three minutes, halted it completely in about ten."

"He may have even been dead already when he went off the road," Beau said.

"Quite possibly."

"No way he gave it to himself?"

"Not that I can tell. Plus, why would he?" Winston said. "Anyway, we kept tissue and blood samples here at the lab, and I realize I'll probably be called to testify about this in court. I tried to make my report thorough enough that any expert medical witnesses who need to look it over can tell how and why we drew our conclusions."

"Was Doctor Plante in agreement about releasing the body?"

"Completely. We documented everything."

Beau thanked the toxicologist for the information and slowly set the phone back in its cradle. Reed was already a step ahead of him. He had done his job thoroughly, having realized the simple traffic accident was now a murder.

The word hung in his mind and he felt a moment's panic. Always one to sweat the details, Beau scrambled to remember whether he'd gathered sufficient evidence and made enough notes about the victim at the scene. He'd been focused on the vehicle's position, calculating its speed when it left the road, and of course concern for the other drivers who had come so close to being entangled.

If he got over to Sanchez Mortuary quickly enough maybe he could take another look and add last-minute notes. He called to see whether the hearse had arrived back from Albuquerque yet.

"Our driver just returned," Monica Sanchez told him, "but we don't have the Lukinger remains. When Victor got to Albuquerque and met with the widow—her name is Ramona Lukinger—she said her husband's wishes were for cremation. Since we don't do that here, Victor drove the body over to Sunrise. Once they have the cremains for us, we'll do a small memorial service, as per Mrs. Lukinger."

"I haven't had any luck reaching her. Do you have a phone number for her?"

"Sure, Sheriff." Monica read off a local number. From the prefix, he thought it was most likely a cell phone.

"Thanks." Beau fidgeted at the change of plans now that he couldn't make any more notes about the body. He hung up the phone and paced the width of his office twice before making himself stop and take stock. The OMI's report was on his computer screen. The folder of photos sat on his desk, along with two bags of personal effects—the clothing removed from Lukinger's body at the morgue and the small items collected at the accident scene.

Somewhere among them must be the right clues.

He picked up his desk phone again and punched the digits for Ramona Lukinger's number. One ring. Two rings. It took a moment to realize what he was hearing—Percy's cell phone in its plastic evidence bag was ringing. When he picked up the bag and looked closely, it was his own number showing on the screen.

Okay … was this a case of a flustered widow in shock, automatically reciting her husband's number instead of her own? Or was something more devious going on?

Chapter 14

Sam wheeled the nearly finished wedding cake into the fridge. Once the sugar paste flowers were completely set, she would do the final assembly and it would be ready to deliver. She stood beside her desk, flipping through the orders for the rest of the week, prioritizing by due date and difficulty. Becky's return would be a huge help. It was all doable. Then the phone rang.

"Sam, it's Benjie." By his tone of voice, Sam could tell he was near panic.

"What's up?"

"It's the furnace. Yesterday we were freezing in here. Now it's so warm the chocolate in the packing room is starting to melt. The girls can hardly handle it without their fingers getting messy."

Not a good thing. Sam's mind raced.

"Okay, have you tried turning down the thermostat? Opening some windows?" *Come on, it's January—there's got to be an easy way to cool a place.*

"Tried the thermostat. The furnace isn't cutting off. I'll get to the windows right now."

Sam promised she would be there in a few minutes and tossed the order forms back into the basket.

"I'm heading for the chocolate factory," she called out to Jen. "I'll be back in time to get the wedding cake delivered, but otherwise don't count on me for the afternoon."

Julio gave a questioning look.

"If you run out of other things to do, start baking the cakes needed for the first four orders in that stack," she told him, with a nod of her head toward the basket on the desk.

He nodded and went back to spreading icing on top of a Bakewell tart, the newest in their line of European pastries. The almond crust and raspberry filling had made it a new favorite with the afternoon tea crowd.

Behind the bakery, Sam started her delivery van and let it warm up for a minute while she pulled out her cell phone. Somewhere in the contacts, she had a number for a guy who knew how to work on the boiler and heating system at the chocolate factory. She debated—call him and try to get him out there immediately, or assess the situation herself first? Decided it would be better to have an idea what was going on. After all, it could come down to a momentary panic among the employees over a situation Sam could easily remedy. She pulled out of the alley and took a left, heading north.

The blue-gray Victorian house, with its slate roof and

turret at one end, sat stately as ever on the rural lane where she'd found it five months ago. When she'd first gotten the lead on the old place, she had been underwhelmed by the idea of moving a whole segment of her business there. But mild intrigue had grown to interest and had become downright love once she saw how the spacious rooms could be adapted to her needs.

The quality of the structure had come through in solid framing, good woodwork, along with reasonably good heating, plumbing, and electrical systems. Although the interior now held worktables, shipping cartons, shelves of cocoa and flavorings, and the kitchen was more like that of a high-end restaurant than any Victorian could have ever imagined, the exterior still held all the grace and charm that the original owner—an eccentric writer—had ever imagined.

Sam pulled the van up the long drive and came to a stop under the portico by the kitchen door. Windows were raised in the packing and shipping areas, where chocolates from the kitchen were placed in decorative boxes and then packed for shipment to Book It Travel's operations center.

She always loved to imagine the candy aboard private jets being enjoyed by people with so much money that truffles and bubbly were probably a daily part of their lives. It was no easy challenge to keep her chocolates unique and special enough to please such a clientele.

Sam walked through the short vestibule into the kitchen, immediately peeling off her coat at the balmy indoor temperature.

"I see what you mean about the heat," she said. "I'll be in the basement."

She walked through the packing room, where the open

windows kept the temperature bearable, but it was a battle between the radiator pumping more hot water through the system while icy January air came through. The thermostat was turned as low as it would go. Same situation in the back of the house, where a second thermostat near the storage room should have been keeping supplies in the sixty-degree range.

Sam opened the door to the basement and descended to face the boiler, the horror scene from *The Shining* flashing for one terrible moment through her head. What she faced was nothing like that—big relief. The benign-looking metal box hummed along, quite content to keep running, even though Sam had switched off the thermostats along her way.

Aside from the melted chocolate, the sheer amount of propane being used could soon bankrupt her. She pulled out her phone and tapped the number for the service guy. The last time she'd dealt with him was in the early autumn when she'd had him check the system in preparation for the upcoming winter.

"Sure, Ms. Sweet, I remember the place. Big old mansion out on Tyler Road, right?"

She described the problem.

"Are all the thermostats off now? Nothing at all turned on?"

She'd forgotten about the one upstairs. He stayed on the line while she climbed the two flights to get to the upper hallway. Turning the dial down on this one, she heard the soft hum of the boiler wind down and stop.

"Sounds like either you've got two bad thermostats or a couple faulty valves," he said when she reported what happened. "I'm in the middle of a job right now … let me see what I can do."

"I've got expensive chocolate that'll turn to syrup if I don't get this thing fixed." Not strictly true. They could shut the power completely off and risk things freezing. "I'll pay overtime, a bonus, whatever it takes."

At the magic words, he said, "Give me an hour."

Sam drummed her fingers on the phone's case after the call ended. An hour wouldn't mean the end of the world. They could play around with opening and closing windows, turning the upstairs thermostat on and off, any number of ways to make the situation workable for the short term. She hoped and prayed he would have any necessary parts with him; this solution wouldn't be a good one if they had to wait days for something to be shipped.

She went back to the kitchen and reported. The girls who'd been packing chocolates in the on-again, off-again temperatures weren't thrilled that there wasn't an immediate fix, but Benjie showed his compassion as a manager by getting in there with them and setting a quick pace. While the other two chocolatiers continued forming delicate truffles, Sam went into the storeroom and took inventory. Packaging supplies were once again running low, so she placed an order for more, along with shipping boxes and tape.

The boiler guy, Hal, showed up thirty minutes later than he'd estimated. The good news was, after taking a look and commenting over the age of the heating system, he did have valves that would work.

"They're not the originals for this model. Nothing's probably original on this old baby," he joked. "But the beauty of this older equipment is that things were made generic. You could interchange parts and such. Not like the new systems today where the wrong computer chip just won't do."

While he took panels off and pulled a hefty looking wrench from his toolbox, Sam sneaked a glance at her watch. Yikes. She'd promised delivery of that wedding cake fifteen minutes from now. She left Hal wrenching away and told him to leave his invoice with Benjie. She would drop a check by his shop tomorrow.

Back at Sweet's Sweets, Sam washed her hands and started placing the full-blown roses strategically on the cake. Thank goodness she'd made them in advance. This day hadn't exactly offered a spare moment. Rechecking the address of the wedding venue, she got Julio's help to set the cake in her van, and off she went.

Her destination was a block off the plaza, only a couple of streets away from her best friend Zoë's B&B. She hadn't seen Zoë in more than two weeks, and she realized her chum's birthday was tomorrow.

Okay, Sam, get your head organized here. Can't let constant work get in the way of friendships and a semblance of a social life. In the past, she would have planned a nice dinner at home with cake and gifts but looking ahead she knew it wasn't going to happen this time. A restaurant lunch and a gift would have to suffice. She pulled up to the back entrance of the small inn where the cake was due, tapped at the kitchen door and checked out the banquet room before loading the cake onto a wheeled cart and taking it inside.

Ten minutes later, that obligation out of the way, she sat in the van and phoned Zoë to suggest the lunch.

"Sam, you're working too hard. Remember, Darryl and I invited you and Beau here for dinner tomorrow night? I mean, lunch out is always nice, but Darryl's already got a rack of ribs marinating and he even pulled out the grill."

"Oh, god, Zoë. You're right—I *am* working too hard.

My brain's been mush this week. Forgive me."

"Hon, there's nothing to forgive. As long as you show up around six, it'll be great. Although, if you want to bring along a little something from your bakery case, I'm always good with that."

They both laughed. Sam knew she would put Zoë's birthday cake at the top of the order stack for the morning, and she would make her friend something perfect. She would just have to think of what that might be. Now, for a gift.

One of Sam's favorite shops on the plaza carried a variety of jewelry and accessories, so she headed that way. Zoë's taste went toward beads and natural-fiber items, and Sam was certain she remembered seeing those styles at Clarice's. A small bell over the front door chimed when she walked in.

Clarice, the owner, was standing behind a display case counting little square jewelry boxes. She greeted Sam with a tight smile. "I swear, I'm going to have to put these inside the case. A couple more have disappeared."

"And it's not even tourist season," Sam said.

"Yeah. Usually it *is* the tourists who help themselves. I know most of my regulars and they'd be too embarrassed to pilfer something, right under my nose."

Sam had spied a metal tree-shaped display with beaded necklaces hanging from it, but she glanced down to see what was in the small boxes Clarice was fiddling with. Each one held a delicate gold chain with an emblem of an astrological sign. She'd seen these before—where?

Jen. A picture flashed in front of her. Jen, holding up a necklace identical to these. She'd said Missy Malone gave it to her. And that wasn't the only time Missy had shown up with little gifts. The day after their first meeting, Missy had given Jen and Sam carved stone trinkets. She glanced around the shop and saw similar ones—it surely must be the work of the same artist.

A thread of distrust wound its way through her.

Chapter 15

Beau had worked late the previous evening and they'd barely exchanged an I'm-so-tired greeting before they headed to bed and fell instantly asleep. Sam had dreams of forgetting Zoë's birthday and rushing around the bakery near closing time in search of a cake. When she awoke at four-thirty, she took it as a sign she'd better get an early start on the day. She tiptoed around the bedroom, getting ready, going downstairs, where she left Beau a note beside the coffee maker, suggesting it would be nice if they could both break away for lunch together.

She parked in the alley behind her shop and was thumbing through the keys on her ring when Julio came rolling up on his Harley. They'd had the conversation more than once—Sam offering him a ride on winter days when he arrived looking half covered in frost. He always declined, and she'd already learned that he didn't talk about his home life or personal circumstances. He swung his leg slowly over the seat and tried not to look as if his legs wouldn't straighten. Sam looked away and busied herself opening the back door and turning on the lights.

Julio greeted her with his customary half smile, then each turned to the earliest-morning chores—he turned on the bake oven, she headed for the front to brew the first pot of coffee. He was measuring flour and butter into the Hobart's big bowl when she returned.

By the time the door opened again and Becky's cheerful face appeared, Sam had reviewed the orders in her basket, and was online at their wholesaler's site to place an order for flavorings and colors that were running a bit low.

"Hey, look at that tan!" Sam commented when Becky slipped off her jacket. "You guys had a great time?"

"Mexico was wonderful. Simple flight, easy to get to the condo we rented, and the kids had a blast."

"I'd say you spent a little beach time yourself. How did Don like it?"

Becky blushed slightly as she admitted how they sneaked back to the room for a while when their sons got busy building a huge sand castle with some other American kids they'd met.

"Hey, a second honeymoon never hurt anyone."

"It was nice, but I'm ready to get back to work. I forget how non-stop the kids can be, especially when they're all wound up with excitement."

Sam handed her the entire sheaf of order forms.

"This isn't so bad," Becky said, studying them. "A lot of these aren't due until later in the week, right?"

"I won't work you to death your first day back. You'd probably head for Mexico again and just stay there."

Becky laughed. "Little chance of that. I'd miss you guys too much."

"I've got a personal order to work on," Sam told her. "It's Zoë's birthday and I'd nearly forgotten about it. Any ideas for a knockout design she'd love?"

Becky pursed her lips. "Well, she loves gardening, and since it's winter she could be missing her flowers. Some version of our flowerpot design might work."

Sam nodded slowly, but she remembered making the flowerpot cake for Zoë last year. "It should be a little different ... I saw a wedding cake in a design magazine awhile back. Sort of rustic with woodsy flowers and pine tree elements, plus some little woodland creatures. I'll think about that. Meanwhile, the cake has to be chocolate, Zoë's very favorite. Julio, do we have a couple of eight-inch layers with the 80% cacao?"

"I baked some of those yesterday," he said. "In the fridge."

"She'll love it," Becky said as she tied her apron around her waist.

Sam located the magazine with the rustic cake designs and figured out what she would do. The cake would look like a slice of a sawed log. Around the sides, she would create the appearance of bark with decorative chocolate; the top would be iced in light tan, with circles piped to represent the tree rings. Then she could use chocolate to shape a squirrel and a baby rabbit. She set to work on the little critters while Becky started with the most difficult of her orders for the week, a five-tier wedding cake.

Sam found herself in her decorating zone as she added

small details—a rustic branch made from edible chocolate and slender pine needles of hardened sugar, which had to be handled very gingerly with tweezers. Wood roses and delicate pastel columbine came together under her skilled hands as she formed the petals and hung each flower upside down to harden before it could be placed on the cake. When her phone rang, it startled her.

"Did a very pretty lady leave me a note with a lunch invitation?" Beau asked.

"Hey, is it already—?" She glanced at the clock above the stove and saw it was after twelve. She'd barely been conscious of the fact that Julio had taken his lunch break already, and Becky was nibbling a sandwich as she piped roses for a birthday cake.

"Can you get away?" he asked. "I've got thirty minutes if I'm lucky, and you're the one I want to spend it with."

Well, who could turn down an invitation like that? They agreed to meet at the deli across the street from the sheriff's department. Beau would walk over and place their orders while Sam washed icing from her hands and got out the door. When she walked into Bert's Place ten minutes later, a steaming bowl of tortilla soup awaited.

"Glad you put in your note that we were invited out for ribs tonight so I knew to order a light lunch," he said, after placing a kiss on her cheek.

"This is perfect." Sam tore a flour tortilla in half and filled him in on her surprise idea for Zoë's birthday cake. "You seem very distracted, hon. What's going on?"

"That traffic fatality a few days ago—well, now it's looking like a murder."

Her spoon clattered against the side of her bowl. "What?"

"Yeah. I have almost no clues to go on, so all I can

think to do is start tracking through the victim's life and see what comes up."

"Tell me whatever you can. I'll be glad to help."

"Percy Lukinger is his name, he'd been in Taos about four months, no job records or employment information. I'm looking for bank records to see if he got a disability income or retirement of some sort, although he wasn't really old enough for the typical pension."

"Maybe he won a lottery or a lawsuit or was extremely lucky at gambling?"

"It's a good idea to look at all those possibilities. He didn't live the lifestyle of someone with vast wealth—had a little adobe two-bedroom rental, and drove a ten-year-old Mitsubishi. I haven't come across anything yet that points to found-money, but you never know."

"A lot of millionaires live quiet lives under the radar," she said.

"Sure—people who work hard, save money, invest well. But this guy seems too transient for that. And those quick winners usually take their jackpot and blow it all quickly, living high and flashing it around. Of course, maybe he did that already and we caught up with him at the end of the cash." He set his spoon down and wiped his mouth with a napkin. "Whatever the story, I still have to figure out who killed him."

"Any idea where to start?"

"None. But there's always a trail of some kind. I feel like I'm stretching my muscles on this one, but I *will* find the answers."

Sam smiled at her husband. If there was one thing she'd learned about Beau in their few years together, it was that this guy was sharp and he didn't give up.

Chapter 16

Beau gave Sam a kiss when they parted outside the deli and watched her get into her bakery van. His commute was to walk across the street. He punched in the digital code for the back door into the squad room. Until the shift change in an hour it would be fairly quiet, so he headed for his desk and stared at the file and evidence bags he'd locked in his office.

Examining the autopsy photos, he couldn't spot the injection site the toxicology expert had told him about, even though he knew where to look. It was amazing the medical investigator had found it. Whoever administered the drug either knew precisely what they were doing or got extremely lucky. Just not lucky enough to go undetected.

The physical evidence was in. All he could do was to

look for the killer, and he would have to dig into Lukinger's life to find answers. It always went back to the central three objectives: Who out there in the world had motive, means, and opportunity to murder Percy Lukinger? So far, Beau didn't know enough about the victim or his recent movements to hazard a guess at any answers.

He got his computer to wake up and checked email. Winston Reed had said he was emailing some documents. Sure enough, his secure mailbox held several messages with attachments. He opened each one and studied it. On a yellow legal pad, he began making notes. By the time his deputies began gathering in the squad room for their afternoon briefing, he had assignments lined up for them.

Voices and the jangle of keys and equipment told him the day shift guys were coming back and the evening shift had begun to arrive. Beau stepped to the open doorway.

"I need everyone to stay a few extra minutes," he said.

He ignored groans from a couple of the men who'd already put in their eight hours. Too bad. It wasn't worth repeating the briefing again tomorrow. A murder case brought special demands and they all knew it. Updates would happen, like it or not.

Beau carried folders with him into the squad room and began tacking photos to the cork board on the north wall. The department was too small to have the luxury of a separate briefing room or a command center that could be assigned specifically to high-profile cases. As the board filled with additional information on Lukinger, less urgent cases would get squeezed to the edges. Every law enforcement officer on earth wished he could give full attention to every case, and all departments in the country wanted to solve every crime and tie up each loose end. But that didn't always happen—cases overlapped. The best he could do was to act upon the information he had as quickly as possible.

"Okay, gather around," he announced.

Desk chairs were pulled out and swiveled to face Beau. He began with the victim's name and the autopsy results, then filled them in with the little he had discovered at Lukinger's home.

"Now that this whole thing has become a top priority, I want a team out there to go over the property with a fine tooth comb. Just because I didn't spot anything at a glance doesn't mean it's not there. I don't care if it's a loose floorboard or a hidden panel somewhere, or an envelope taped to the bottom of a bathroom drawer ... Rico, I'm putting you on this one. Martinez and Salazar, you're with him. Get Lisa and her forensic kit and scour the house and the whole property. We want something—anything—that will tell us who disliked this guy enough to kill him."

Rico nodded and made notes on a pad.

"Travis, I've uploaded the file with Lukinger's fingerprints digitally scanned. I need you to run them through every national database. Maybe he's been in trouble in another jurisdiction and we can find an enemy out there somewhere."

Travis was his youngest deputy, but savvy about computers and up to date on the latest ways to gather information quickly. He liked digging through digital records and wouldn't gripe about it the way a couple of the older men would. Beau had assigned those tradition-minded guys to accompany Rico.

"There's a wife," he told them. "Travis, while the computer is chugging through fingerprint files, I need you to find background information on a Ramona Lukinger. From what I could tell, she doesn't live in the house on

Montaño Lane, but she has to live somewhere. His house here is pretty sparse so it could be Percy's important stuff is with her. Get an address and we'll pay the lady a visit."

The funeral home had said Ramona requested a small memorial service for Percy. Beau wanted to find out when that would be, and he planned to attend. Friends of the deceased would be of interest—enemies even more so.

He dismissed the men. Those going home for the night seemed relieved they'd not been pressed into working a double shift. Travis rubbed his hands together in anticipation and turned to his computer keyboard. While they waited for Lisa, the forensics technician, Rico's team gathered evidence bags, powerful flashlights, and latex gloves. Beau went back into his office and quickly sent the fingerprint file to his eager young computer expert.

A call to Sanchez Mortuary got Monica Sanchez on the line, and he asked whether the Lukinger service had been scheduled yet.

"Yes, I just spoke with Mrs. Lukinger," Monica told him. "She said it wouldn't be a large attendance, and our smallest chapel was available, so we've scheduled the memorial for five o'clock tomorrow afternoon."

"Thanks. Do you have her file handy? Could you give me Mrs. Lukinger's number and address?"

"I can look it up," she said. A half-minute passed. "Okay, here it is—it's fifty-four Montaño Lane, here in Taos."

Beau swallowed his disappointment. Clearly, Ramona Lukinger was keeping up the pretense that she and Percy lived together in that house. However, the phone number she'd given the funeral home was different from the one she'd given the OMI's office. He thanked Monica for the information and hung up.

He started to dial Ramona's number but stopped part-way through the digits. Her caller ID would likely show the call coming from the Taos County Sheriff's Department, and he didn't want to alert her. His personal cell phone would show his name and, being an elected official, he might be recognized. It was much too easy for a suspect to ignore a phone call—making initial contact face-to-face would be better. He would have to think about the best approach. At least he had until the following afternoon to decide.

While Travis watched data flicker across his computer screen and the other deputies examined the adobe house he'd already searched, Beau felt a little at loose ends. Until they had further evidence, this was the lull before the storm, in a way.

"Sheriff?" Travis called out. "Want to take a look at this?"

Beau went to the deputy's desk for a look at the computer screen.

"There's a Lukinger in Albuquerque, but the names are Ron and Bobbie. Could be related?"

"I'll give a call." He jotted down the number. "Any hits on the fingerprints yet?"

Travis toggled to the screen where his query was still racing through the database. "It'll make a ping sound if there's a match."

Beau knew that—he was just becoming impatient. In his office, he dialed the number Travis had given him. The woman who answered sounded at least in her sixties.

"Mrs. Lukinger?"

"Speaking."

"This is Beau Cardwell, sheriff of Taos County."

"We already donated, just last week." She sounded

short and ready to hang up.

"Wait, it's not about a donation." Damn those organizations that called people about some group loosely connected to police work. "We're investigating a traffic accident up here near Taos, and I have some questions."

"Taos? Well, I sure as heck haven't been anywhere near Taos in a long time."

"That's fine. I'm actually looking for a Ramona Lukinger—is she related to you?"

"Ramona ... no, nobody named Ramona at this end of the Lukinger family."

"Or a Percy Lukinger—is that a relative?"

"Sorry, no."

He asked her to write down the department number in case her husband might know of someone or if either of them thought of some pertinent information later. It was a complete longshot, he knew.

His personal phone rang and Sam's picture appeared on the screen. The time showed 4:18.

"I haven't forgotten about dinner at Zoë's tonight," he said immediately.

She laughed. "I knew you wouldn't."

Actually, he wouldn't admit it but a birthday dinner was a little low on his priority list right now. Still, he'd said he would go.

"I'm going to leave the bakery van here at the shop so Becky can deliver a cake on her way home. Can you come by here and pick me up?"

They discussed whether they would go home and change into civvies or just show up at Zoë's in their work clothes. Decided it would depend on whether each could get away from work within the next ninety minutes.

"Try to leave in an hour if you can, Beau. We've stood

up our friends a few too many times."

He assured her he would do his very best. Once the call ended, he decided to take his chances with Ramona Lukinger's cell phone. Worst case, she would hang up, but maybe by using the "wrapping up a few loose ends on the car crash" excuse she would agree to see him.

He was surprised when she answered, more surprised when she didn't brush him off after he introduced himself. She seemed friendly and agreed to stop by the office first thing in the morning.

Chapter 17

Beau was on his phone when Sam set Zoë's birthday cake on the back seat of his cruiser and climbed in the front.

"Okay. Got it." He jotted notes in his small pocket notebook. "Start tracking those, see if any have local addresses."

She sat patiently, wondering how long the call would go on; they had thirty minutes to get home and change clothes before turning around and coming back into town for Zoë's birthday dinner. She'd just learned that Kelly and her boyfriend Scott were also invited, and a purely social evening suddenly sounded like great fun after the harried week she'd spent.

Beau ended his call and turned toward her. "Sorry,

darlin', but it looks like we may have just caught a break in this case."

"A good one?"

"Yeah. Travis got more than one hit on the fingerprints of our victim. Turns out he's been arrested in several jurisdictions—under several different names." His eyes had a sparkle that hadn't been there the past couple of days, and he handed her the notebook while he put the SUV in gear.

Sam read his precise block lettering: John P. Lukinger, Percival Johns, Johnny Luck.

"Johnny Luck?" She felt a chuckle building inside her.

"Yeah, that one was in New York where he was apparently running a street game of three-card Monte."

"That's a con game, right?"

"Yeah, all the charges we've found were con games. He's got long rap sheets in New York, New Jersey, and Southern California."

"So … now there are almost an infinite number of people with motives to be angry at this guy."

"That's what I'm thinking." He'd taken the back route northward, toward home. "This morning I was scraping around for a motive and now suddenly I have a bunch."

"But to kill a guy over losing some cash in a street card game?"

He sent an indulgent smile her way. "There's got to be more to it than that, but I feel like this is just the outer layer of a very complicated onion that I'm going to have to peel away."

He tapped the face of his phone to make a hands-free call and soon had his senior deputy, Rico, on the line. Beau repeated the aliases Percy Lukinger had used, telling Rico to have the search team look for anything in connection to those names.

Sam saw his lingering glance when they passed Civic Plaza Drive and knew she'd be lucky to have ten percent of his attention tonight at the birthday party. He ended the call to Rico when they turned onto the final stretch for home, and she could tell his mind was zipping along at a million thoughts a second. Although she'd been involved in several of his cases and always found it intriguing to know what was going on, right now it was best to simply let him mull things through.

At home, she left Zoë's cake and gift in the cruiser while she raced through the routine of feeding the dogs their evening meal and turning on some lights around the house. A quick swipe of the washcloth took off the dusting of powdered sugar she always brought home on her face and arms. While Beau unburdened himself of his belt full of lawman gear and searched the closet for a casual shirt, she slipped into the dress slacks and cashmere sweater she'd set out for herself that morning. In under fifteen minutes they were ready to head to Zoë and Darryl's place.

Sam felt her mood lighten during the drive. Becky was back at work, which helped tremendously, the furnace situation at the chocolate factory had been repaired, and although the break-in house loomed as a project to finish, she refused to think about it until she absolutely had to. When they pulled into the driveway at Zoë's, she spotted Scott's Subaru.

Her daughter had met this wonderful man last year. A history professor at the Taos UNM campus, Scott Porter was interesting and, best of all, level-headed and stable—a first in Kelly's love life. Their happy relationship was another cause for Sam's peace of mind.

The smell of barbeque sauce reached them before the back door had opened, and Zoë greeted them, looking radiant in one of her standard long gypsy skirts and a gauzy top. Her graying hair was pulled back into a braid that reached halfway down her back, and she held a glass of wine in one hand.

"That barbeque smells good enough to make my knees weak," Beau said with a grin toward Darryl. "I didn't realize how hungry I was."

Sam seconded the sentiment as she handed the cake box to Zoë and they shed their coats. The big round kitchen table was set for six, with a bright Mexican-blanket tablecloth and vivid cloth napkins to match. Talavera plates shone at each setting and glassware sparkled from the light of slender candles in the center of the table. Sam added the small wrapped box containing the beaded necklace to the stack of gifts on the sideboard.

Darryl carried a huge pan covered in foil to the table and set it in the middle. Bowls of coleslaw, veggies and a basket of cornbread already awaited. He turned to Sam, still wearing his monster oven mitts, and gave her one of his standard teddy-bear hugs.

"Good thing everyone's hungry," he said. "This is enough to feed the army."

"Or our B&B guests for another solid week," Zoë added.

"Huh-uh," said Darryl. "They get your breakfast burritos and homemade muffins. Ribs—these are mine."

Sam noticed Kelly and Scott hanging to the side a bit as Darryl and Zoë gave the table a final scan and asked each other if everything had been set out.

"What's with you two?" she chided her daughter. "You look like you're keeping a big secret."

The minute she said it, her breath caught and she glanced at Kelly's stomach.

"No! It's not that, Mom," Kelly said. "Not yet."

Realizing everyone in the room had stopped to stare, Kelly blushed clear to the roots of her cinnamon-colored curls. Scott ushered them toward the table and raised his wineglass. "I have the honor of telling you that this very beautiful woman has accepted my proposal."

"We're engaged!" Kelly squealed. She held out her hand and flashed a diamond solitaire.

Chapter 18

"Well, the evening sure took a turn," Sam said, smiling and leaning back in her seat in the cruiser.

"Yeah, it did," Beau agreed.

Once the word *wedding* had escaped Sam's lips, the three women had gone into some kind of feminine planning frenzy. Words like bridesmaids, wedding gown, venue, and cake bounced around the room like ping-pong balls. He didn't recall Sam getting this worked up over their own marriage ceremony. Zoë didn't seem the least bit upset that her birthday celebration had been usurped, although Kelly kept saying how she'd planned to hold on to the news until later, for that reason.

At one point, Beau had received a call from Rico, which he excused himself to take in another room. The investigative team had made no big discoveries at the Lukinger home—no surprise, really—and Rico said the few items they'd picked up were now bagged as evidence and would be ready for Beau in the morning. Lisa had taken fingerprints from a variety of surfaces and bagged hair brushes and toothbrushes from the bathroom so they could establish a chain of evidence proving the home was the residence of the dead man. It was all they could accomplish tonight, and Beau told Rico to release the other deputies for routine calls, to get some sleep, and to be ready to review all the evidence together in the morning. He also had the appointment with Ramona Lukinger to look forward to.

He tossed and turned in bed that night, suspecting Sam was doing the same. The rich food and news of Kelly's engagement no doubt accounted for his wife's restless night; his unrest had to be chalked up to the frustrating lack of clues in his new case. By four a.m. he'd given up on sleep. Dressed in flannel-lined jeans, and several layers of shirts and jackets, he walked the crackling, frost-covered path to the barn. Scooping oats for the horses and talking to them, feeling their hot breath on his hands brought the familiarity of routine to his morning. He chopped the layer of ice from the water trough, performing his duties quickly.

The sky was black and glittered with the reassuring silver pinpricks of stars. Orion had traveled across the sky and the Big Dipper sat at its early morning angle beneath the North Star. He breathed deeply, feeling the below-zero air freeze the moisture in his nose, tickling the tiny hairs there; on the exhale, his warm breath unfrosted them. He listened to the silence of the early morning, disturbed only by the sound of a single vehicle somewhere on the road more than a mile away.

A light came on upstairs and he knew Sam would be starting another early morning at the bakery. He missed having her input on his cases since she'd opened the chocolate factory. Her two separate-but-related businesses kept her running, and he wondered if she wasn't stretching herself too thin. The upside, as she'd reminded him on several occasions, was that the contract with the travel company was helping to pad their retirement fund quite nicely.

Retirement. What would that be like?

No picture came into his head—no vision of a fishing pole and riverbank, no golf clubs, no television binges of old Westerns. If anything, he wouldn't mind tackling the library of unread books that lined the living room walls. Travel held some appeal, but only if Sam hung up her apron at the same time and they found places to explore together. He shook off the thought. He was a long way from being ready to turn in his badge.

The house felt warm, as it always did after the brisk outside air, and he quickly shed his heavy coat and fleece vest. The scent of Sam's shampoo came wafting down the stairs. He could hear her moving around in the bedroom. The coffee machine had already brewed a pot, thanks to the timer.

"Sam, would you be up for some bacon and eggs if I cook them?" he called out.

Her face appeared at the doorway. "I'd better not today, honey. It's already five."

He sighed. No point getting grease on the stove, messing up several pans, and clogging his arteries. He spooned oatmeal into a bowl, added water, and put it into the microwave. Sam bustled into the kitchen as the timer dinged.

"Hey, handsome," she said, her smile warming him as always. "I'm surprised you aren't already at your desk, considering what you said about the new developments with your case yesterday."

"I'll be there before you know it." He pulled her into his arms and they kissed. "Unless we both want to go back upstairs and start the morning in a more fun way."

She laughed. "Umm, that would be *so* nice."

But neither of them made a move toward the bedroom. They had definitely settled into routine married life.

"I don't have to dash out right this minute," she said, pulling two mugs from the cupboard and filling both from the carafe. She had read his thoughts.

"So, anything new on your case overnight?" she asked, while he took his oatmeal from the micro and set it on the table.

"Nothing. Didn't really expect it though." The coffee was on the bitter side and he added a spoonful of sugar. "I'm hoping to talk with the widow this morning. Finally reached her and she agreed to come by my office."

"You said there were a ton of unanswered questions?"

"We basically know nothing about this Percy Lukinger's life, so there's nothing to go on. We believe the murder was premeditated—as opposed to accidental or done in the heat of a fight. Usually, there's either something at the scene of the crime, some witnesses who can tell us what was going on in the victim's life, or some clues in their personal belongings. I sent deputies to the home yesterday. Today I'll have forensics go through the vehicle with a magnifying glass, but I don't hold much hope. I looked through it at the time of the accident and didn't find anything."

Sam gave him a sympathetic look, but he could tell she was eager to get moving. No doubt some new cocoa emergency. He pushed back the thought that her work was frivolous compared to law enforcement—that wasn't fair.

He kissed her goodbye and watched her red truck pull down the driveway, but his mind was quickly back on his case as he went upstairs to put on his uniform. Twenty-five minutes later he was pulling into the parking lot at the department. His first stop was the evidence locker, where Rico and his team should have left everything they found at the Lukinger home.

Beau wanted to go through it all in preparation for his meeting with Ramona Lukinger. She had agreed to come by the station, but only said 'first thing in the morning.' Now he was wishing he'd been a little more firm in setting an exact appointment.

Now that the case went beyond a file-folder's worth of reports and photos, a box had been created with the label 'Lukinger, P.' and the date of the man's death. Beau carried it to his desk and opened the lid. He was pleased to see Lisa had left documentation showing she'd taken hairs and toothbrushes to have evaluated for DNA. It was becoming standard procedure to test and document everything. There was no telling how the case would eventually go, who their suspects would be, what type of denial defense those suspects would present in court. Always good to have their evidence lined up well before the prosecutor asked for it.

He pulled out the small collection of plastic bags, disappointed but not surprised that there wasn't more to show for two searches of the house. A business card, dingy and frayed at the edges, a couple of lottery tickets, a gas receipt dated the previous October. The Player's Club card from the Indian casino might turn out to be valuable. If Percy was a regular gambler, patterns of his casino habits might provide clues. Beneath the paper items his fingers encountered a small, hard nugget.

When he picked up the tiny plastic bag holding it, he saw what appeared to be a diamond. Beau felt its contours then held the bag to the light. He knew almost nothing about gemstones, but guessed this one must be at least two or three carats in size.

"I found that loose in a dresser drawer, jammed into the corner." Rico's voice startled Beau.

"Hey. Didn't realize you were here yet." He held up the baggie. "You think this is real?"

"Doesn't make any sense to me, boss. A diamond that big thrown into a drawer?"

"Yeah, you're right."

Beau decided he would take the stone by a jeweler, though, just for verification. He looked at the diamond's many small surfaces—too small to read a fingerprint from, for sure, although he wished it were possible. For all they knew, the stone had been in that dresser for years, through many tenants in the house, maybe even a garage sale or flea market where Charles Romero purchased the furnishings for the rental. A heartbroken woman may have been wondering, for years, whatever happened to the precious stone from her ring.

"The rest of those things, the tickets and that casino card, I found those in the pocket of a jacket hanging in the closet," Rico said, breaking Beau's wandering train of thought.

Beau set the stone aside and picked up the bag with the business card and receipts. "Grant Mangle. Grant Mangle Enterprises, Inc. Doesn't tell us a whole lot."

"The card is pretty worn," Rico said. "Maybe Lukinger carried it around for a long time?"

"Could be. It's worth a call. See if you can reach Mr.

Mangle and find out how he knows Percy Lukinger." He handed the bag to Rico.

Alone in his office, Beau glanced at his watch. The widow Ramona should be showing up any time now. He picked up his desk phone and told the front desk officer to buzz him the minute she arrived. While he waited, he could check a few other facts on his own. He picked up the casino card.

It took a few minutes to track down the casino's security chief, after being told the manager of the establishment only worked nights. Not a problem, Beau assured himself. Security could likely answer his questions. The man who came on the line introduced himself as George Stennis.

"We're investigating a death," Beau told him, "and we think the man carried one of your Player's Club cards. If I give you the number, can you verify that for me?"

"Sure thing."

Stennis came back with a name—Johnny Luck. One of Percy's aliases.

"Sounds like a made-up name to me," Beau said. "Do you require ID when you issue these cards?"

"Not to get the card. If somebody wins a big jackpot, something we have to report to the IRS, then yeah, we get identification, social security number, the whole bit. People have funny beliefs about gambling, and it isn't uncommon at all for them to choose a name they think will be lucky."

"Can you trace the gambling habits of a customer through this card?"

"Oh, yeah, that's the whole point. We want to know how often they visit, how much they wager, and who our high rollers are."

"Can you tell me the last time Mr. *Luck* used his card?"

"One minute ..." Computer keys tapped in the back-

ground. "Looks like he got the card back in October …
Then he gambled pretty steady and was in here quite a
bit in December." A chuckle. "Lots of people think they'll
earn their Christmas spending money at the slot machines.
Hmm … New Year's Eve was the last time he was here."

More than two weeks ago. "No activity at all since
then?"

"Nada."

"Okay, thanks." Beau was about to hang up when he
thought of something else. "How long do you keep your
security videos?"

"Thirty days. Anybody with a dispute over his winnings
usually raises a question right away, but sometimes
he'll come back later. But, if we suspect employees of
shenanigans, we'll keep watch on them a while, then make
copies of certain tapes that might prove a legal case against
them."

"I need you to hang on to the tapes from the dates
Johnny Luck was there."

"Uh, that would be up to the manager."

"I can get a subpoena." He hoped he could. "Or you
could just do me this favor until I have a chance to come
by there and review them."

"You realize we've already erased the ones from early
December."

Beau knew he would have to take his chances. "I'll
come out there this afternoon."

By anyone's clock it was now midmorning and he
hadn't heard a peep from Mrs. Lukinger. He found her
number again in his notebook and dialed.

"Did you forget our appointment this morning?" he
asked when she answered. "If it's more convenient, I can
come to your place."

"Sorry, Sheriff, today's not going to work for me."

"When—?" He realized the line was dead.

Chapter 19

Sam looked up from the elaborate, ruffled hydrangeas she was creating for a cake, stretched her shoulders, and decided a cup of tea was what she needed. She'd been working steadily at the multi-toned flowers for more than two hours and every part of her body felt stiff. Kelly had come through before her workday began at Puppy Chic, flashing her ring and her news to the girls in the bakery.

By the sounds of voices from the sales room, Sam suspected her daughter was still around. She draped a sheet of plastic over the mound of sugar paste she'd been working with and walked toward the doorway, stretching her arms, rolling her neck and shoulders.

"… since my husband's in the business. Really. He'll get you a great deal on it."

Sam took in the little tableau. Jen behind the counter, Missy facing the door where Kelly stood with one hand on the knob. The statement had clearly come from Missy, most likely directed toward Kelly.

"What business is that?" Sam asked, sending a little smile toward the three younger women.

"Oh, hi, Sam. Jewelry. I was just telling Kelly when it comes time to get Scott's wedding band, we could get her a good deal. Too bad I didn't know you guys sooner. Scott could have saved a bundle on your diamond."

What kind of thing was that to say to a newly engaged woman? Sam tried for what she hoped was a reassuring look toward her daughter. Kelly seemed to laugh it off, though. She gave a tiny wave to the rest of them and breezed out the door.

Sam went to the beverage bar and made herself a cup of tea, stifling the urge to say anything. Missy was actually becoming a regular customer, as evidenced by her coat draped over one of the bistro chairs. A plate with the remains of crumb cake, a crumpled napkin, and an empty mug with a pink lipstick mark on the rim sat on the table. Sam hoped Missy was paying for her daily indulgences, that Jen wasn't footing the bill just to have a friend to chat with each morning.

"Sam, how is your husband's newest case going? Jen tells me it's a murder case?"

Sam shot Jen a look. Beau's work was not to be discussed casually in the bakery, not to mention Jen truly didn't know anything about it beyond what she might read in the local paper.

Almost reading her boss's thoughts, Jen sputtered. "Sam, I didn't—"

"That's true," Missy said, covering quickly. "I'd heard

something about it elsewhere, I guess. I'm just so fascinated by police work."

"Yeah, I hear you're going to school for your forensic sciences degree?" Sam took a step closer.

"Oh, actually not. I'm going to start writing crime novels." She moved toward the bistro table and gathered her dirty dishes.

"Crime novels. Has writing been an interest of yours for a long time?"

"Um, sort of. I mean, I haven't actually studied it or anything. I just thought—well, look at how much money James Patterson makes. It wouldn't be a bad career choice."

Jen watched the exchange, frozen like a baby deer. She seemed relieved when the phone rang and hastened to answer it.

"Sam, it's Mr. Bookman," she said.

Sam couldn't ignore her biggest customer, but she locked eyes with Missy an additional half a minute. The blonde picked up her coat, suddenly remembering she had to be somewhere. Sam went to the kitchen and her desk to take the call.

Stan Bookman was bubbling with a concept for a new marketing campaign featuring her chocolates, and it was all Sam could do to scribble down the ideas as quickly as the words poured out of him. After a couple of minutes, she caught his infectious enthusiasm, letting thoughts of the irritating conversation with Missy Malone slip away. By the time he hung up, Sam had taken two pages of notes about custom chocolates for his new 'travel the world' campaign.

Her cup of tea had become chilly and she dumped it in the kitchen sink, mulling over everything Bookman had said. Jen walked in, heading for the rack where Julio had just set a tray of freshly iced mocha-cappuccino brownies.

"Sam, I hope Missy didn't overstep—"

"Do you trust her?" Sam asked. "I mean, it seems like a different story every time she's here. Is she making this stuff up as she goes, or does she just not know what she wants to do with her life?"

Jen shrugged. "I honestly don't know. She just seems to want a friend to talk to."

"Maybe that's all it is. But it seems weird, you know. She's talked about this husband who's so successful and rich. They have two homes, they travel a lot. Seems strange her choice of hangouts is a small-town bakery."

"Yeah, I've thought that too. I don't know … as long as she buys something every time she comes in, I'm not complaining." Jen picked up the brownie tray and turned toward the sales room.

With hydrangeas to finish and Stan Bookman's call still running through her mind, Sam had more important things to think about than whom Jen chose to chat with during the day. She went back to her sugar paste flowers. By noon, three large hydrangeas in shades of blue, pink and lavender topped the four-tier wedding cake on which Becky had draped fondant and pressed a quilted pattern, inset with hundreds of candy pearls. They set the cake into the fridge to await delivery later in the afternoon, and Sam decided she was starving.

A quick call to Beau didn't net a lunch date. He was headed to the casino, and she couldn't figure out what that would be about. With a hundred things to think about, maybe it was better she didn't add a whole new conversation to the melee that was going on inside her head already. She asked if the others wanted anything; they all declined, so she grabbed her coat and went out the back door. McDonald's was closest. When she saw the length of the drive-thru line, she parked in the lot and dashed inside.

The woman at the head of the line started adding stipulations to her order—no pickles, mayo instead of ketchup—and Sam saw this dragging out for a while. But the clerk was courteous and finally figured it out. When the woman turned, Sam knew it was a familiar face. Most likely a bakery customer, but Sam couldn't quite place her. She smiled.

"I know you, don't I?" the lady said as she stepped to the side to wait for her food. "Don't tell me."

Sam wanted to say "Sweet's Sweets" but she didn't.

"My father's neighbor. No … you were *working* at the house next door."

Dolores Zuckerman. The name clicked into place.

"Yes. How is your father doing? Any luck with the retirement home idea?"

Dolores rolled her eyes. "Not a bit. I'm putting it on the back burner for a while. His wife has been around a bit more these past few days, and he seems happy enough."

Two people had finished placing their orders and it was Sam's turn. When she turned around after requesting chicken nuggets, Dolores Zuckerman was on her way out the door. Just as well. Sam hadn't really wanted to linger over a conversation about an irascible old man and the dynamics with the daughter who was trying to control his life.

She decided to head for the Victorian, where she could see how the factory crew was getting along and also to check her inventory of chocolate molds. She would need a variety of new designs for Mr. Bookman's big plans.

Chapter 20

Few people defied a lawman with as much cheery disdain as Ramona Lukinger, Beau thought as he stewed over the brush-off from Percy's widow. He debated calling back—useless—she would simply not pick up. He missed the old days of landlines. You didn't always catch a person at home or work, but when you did you knew where she was.

Well, he knew where Ramona would be at five o'clock this afternoon. Monica Sanchez had told him that's when Percy's memorial service was scheduled. He glanced into the squad room where Rico was sitting at his desk, seemingly deep in thought.

"Any luck reaching the guy on the business card?" Beau asked.

"Grant Mangle? Yeah. He answered. Claimed he didn't remember any Percy Lukinger. Hung up before I had the chance to run the other aliases by him. It really felt like he was dodging me."

"There's an address on the card, right?"

Rico picked up the card and nodded.

"Okay then, let's go." Now *this* was what law enforcement should be like.

Grant Mangle Enterprises, Inc., occupied a corner slot in a strip center that also housed a satellite TV service, an insurance agency, and a small jewelry store. The latter reminded Beau of his other errand, and he patted his shirt pocket to be sure he'd carried the diamond with him. Nothing about the signage on Mangle's office specifically stated the nature of his business, but small clues hinted that it had something to do with real estate. Through large windows, he saw two desks in the small room, which seemed to be the sum total of the operation; a man sat at one. His focus was on the computer screen in front of him. The other desk might have belonged to a receptionist, but he or she was not present.

"Grant Mangle?" Beau asked, as soon as he and Rico walked in.

The man was in his late forties with dark brown hair cut very short, blue eyes, and a deep crease between his thick eyebrows. He automatically nodded before looking up to realize who had asked. When he saw the uniforms, his hands fidgeted nervously over the items on his desk.

"My deputy here called awhile ago but he seemed to have gotten cut off. We thought you might remember things a little better if we dropped by." It was said with a smile, but Beau knew the man received his message.

Mangle put on a salesman's smile and stood to shake

their hands. He stood almost six feet tall and was slim for his height. "What can I do for you, Sheriff?"

"Rico asked whether you know a Percy Lukinger."

"No, I'm afraid that doesn't ring a bell. I told you that, deputy."

"What he didn't get the chance to ask was if you might know a couple of other names." From his folder, Beau pulled out the driver's license photo of their victim.

"Well, you know how bad license pictures are. A person never really looks the same," Mangle said with a weak little smile.

"Take a close look. Maybe John Lukinger is how you knew him? Or Percival Johns, or Johnny Luck?"

"John something. Yeah, I think that's the one." Mangle handed the photocopy back to Beau.

"He had your business card in his pocket. What's the nature of your business anyway?"

"Oh. Well, we handle property rentals. I know the office seems small, but ninety-nine percent of what we do is online. All records are on computer, you know, so it doesn't take a large staff to maintain the accounts. Independent contractors handle all the maintenance. We basically just receive and disburse rental income to the property owners."

"And John Lukinger was a customer?"

Mangle glanced toward his computer, obviously knowing any such claim could be verified.

"No, not yet. He, uh … he wanted information about our services and such. We talked for a few minutes and I gave him my card. That's all it was."

"When was this?"

"Whew—maybe six months ago?"

"You must talk to a lot of people in the course of a month, and yet you remember this one. So, am I to assume he came back, talked to you some more? Was he interested in renting, or did he have a property he wanted you to manage for him?"

Again, a sideways glance toward the computer. A bunch of mental ping-pong as Mangle decided what his story would be.

"Okay, I gotta admit I really don't remember him all that well. I swear, I'm sure he only came in the one time. Maybe twice at most. We never did any business."

A lot of protesting. The sheen of sweat on the man's upper lip told Beau there was more to the story.

"Okay, thanks, Mr. Mangle. We'll be back in touch if we have any other questions. If you remember anything more, you can always call us." Beau handed over one of his cards.

Outside in the chilly air, Beau and Rico stood in sight for a couple minutes.

"He's totally full of it," Rico said.

"Yeah. Let's give him a little something to sweat about." Beau stared at the plate glass windows fronting Mangle's office. The man had not gone back to his seat. "Come on."

He and Rico walked to the business next door, the satellite TV place, and he made a show of having Percy Lukinger's photo in hand. The clerk at the front desk looked about nineteen and the eagerness with which he greeted them told Beau the young guy probably earned most of his pay through commissions. When he showed the photo of Lukinger, it drew a blank look.

"Sorry, I've only worked here a couple weeks, so I'm not really familiar with the customers yet."

Beau hadn't actually expected recognition. He spent a few more minutes asking about satellite dish plans, just enough time to really make the guy next door sweat if he had reason to. When the lawmen walked back out to the cruiser, he saw through the window that Mangle was on the phone at his desk, speaking rather intently to someone.

"I'm going to walk down to the little jewelry store at the corner," he told Rico. "Watch Mangle and see if he makes any moves. I shouldn't be long."

He left Rico to the warmth of the vehicle and headed toward the small jewelry shop. A sign on the window said "Certified Gemologist" so he figured he could get a quick answer to his question. He pulled the small plastic evidence bag from his pocket. The man who greeted him was in his fifties, with a thick head of gray hair and mellow brown eyes.

"I've got this piece of evidence in a case," Beau said. "Can you tell me if it's a real diamond or one of those synthetic ones?"

"Sure. I'll need to take it out of the plastic."

Beau removed the stone and handed it over. The man polished it with a cloth then carried it over to a machine that looked like a huge microscope. Setting the stone carefully in place, he stared down through an eyepiece.

"Nope, it's a cubic zirconia," he said, without looking up. "Nice one though. Nicely shaped and it has good sparkle. I can see where it could fool your average consumer."

He removed the stone from the clamps and handed it back to Beau.

"Sorry. I hope you haven't bought it for your wife."

"Nope. It's just another piece of evidence in a case. Say, is there any way to tell the age of this stone or where it came from?"

The gemologist just gave him a look and a tiny shake of his head.

Okay, it's probably a dead end, since we don't even know whether Percy knew the stone was in his dresser drawer, but it was worth a shot. He thanked the jeweler and left.

Back at the cruiser, Rico reported that when Grant Mangle noticed him sitting out there he ended his phone call and went into another room at the back of the office, probably the restroom. Beau started the SUV and drove around the side of the building where there was a narrow alley with a trash dumpster for each of the units. Each business had a hardy-looking steel door to the alley, but there was no sign Mangle had left. A Cadillac SUV was parked there. Since he hadn't locked his front door, most likely he was simply hiding out of sight until the officers went away.

"Let's check in at the station," Beau said. "I'll leave you there to go through the rest of those pieces of evidence, while I run to the casino to find out what I can about Percy's card. I'll be back in time to change out of uniform and attend the memorial service. You should probably come along."

The drive to the casino gave Beau a chance to touch base by phone with Sam. He invited her to go with him to the memorial service, but she begged off saying she had a lot going on at the chocolate factory. He didn't blame her. Although she took an interest in his cases, had in fact been deputized to actively help him on a few, her business needed her full attention in recent months.

He made the angular turn off Highway 64, taking the road to Taos Pueblo, coming to the casino a little over a mile down. The unprepossessing adobe-styled building could have passed for a large restaurant or small inn—

nothing like the establishments along the interstate, the tribes who brought in enough business to put up rambling five-story hotels and invest in flashy Vegas-style lighting. He pulled his cruiser under the portico, where simple red letters spelled out the fact this was a casino. Aside from the fabulous sunset, the most impressive thing about this one was the fact that it was a non-smoking facility.

Late afternoon looked like a busy time, he thought, as he walked through the main room, assaulted by the constant pinging and electronic clatter of the slot machines. George Stennis had told him to go to the cashier's cage and he would come right down.

Beau expected someone with the look of ex-military or ex-mobster, a man with an intimidating air, but Mr. Stennis came across much more like a giant, bald teddy bear. Six feet tall, with a wide middle as if there was a basketball under his shirt. He wore the casino's logo on the chest of his polo shirt, along with khaki pants and a pair of black Skechers.

They shook hands and Stennis motioned Beau to follow him into an alcove and through a doorway concealed by a poster for the headliner in the bar this week.

"Bet you thought I'd be armed," Stennis said. Before Beau could respond, he continued. "Our guys on the casino floor are, and the men who usher the daily take to the armored cars. Me, I'm just a computer guy, a desk jockey."

Beau had seen documentaries on the lengths to which casinos went to protect their business, which was ninety-nine percent cash and a prime target for cheaters and armed robbers. He pretty much knew what to expect when he walked into George Stennis's darkened roomful of video monitors, but the security man was proud of their setup and wanted to show it off anyway. He flopped down into his chair and demonstrated how he could zoom a camera to a close-up of any particular table or area of slots.

"There's hardly a blind spot in the whole place," he bragged.

Beau had spotted one, but didn't say anything. Critiquing the casino's system wasn't what he was here for.

"We had talked about your recorded video footage from December. Is that stored on the computer, or are there physical tapes?"

"We're still a little old-school on that. We've got tapes." Stennis got up with effort and went to the open doorway of a small side room. Squeezing sideways, he ran his fingers over the labels on boxes until he came up with what he wanted. "There's one for every camera for every day. You can see why we can only keep them a short time. Just don't have the space."

Beau stifled his impatience. Casino management must be run by a team of ninety-year-olds to put up with this. He'd hoped they would have facial recognition software and the identification process would take a few minutes. He could see he was in for hours of staring at a monitor. Bizarre, considering they issued electronic cards and knew their customer's gambling habits.

"You told me Percy—um, Johnny Luck—was here on New Year's Eve. Can we start there and then just backtrack to the dates he came in?"

"Good idea. Gamblers are a superstitious bunch. If he got lucky at a machine, odds are good he went to it every time. We can narrow down the number of cameras we need to monitor."

"Does the data from his player's card show which machines he used?"

"It does. I'll get that real quick and we'll be in business." Stennis moved to his computer once again and Beau recited the number he'd written in his notebook.

It still wasn't going to be a quick process. While the security man fiddled with video tape and the machine, Beau reminded himself that nothing in law enforcement was instantaneous; it was a matter of finding clues and meticulously following them. Still, this was bordering on the ridiculous.

With the first tape rolling, the time stamp in the corner showed it was 12:01 a.m. Stennis checked his record again.

"Mr. Luck swiped his card at eight p.m. so we'll fast-forward to that."

Thank you!

They managed to get the right camera on the third try. There sat Percy Lukinger at a video poker machine, jabbing buttons for all he was worth. The video had no sound, but the lights on the machine were blinking like crazy.

"Okay, that's our guy," Beau said.

They watched for a while, fast forwarding so Percy's movements took on a cartoon-like silliness. The man never took his eyes from the screen, never left his seat. This could end up being a complete dead end, Beau realized. Twenty minutes into it, by the time stamp, a woman approached Percy. She had red hair, cut in a pageboy, and wore a spangled dress and one of those silly Happy New Year headbands. She stood at his shoulder for a few minutes but the two didn't interact. Beau couldn't tell whether they actually spoke to each other. If Percy minded her watching him play, he didn't indicate it. Beau sneaked a peek at his watch. 4:37. He needed to get out of here now, to be on time for the memorial.

He gave Stennis quick instructions to pull the tapes from each of the days and times Percy—Johnny Luck— had gambled. He would send a deputy by to pick them up first thing in the morning. He could already predict that tomorrow would be a long day, but he needed to know. Did Percy Lukinger meet up with someone in the casino who eventually killed him?

For the moment, he needed to get to the funeral home. He hit his lights and siren and got to the station in six minutes, dashed inside to change his shirt and jacket— after all, he hoped to blend into the group of mourners and get a look at the widow before she spotted him as a lawman. Five minutes later he and Rico were on Paseo del Pueblo Sur in Rico's private car. They walked into Sanchez Mortuary at one minute to five. Things seemed a little too quiet.

No mourners, no sad music, no greeter at the door.

He found Monica Sanchez in her office.

"Sorry, Sheriff, the Lukinger service was cancelled."

His surprise must have registered. Who ever heard of a funeral being cancelled?

"Mrs. Lukinger stopped by earlier today and picked up the cremains. She was quite upset, apparently because she felt no one would be here to mourn her husband. I assured her we often have very small services—it's not about the crowd size but about remembering the deceased. She said she just wanted to take her husband home."

"I was hoping to have a few words with her," he said. "It's strange, but we've never even met."

"Oh, you would know her in a minute. She's got long, beautiful black hair. This time she wore a black dress and veil. Classy, like Jackie Kennedy, you know."

Beau thanked her but his patience was wearing very thin and the day had proven entirely frustrating. He felt like kicking something as he and Rico went back out to the car.

Chapter 21

I guess I'm going to have to treat the widow as a suspect. She's obviously dodging me," Beau told Sam that evening at home. "She didn't live in the same house as Percy—I mean, I never ran across a woman yet who didn't own a bunch of clothes and makeup and stuff. The whole bare-bones house bugs me. Hardly anyone these days lives so minimally they can fit all their possessions into one suitcase."

Sam was stirring chicken noodle soup in a large stockpot on the stove. "Maybe they were estranged and she has an apartment somewhere else. Or, she might have a job in another town. Most of her things would be there and she commuted to be with her husband on the weekends. You said there were two toothbrushes and a few women's clothes, right?"

"Right. It could explain where the rest of his stuff is, too. I had Travis search for her locally, but she could be living in Albuquerque or someplace else. Could even be out of state." He pulled a beer from the fridge. "Tomorrow, I'll put Travis on it. I have about a month's worth of casino video to watch."

"Did you bring the videos home? I could help you go through them," Sam said. She pulled a sheet of biscuits from the oven.

"Nope. It's been a long enough day already and I'm beat. That soup smells great, and I'm doing nothing more than having a good dinner with my wife and maybe watching the game on TV."

Sam ladled soup into bowls and put four biscuits into a basket with a light cloth over them. They sat at the kitchen table and conversation dwindled. Beau found his thoughts drifting back to his case, despite his determination to leave work behind. By the time he'd settled in his favorite recliner to see how the Cowboys would play against the Patriots, his early-morning awakening had caught up with him. He jolted awake in mid-snore as the TV commentators went crazy over the game-changing touchdown he'd missed.

Sam looked up from her book and smiled at him. "We should just go to bed." It was eight o'clock.

They climbed the stairs together slowly. Were they really becoming this old? He'd been in law enforcement more than twenty years. He shook off those thoughts. No way was he ready to sit with a fishing pole all day, and he couldn't think of another career he could embrace with the enthusiasm he felt for his duties as sheriff. Nah—he was just tired because he'd awakened too early. A hot shower and a good night's sleep would fix everything.

It did. He woke up at five-thirty with a new idea. Ramona

Lukinger had missed her chance to come forward. He would take his search for connections in another direction. Sam wasn't in bed and her pillow was cool to the touch. She was working too many hours, becoming stretched thin with responsibility, and he worried about that. He dressed quickly and rushed through his ranch chores while ideas for his Lukinger investigation raced through his head.

The squad room was quiet at 6:19 when Beau walked in. Just as well. He wanted some time to put his ideas in motion. He found fresh coffee; obviously the desk officer had started a new pot. He settled at his keyboard and began drafting a statement. Within thirty minutes, he'd prepared a public plea for information that could help the Taos County Sheriff's Department in the unsolved death of Percy Lukinger. He actually included the word *mystery*, although it wasn't really a law enforcement term. With luck, it would appeal to the audience he wanted to reach.

He faxed the statement to the three major Albuquerque television stations, along with Lukinger's license photo. Apparently, it was a slow news day. All three news directors called within minutes to ask clarifying questions, and when he switched on the squad room set, Channel 4 already had its picture-perfect news duo talking about it.

"What's this?" Rico asked, sauntering in with coffee in hand.

"Hoping I'm on the right track with this. We're pitifully short on clues here."

"They didn't say anything about our victim being murdered," Rico said when the segment ended.

"I figured that could scare off a lot of our information pool. Decided we'd go with the 'seeking information about this man' tactic." Beau pointed to the stack of videotapes he'd placed beside the TV. "Feel like watching a different kind of programming for a while?"

Rico stifled a groan.

"Here's a list," Beau said, handing him the casino security man's list of dates and times Percy's card was used. "Hey, at least you can fast-forward through a lot of it."

"It beats watching it all in real time, I suppose."

"I like your bright-side-of-things attitude." Beau gave him a pat on the shoulder and headed back to his own office, where the phone was ringing.

"Lines one, two, and three are calls pertaining to something they saw on TV," Dixie said when he picked up.

"That guy they showed on the news? I know I've seen him somewhere, just can't remember where," said an elderly male voice.

"Would you mind holding for a moment?" Beau asked. "Rico! Pause the video and help me take some of these calls. Get line two. They're all calling about the news story, so just see what info they have. Be sure to get contact information from everyone we talk to."

He pressed the button for line three. "Sheriff? I know that guy from the news. He's the leader of this UFO group in Roswell. Every one of them claims they've been abducted by aliens."

Beau took a phone number and promised to get back to the caller. Switching back to the elderly man on line one he said, "Sir, thanks for holding. Did you happen to remember how it is you know Percy Lukinger, the man they showed on TV?"

"Well, I can't say as I exactly know him, but I do know his name isn't Lukinger. He's Percival Johns. I remember that clear as day because it sounded so English. He has an English accent and he convinced me to give him money because he could invest it for me at an excellent rate of return."

It was one of Lukinger's aliases, and the fact it involved a con made a lot of sense. Beau's attention perked up, even though he noticed two more lights had begun to blink on his phone. He asked for his caller's name, address, and phone number, then suggested he start from the beginning to describe his connection to this Percival character.

At the periphery of his attention, he noticed Rico writing notes, hanging up the phone, picking it up again to take another call. When Travis walked in, Rico said something to him and the second deputy immediately picked up his desk phone as well. The calls came in steadily for a half hour then began to taper off. Beau stood up to stretch and walked into the squad room. Three more deputies had reported for duty in the meantime.

"Rico, what've you got?" Beau asked, gathering everyone around to compare notes.

Rico shuffled pages, having kept a separate sheet for each call. "Two obvious nuts. One says his brother is in Bernalillo County jail and says Percy was in the same cell yesterday. One claimed Percy was part of some UFO group."

Travis laughed. "Yeah, I got that one too."

"Gotta give him credit for persistence—he called three times," Beau added.

Rico continued. "Otherwise, I have two who might be legit or they could be grudge cases. Both are local. Both claim to know the man and said he was dealing drugs to a relative. One sounded like a man desperate to stop some slimeball from selling coke to his son."

"Okay. We'll need to interview them. Travis? What's on your list?"

The other deputy described similar results—a few callers obviously were either delusional or were seeking the limelight by having information on a news story. "The one that could be for real was an elderly woman who said the man came to her home and offered to repair a fence that had fallen down. Said he needed six hundred dollars to buy the materials and would be back the next day to start the work. She couldn't understand why he never came back."

"Because he'd been killed in the accident?"

"No, this was three months ago."

"Sounds like a classic home-repair scam. Older people are frequently targets of such things." It was a con that never seemed to run dry, Beau thought, remembering his parents talking about how his grandparents had been taken in by nearly the same line.

He and the deputies sorted their notes into classifications: the impossible, the grudges, and the scams.

Chapter 22

Travel The World was the name Stan Bookman had given his new program, and the way he'd explained it to Sam was that he envisioned a deluxe tour package based on chocolate, history, and art. Sweet's Chocolates had provided such a wonderful amenity to his regular charter flights, he now wanted her to come up with an international palette to represent it.

He'd been vague on specifics but she could tell he had something definite in mind. The clues pointed to her needing to learn a variety of specialties from the countries he meant to include in the itinerary. She could foresee a daunting amount of work to accomplish it, but at the same time it was exciting to add a new dimension to her business. As she drove toward the bakery, she needed her creative side to rev up—she was feeling low on ideas at the moment.

Kelly's little red car sat outside the rear entrance to Puppy Chic, and Sam spotted her daughter emerging. She was trying to pull her puffy coat more tightly around her while balancing a coffee cup and oversized handbag, and she was having a little difficulty pressing the button on her key fob lock while wearing bulky mittens.

"Looks like you need a hand," Sam said as she stepped out of her truck. She stepped over and took the coffee cup.

"Thanks. I should have just come over to your place— your coffee's better, but I was at the bank and they had a pot going."

"Come over when you get a break and we can talk about ideas for your cake."

"Don't stress, Mom. The wedding won't be until sometime this summer. We have to wait for the end of the semester for Scott to have a break, anyway."

"I know. Just please don't be one of those girls who shows up two weeks before the wedding wanting something really elaborate."

"I've heard the tales, Mom. I know how they stress you out."

"Just sayin'." Sam lifted the strap of her pack to her shoulder. "Did I tell you about the call I got from Mr. Bookman, about the huge international chocolate campaign he wants me to put together?"

Kelly's smile brightened. "And he wants all this right about the time the wedding season is in full swing ..."

"Pretty much. Well, I'm not sure. He just said it would be this summer."

Kelly reached over for a one-armed hug. "The campaign will be amazing, and everything else will work out.

Don't worry."

Sam handed her coffee cup back and watched as Kelly turned toward the grooming salon, then Sam headed into Sweet's Sweets, where the familiar scents of cinnamon, chocolate, and sugar greeted her. Julio was pulling a huge sheet of cinnamon rolls from the oven. He'd come up with a recipe that literally melted in the mouth and surpassed everything the popular chain restaurants had ever devised. Even though she spent every day surrounded by these delicacies, Sam couldn't resist plucking one of the warm rolls from the tray and carrying it to her desk.

"Didn't grab any breakfast at home," she said, a little sheepishly, to Becky.

"You warned me, it's one of the dangers of the business," Becky said with a grin. She turned back to the elephant she was creating from modeling chocolate for a kid's zoo-themed birthday cake.

Sam checked messages and saw Stan Bookman had called this morning already. He wondered if she'd given any thought to the new designs. She felt a moment's panic. Surely he didn't think she would have a campaign ready to present yet. She dialed his number and felt lucky when the voicemail message came on.

"I'm working on design ideas right now," she said to the machine. "Hoping to have something to show you within a day or two. Let me know whether I should email them or if you'll be in town."

"Design ideas in a day or two?" Becky said.

"I know, I know. I was never the kid in school who waited until the last minute for anything, and I've done my best in business not to over-promise, but my idea machine isn't focusing very well right now."

"Want to brainstorm? I think I can pipe bright stripes

and talk at the same time."

"Sure. The theme is 'travel the world' but he hasn't told me specifically what countries will be on the itinerary. I think I need to plan on several European capitals and maybe a biggie like Cairo or Istanbul, but he might also be planning on a Far East element. What if I have to come up with something for China or Japan or Thailand? I have to admit I'm getting a little panicky."

"So, we start with the obvious ones," Becky suggested. "Paris—gotta have the Eiffel Tower, right? London—Big Ben."

Sam jotted notes but worried that the obvious ideas would be too cliché for Bookman's taste. Still, any place would at least be a start. She added a Great Pyramid for Egypt and a minaret for Turkey. Choosing the flavors would be a bit more tricky, as she wanted something unusual for each location but also wanted the chocolate flavors to represent something about the place. She turned on her computer in hopes she could pick up clues from the internet.

A message from Book It Travel waited in her inbox: Sam, thought it would help if you had a list of our destinations.

Peru, Machu Picchu
Chile, Easter Island
Australia, Great Barrier Reef
Cambodia, Angkor Wat
India, Taj Mahal
Tanzania, Serengeti
Jordan, Lost City of Petra
Morocco, Marrakech

Holy cow! How will I figure out chocolates to fit these places? She read the names twice. This would take some thought.

No Eiffel Tower or Big Ben for this crowd.

Jen bustled in as Sam was printing the list. "Another wedding cake for you ladies," she said, handing the order form to Sam.

Sam set aside the mind-boggling list Bookman had sent and looked at Jen's sketch for the wedding cake. She flashed the sketch in front of Becky. "A Valentine theme. Are we getting this close already?"

"Afraid so," Becky said with a nod. "It's going to be a busy year for weddings, since Valentine's Day falls on a Saturday."

Sam had noticed several such orders but had put them to the back of her mind since the holiday seemed so far away. When it came to wedding cakes, having a month's lead time wasn't too far out. She headed for the shelves to check supplies. It was important to be sure they didn't run low on flour, sugar, or red food coloring right now.

When she sat down at her computer to place her supply order, a new email from Bookman awaited.

Meant to say, those are our global destinations. Later in the year we'll add a European itinerary:

Transylvania, Croatia, Slovenia, Montenegro, Siberia

We are still fleshing out the exact locations to be visited. Thx—Stan

So much for London and Paris. These were obviously folks who would be going for somewhat more exotic locations. She clicked over to a website that described one company's similar vacation trip, and she nearly choked. Fourteen days cost more than she'd paid for her first house! There must be a lot of super-rich people out there.

Well, the super-rich would get what they paid for, she

decided. Her line of chocolates for Book It Travel had to surpass anything she'd ever done. She browsed further and came up with a few images that might translate well to chocolate.

Now she needed inspiration for recipes and techniques. It would help to be at the chocolate factory where she and Benjie could brainstorm ideas and she could browse her ingredients for inspiration. She checked Becky's orders to be sure she wasn't leaving her decorator with anything she couldn't handle. All seemed well.

Leaving the world of wedding cakes and dessert pastries, Sam drove toward the Victorian. She admired the blue-gray siding and black shutters as she turned into the driveway. With the recent coating of snow still on the ground, the place would fit into any tiny New England village of a century ago. Now, if she could only get the business to run on automatic so she had a bit of free time now and then.

Chapter 23

We didn't find any of the usual signs of drug activity at Lukinger's house," Rico said, setting aside the notes from the few tips they'd received on that subject. "No product, no cash, no burner cell phones."

"Yeah, and if you'll notice, most of those calls sound like the type where a distraught relative is hoping the cause of their family problems is now off the street. If parents really believed Percy was dealing drugs to their kid, they certainly wouldn't kill him and then call us to provide information."

Travis held up the pile of scam reports. "To me, this is what feels like our guy—a con artist. Think about it—no job, no history in town, no paperwork trail beyond one receipt for gas at the Allsups."

Beau nodded. "And, the easy-money type who might spend time in the casino. Rico, sorry to say this, but I need you to get back to those tapes. When you spot Lukinger, watch for him interacting with other people. See if he chats them up or if anyone hands over money to him. The casino might be where he hung out to target his next victims."

It seemed a far-fetched idea. Most casino patrons were simply there with a hope of winning at the machines. But con men looked for easy marks, and a casino could be a hangout for all types. Maybe it wasn't so far-fetched, after all.

"Travis, run a background check on Ramona Lukinger and see what we can learn about her. The fact she showed up twice to claim Percy's remains makes it seem she cared for him, even though she didn't live with him."

Travis nodded. "Now that we have the idea he might be a scam artist, his not having a whole lot of possessions makes more sense. But I'm also thinking maybe the wife has most of his stuff at her place. I'll get right on it."

Beau picked up the reports from callers whose knowledge of Percy seemed related to being conned by the man. At his desk, he picked up the phone and began dialing. First call went to the lady who'd said the man took money for a fence repair. He realized all six calls on his list could lead to Percy Lukinger, or they could open up six new cases if it turned out the perp wasn't Percy.

"Mrs. Baca? This is Sheriff Cardwell, following up on a call you made to our department this morning."

"Sheriff, thank you for calling back." The frail voice of an elderly Hispanic woman brought home to him how real the victims of these types of crimes were.

"My deputy took notes, but I'd like to verify a few things and then one of my deputies will come by your house and have you sign the report."

"Oh, thank you! That money was half of my social security for the month. I'm eighty-five years old and barely paying my heating bill as it is."

He made a note to contact the gas company and see if there was something in their budget to help. He knew they had a program for elderly people, to keep them from freezing in their own homes.

"Tell me how the man approached you," Beau said.

"Well, I was watching *The Price is Right* on TV and the doorbell rang. My little dog went crazy—she always does."

Obviously, this lady had no problem remembering details.

"This man was at the door. He wore tan workman's clothes, and there was a patch above the shirt pocket that said 'John.' He handed me a card and said his company did handyman work and repair jobs. He had noticed that my wooden fence beside the house was falling down and wondered if I wanted it fixed. He bent down and petted my doggie and said, 'We wouldn't want this little angel getting out in the traffic, would we?' I thought that was so nice of him, that he cared to keep Bitsy safe."

"He asked for money before doing the job?"

"Well, yes, he said it was customary to pay half up front—to cover the materials. He showed me how most of the boards were rotted."

"What kind of vehicle did he drive? Did you notice a sign on it? Tools, or anything like that?"

"Well, that's kind of a strange thing. I didn't see a vehicle. I think he said he'd parked up the block where he was doing another job. He'd noticed my fence when he drove by."

"And you're sure it's the same man whose picture you

saw on the news this morning?"

"Pretty sure. I mean, that was just a snapshot and not a great one, but he had the same receding hairline and a sharp nose. He was tall."

Lukinger was five-nine, not exactly towering.

Mrs. Baca giggled. "Everyone seems tall to me. I was five-one in my teens but I think I've shrunk a bit."

Beau assured her they would show her another picture of the man they were looking for when the deputy came by to get the report signed.

"Do you think you'll catch him, Sheriff? I'd hate to think of him out there doing this to a lot of other old people."

Beau assured her this man wouldn't be taking anyone's money again.

Travis had been hovering outside Beau's office door, and he stepped inside as soon as Beau hung up the phone.

"Ramona Lukinger doesn't have a New Mexico driver's license," he said. "She probably never updated it after moving here. Should I start searches in other states?"

"Yeah. Although it could take a while to get results, we'd better do it. We still don't even know what she looks like or where they came from before moving here." Beau drummed his pencil on the desktop. "You know what— run her name through NCIC and see if anything comes up."

Beau wasn't sure whether to be hopeful or not. The woman could have used any number of aliases, just as her husband did. Ramona, so far, had shown a tendency toward trying to con him—the *mistaken* phone number at first, the times she'd shown up to claim Percy's body, and then his ashes, while neatly managing to dodge questions, the appointments to talk to authorities and then skipping the meetings. It wouldn't be the first time a husband and wife teamed up to perpetrate their shady games.

Travis had gone back to his desk, and Beau returned to his list of complainant calls. The first three went almost identically to the call with Mrs. Baca—someone came to the door, had spotted something that needed repair, took money as a deposit and never came back. One was for a cracked concrete driveway, one house had damaged roofing shingles, and the other needed overgrown shrubbery trimmed. In each case, the man at the door quoted a price that seemed high and claimed it was standard to pay half up front. Two people couldn't remember the exact date it had happened to them, but all were sure it was in the fall, October or November time frame, because the repairman made a point of how the work should be done right away because winter was coming soon.

A couple of the men ranted in anger, the sting of being gypped still very fresh. Beau might have considered them suspects in Percy's death, but both had admitted to being over eighty years old. He had a hard time envisioning either of them in a physical confrontation with a man in his forties.

In no case had the victim seen the man's vehicle, even when they walked outside with him so he could point out the repairs he wanted to make. On the fourth call the woman, a Helen Flagler, added a new wrinkle.

"There was a woman with the man," she told Beau. "They were handing out religious tracts and I told them I already attend the church of my choice, but they wanted to leave their literature with me anyway. Then the woman apologized and said she really needed to use the bathroom, and since they'd left their car two blocks away while they walked door-to-door, could she use the facilities at my house? Well, I felt sorry for her and said yes."

"And you discovered something was missing after they left."

"Two bottles of my prescription medicines and a little necklace my granddaughter gave me for my birthday. I was embarrassed to call the police about it. At first I thought I'd probably misplaced them—I'm getting more forgetful all the time."

"Can you describe the woman?"

"Well, let's see. She had blonde hair that was kind of short ..."

He'd been told Ramona's was black, but one or both styles could be wigs. "Could you identify her from a photo, if I bring one by?"

"Hm ... maybe. I didn't spend much time with her. It was the man who talked to me the whole time. They left almost as soon as she came out of the bathroom."

"Did you keep the religious tracts they left with you?"

"They're probably here somewhere. I never got around to reading them, and my daughter teases me about not being able to throw anything away."

"We're working on finding a photo of the man's wife. When I get one I'd like to bring it by for you to take a look. I'll call first to be sure you're home, if that's okay. Meanwhile, if you locate the pamphlets they left, could you set them aside? Try not to touch them much."

"Because you could get fingerprints off them, right?"

He would bet Helen Flagler was a big fan of *Murder, She Wrote*. They ended the call on a friendly note, and she said she had baked sugar cookies, in case he came by this afternoon.

Beau felt his pulse rise as he read over the notes he'd scribbled. This was their first lead that involved Ramona

Lukinger in Percy's crimes. If he could come up with a picture of her, it would help. If Ramona had touched the pamphlets and *if* she had a record, it might give them more ways to track her down.

He stood and stretched, working the crick out of his neck from holding the phone against his shoulder. Through his office window he could see Rico sitting in front of the video monitor, intent on casino footage. He walked into the squad room to check on progress.

"I'm less than halfway through the list," Rico said, pointing to the printed page with dates and times of Percy's casino visits. He had crossed through some of the entries. "Those are the times he sat alone and played one machine for a while. No contact with any other person, as far as I could tell."

He paused the video as it fast-forwarded.

"Now these are cases where he spoke to someone or they spoke to him." He indicated about a half-dozen lines where he'd made short notes. "W is where a waitress approached and offered him a drink. Each time it seemed to be a different girl, so I didn't think they were significant. This one, marked RH was when a redheaded woman came up to him. They talked a bit, maybe two or three minutes, and she left. Something felt a little odd about it, but I'm not sure how to define my feeling. She seemed aware of the camera because she gave a quick glance upward as she walked up the aisle of machines toward Lukinger, then she turned and approached from another side and stood with her back toward the camera. I don't know ... I could be all wrong."

"We can go back and review it," Beau said. "Any others?"

"Yeah. My note here—GM. Remember Grant Mangle,

the guy we talked to about Percy, the one who claimed he'd met Lukinger once and it was more than six months ago? Well, he seemed to know him well enough on January eighth—less than two weeks ago."

"Show me that one."

Rico put another tape into the machine. He had paused it at the point he wanted to show Beau. When he started it, the monitor showed Percy Lukinger at a video poker machine at the end of a row that was otherwise empty of players. The clock in the lower corner indicated it was a Thursday at eight a.m. No surprise the casino was virtually empty. And what a good time for a meeting between two people who didn't want their conversation overheard in a setting where the encounter could appear completely random.

"Mr. Mangle comes into the picture right about here," Rico said. Mangle walked into the frame from the left side, glanced over his shoulder and down the aisle where Percy's machine was, then stepped in close to their subject.

"Can we zoom in closer to their faces?" Beau asked.

"Not on this tape. Unfortunately, controls like that are only available there at the casino while the video cameras are live. This is only a static recording."

Mangle loomed over Percy, his stance firm and his body tense. At one point he shook his index finger in Percy's face. Lukinger reacted with a laugh. Mangle reached inside his jacket and pulled something from a pocket. When he held it out to Percy, it looked like a small paper envelope, the kind that might hold a single key or perhaps a bank receipt. It was much too small to be a letter that could go through the mail.

"We never do find out what's in it," Rico said.

Sure enough, Percy squeezed the envelope so he could

peer into it from one end, closed it again, and folded down the small flap. He slipped the tiny packet into his own pocket.

Percy smiled largely and reached to shake hands with Grant, but when the other man turned to leave, Percy's smile morphed to a sneer and he stared at the other man's back until he was out of sight.

"Interesting," Beau said. Another visit to Grant Mangle Enterprises seemed to be in order.

"Yeah. So much for the story he gave us."

Chapter 24

Beau straightened the items on his desk, put the stack of reports from their recent phone calls into a manila folder, and grabbed his heavy coat. With luck, he would catch some of these older folks at home. He instructed Rico to stick with the tapes and keep making notes about any other contacts Percy Lukinger made. Clearly, their dead guy had used the casino as a meeting spot several times.

"Hey, boss," Travis called out as Beau passed his desk. "Got something for you."

Beau looked at the deputy's computer screen and saw the name Ramona Lukinger on a list. His interest sharpened.

"Looks like she got a driver's license in California eighteen months ago," Travis said.

He clicked her name and up came an MVD record, including a photo. Beau studied the face. High forehead, dark brows, eyes half closed, mouth in a straight line. It was as if she didn't care to impress the camera—for some reason most people tried for a friendly likeness of themselves on their license picture. According to the license data, Ramona was 150 pounds, 5'4" with brown eyes and brown hair. She looked vaguely familiar, but he couldn't think why.

"Print that for me, would you?" he asked.

Travis hit a couple more keys and the printer across the room began to whir.

"Do another copy," Beau said, "and give it to Rico. Maybe this is our redhead from the casino."

Happy to get out of his chair for a stretch, Rico joined them beside Travis's desk and looked at the photo on the screen. "I don't know ... hard to tell. I'll go back to the tape of the redhead and compare. If it's really his wife, maybe she comes back to the casino another time and I'll get a better shot of her."

Beau remembered how the woman in the casino had purposely avoided facing directly toward the camera. Positively identifying her could be a challenge. He folded the license photo and slipped his arms into the sleeves of his jacket.

"I'm off to interview a couple of witnesses. Travis, use the data from her driver's license and run a full background check on her. Call me if there's a sudden breakthrough," he said with a grin.

Out in his cruiser, Beau decided to run by Helen Flagler's house first. As the only witness who'd come forward who might have had contact with both Percy and Ramona, Helen might add information of value to the rest of their search. Her address was south of town in a neighborhood of older homes. A glance through the notes from the other callers showed they all lived in roughly the same area.

It made sense. Middle class homes, older people who would be home during the daytime, easy targets for the sorts of con games it seemed Percy was fond of. He probably worked a neighborhood, picking houses far enough apart that the victims wouldn't necessarily know each other and start comparing notes. Use a different approach with each—the home repair scam about a new roof, a new fence, some landscaping repairs, and finally the 'may I use your bathroom' con—and then move along before any of them call the police. He thought of the scanty possessions in Percy's home and the suitcase large enough to pack on a moment's notice.

Helen Flagler was standing in the doorway when Beau stepped onto her sidewalk.

"Hi, Sheriff. You remembered those sugar cookies, didn't you?" Her gaze took in his uniform and she smiled coquettishly.

He gave the kind of smile he thought an eighty-year-old flirt would want to see. "Yes, ma'am. I'd love a cookie. I brought something for you to look at."

"Well, come on in first. It's too cold to stand out on the porch." She led him into an overly warm living room with green shag carpeting, a brown sofa and recliner set, and about four dozen knitted blankets in bright colors, the kind his grandmother used to make. The house smelled like coffee and sugar, and he realized how much she had been hoping for someone to stop by and spend a little time with her.

Beau tamped down the urge to simply ask his questions and move on to the next interview. Helen insisted he sit at the table and she'd moved to the kitchen already, where the coffee smell became stronger and he could see through the open doorway she'd already set out two cups. The plate of sugar cookies looked enticing, a reminder he'd not eaten lunch.

"Cream and sugar?" Helen called out.

"No, thanks, black is fine." He pulled Ramona Lukinger's license photo from the inner pocket of his jacket and set it on the table.

Helen returned, carrying a silver tray with two delicate china cups on saucers—another distinct reminder of his grandmother. The cups rattled slightly, and it was all he could do not to jump up and offer to take the tray. He moved the photo out of harm's way as she chose that very spot to set down her burden.

"Here we go," she said, taking her time about placing a cup in front of him and another at the second chair. "I hope you like Kona. I've been addicted, ever since my Max and I took a trip to the islands for our silver anniversary. That was a long time ago."

Her wistful eyes told him Max had long since passed. She blinked twice and pointed to the cookie plate. "Help yourself, Sheriff."

He thanked her and took a sip of the coffee, which, by far, beat the brew down at the station. The cookies were a little on the overdone side, but he finished one before getting down to business by holding out the license photo and asking if this was the woman who had come to the house.

Helen adjusted her glasses and stared at the picture

closely. "I don't know … Her hair isn't the same at all. She's not wearing glasses here. The woman who came in was wearing glasses with dark frames."

"She may have been required to remove them for her license photo," he said. "Can you imagine her with the glasses on? Could it be the same person?"

Helen's head bobbed a little. "It could be … but she seems heavier here. If I saw her in person—it's different, you know, when you can see someone move and talk—different than a stiff picture like this one."

Beau felt let down, but reminded himself this was only one tiny cog in the wheel of the investigation. He was really trying to reconstruct Percy Lukinger's life and recent movements. The whole goal was to find his victim's killer.

"Well, that's okay, Mrs. Flagler. If we are able to catch the woman who took your things, we'll have her for you to identify in person."

"Yes, that would be much easier." Helen visibly relaxed.

Beau had finished his coffee while she'd studied the photo. It was time to move along and get out of the stifling warmth of the overheated house.

"Did you happen to find those religious tracts you told me about?" he asked.

"Oh! I sure did. Let me think where I set them." Helen set her cup aside and stood. She glanced back and forth across the cluttered living room a couple of times until her gaze landed on a small table by the door. "I put them in a bag, just like you said."

Beau met her where she stood and accepted the zippered plastic bag, which he saw contained a couple of brochures with ethereal-looking photos of clouds behind a haloed Jesus. He thanked her for her help, for the coffee, and complimented her on the cookies, but insisted he had to get on with several more interviews.

Outside, the January day gave a blast of fresh, frigid air and he breathed deeply. The shoulder mike on his jacket squawked at the moment he reached his cruiser.

"Yeah, Dixie," he said.

"Sheriff, there's a reported 10-31B at the pawn shop on Gallegos Road. The man reporting says he's holding the perpetrator."

"10-4. I'll be right there." He slid behind the wheel and tossed the Ziploc bag on the passenger seat beside him.

Beau remembered the pawn shop when he pulled into the parking lot. There had been an armed robbery here about three years ago. The old guy who owned the place back then had installed all new security systems, but the shock of being held at gunpoint in his own business had been too much and he'd decided to sell.

The new owner introduced himself as Robert Nieto. A teenage girl sat on a high stool in front of the counter, her hands clasped between her knees, a dried mascara trail running down each cheek.

"What happened here?" Beau asked Nieto. He watched the girl and saw a new batch of tears threaten to overflow her eyelids.

"Oh, she's not the thief," Nieto said. "This is Daisy Ruiz. She's a friend of my little cousin."

Beau waited patiently. There had to be more to this story.

"The thief is locked in the gun crib, handcuffed to an 18-gauge wire wall. Don't worry—all the weapons are stored unloaded, and there's no ammo on the premises." From a back room somewhere came a metal-on-metal clatter.

"Do you know him?"

"It's a her."

"Better start at the beginning."

Nieto patted Daisy on the shoulder. "About an hour ago, I'm here by myself working behind the counter and I see these two out front, talking with their heads together, staring at a small object in Daisy's hand. I didn't recognize her at first—it's been a couple years. They come in, and Daisy hands over this ring and wants to know how much she can pawn it for."

Daisy stared at the floor, drapes of her long hair obscuring her face.

"I tell them I'll have to take a close look, so I get out my loupe. It's a real diamond, all right, but while I'm looking through the loupe, the other lady decides to help herself to a nice emerald from the tray I'd been working with. I catch the motion from the corner of my eye and tell her to put it back. She hits the tray and sends the other rings flying to the floor, then makes a run for the door. But all I have to do is hit the switch that's under the counter for the automatic door lock."

By this time the teen girl was mopping tears from her chin.

"Look, Sheriff, I try not to be a hardnose. Kids try to take things. But this other lady is no kid, and she's experienced at this game. I can tell. Soon as she knows I'm onto her, she slips the emerald ring into the hole on that guitar that's on display and then tries to claim she has no idea what I'm talking about. C'mon—the ring is clattering around in there the second I take the guitar down from the wall."

Beau tilted his head toward the teen and gave Nieto a questioning glance.

"I don't know. She won't talk to me. Afraid I'll call her dad, probably."

Beau stepped in front of Daisy. "Okay, what's your side of this?"

Another loud clatter from the back room, and a woman's voice shouted, "Don't you tell him anything!"

"She's locked up," Beau said to the teen. "It's better if you tell me."

Daisy shook her head and wouldn't meet Beau's eye.

"I'll get you a ride to the station and we can talk about it there," Beau said, keying his shoulder mike and requesting a deputy to come by.

He turned back to Nieto, who said, "I think it's some version of the classic Diamond Ring con game. Two people seemingly *find* a valuable item at the same time and decide to either sell or pawn it and split the money. Usually, only the dupe comes into the shop while the pro waits outside."

"Daisy? Is that about what happened?" Beau asked.

She sniffed loudly and nodded. Another loud rattle came from the back room.

"Mr. N.?" Her voice came out thin and scared.

Nieto patted her shoulder. "I'll press charges, Sheriff, as long as Daisy doesn't get in trouble. It's the other woman who instigated this."

"Look, Daisy," Beau said. "You're not being arrested or anything. I just need you to go to our station and help my deputy write a report about this."

Right on cue, another department cruiser pulled up in front of the shop and Deputy Walters got out. Daisy was shaking by this time, and they got her safely stowed in the back seat.

"We'll put the other one in my SUV," Beau told Walters.

"I might use your help to get her there. She sounds like a tiger."

Sure enough, when they approached the heavy wire enclosure in the back of the pawn shop, they got an earful from the prisoner, a petite Anglo woman with wild blonde hair, flashing blue eyes, and the mouth of a sailor.

"What's your name, ma'am?" Beau asked.

"Nonna Yurbidness."

"Cute. Do you have some identification?"

She stared defiantly at him. From the doorway, Nieto spoke up. "She wasn't carrying a purse when she came in."

Beau pulled handcuffs from his belt and ordered the captive to turn around. "You're under arrest for attempted robbery and damage to property." When she didn't move, he said, "We can easily add resisting arrest to the charges, ma'am. You don't want to make this harder than it needs to be."

Nieto unlocked the door to the pen, Walters stood back and covered her with his weapon, while Beau cuffed her wrists. Her hellcat manner turned sullen as they marched her out to the cruiser.

Chapter 25

Sam stared in dismay at the shelf with all her food flavorings. There was not a single thing here she hadn't already used in the chocolates her company was providing for Book It Travel. Now Mr. Bookman wanted 'new and unusual' for his exclusive upscale charter trips that would take the jet set crowd around the world. She chewed on the end of her pen.

Think, Sam, think!

A flash of a vision, the quirky chocolatier from Romania who had showed up unexpectedly several times—Bobul. If only he were here right now, he would surely stare at this shelf and pluck a couple of flavors she'd never think of combining, and his concoction would be fantastic. Or he would have some new magical thing in that scruffy bag of his, some little pinch of wonderfulness that would transform ordinary chocolate into the irresistible delights her client wanted.

She snapped back to the present moment, the one where she was standing alone in the pantry at Sweets Handmade Chocolates. No Bobul. No miracle. And Stan Bookman was due at the airport in fifteen minutes.

She had nothing ready to show, and she wondered if Bookman expected a professional presentation, complete with Power Point slides, on such short notice. If he did, well, too bad. They'd worked together long enough for him to know Sam wasn't that kind of businesswoman. But she wished she had at least come up with one or two new flavors, some real knock-your-socks-off samples to hand him when she picked him up.

She glanced at the clock again and rushed upstairs to her office where she gathered the few notes she'd made, along with some photos from the internet, and placed everything into a folder. This was a preliminary meeting. She would listen to her client's ideas and let him set the tone. Her challenge would be to keep his visions within the realm of reality, as Bookman seemed to think Sam could concoct virtually anything he could dream up. As she put on her coat, a picture of a ten-foot Taj Mahal popped into her head. She could only pray he wouldn't ask her to fit *that* into a gift box.

"I'm leaving to pick him up now," Sam told Benjie in the kitchen. "Make sure this place is spotless and everyone is working efficiently, in case he wants to hold our meeting here."

The travel company owner hadn't actually stated any specific plan, only that his personal jet would be bringing him to the Taos airport and he wanted to spend some time going over the new campaign. Beyond telling her the tours would begin this summer, and the list of countries he had emailed to her only this morning, she had no clue what he had in mind. She bustled out the back door and started her van.

It had turned into one of those bright, clear New Mexico winter days with an intense blue sky lighting the remaining snow on the fields north of town. The high temperature was predicted to be around thirty, dipping into the teens again tonight, so nothing was likely to change much for a few days. She made the left turn off Highway 64 and watched as the private jet lined up with the runway. By the time she parked and walked into the small terminal, the plane had come to a stop on the tarmac and the steps were automatically descending to the ground. She took a deep breath and walked out the door toward it.

Stan Bookman spotted her as soon as he emerged. "Sam! So great to see you." His gray hair had been freshly trimmed, and the silver wire rims on his glasses must have been chosen to match.

She smiled at his effervescent manner. Her being here wasn't exactly a surprise, and yet he acted as if the sight of her delighted him.

"How was your flight?" she asked. As if buzzing into any airport in the world on a whim wasn't something special.

"Clear skies, no turbulence—couldn't ask for any better," he said.

His flight attendant followed them into the building, wheeling Stan's small bag until he turned and took it.

"Where to?" Sam asked. "You hadn't said whether you want to go directly to the chocolate factory, or—how about food? Have you eaten?" Silly question, she realized.

That plane was probably stocked with anything its owner could possibly desire.

"Thanks, I had a snack on the flight. Margie and I closed the house here for the winter. She wanted more time in Houston with the grandchildren. I'm booked at El Monte Sagrado for the night, and then I thought we'd spend the day tomorrow going over our campaign plans." From a zipped pocket on his suitcase, he pulled a glossy Book It Travel folder. "Meanwhile, thought you'd enjoy looking over this."

At a glance, Sam saw it was the brochure his customers would receive when they inquired about the global charters.

"Behind the razzmatazz stuff the clients see, there's a couple sheets with our internal documents, menus for each leg of the trip, and all that."

While they'd been talking, Sam noticed the crew had parked the plane on the east side of the building and apparently closed it up for the night.

"Can I drop you at your hotel?" she asked Mr. Bookman. "And what about your crew—do they need a ride somewhere?"

"We keep a company car here, and they've got rooms at the Holiday Inn, so they're all set. I'd appreciate the ride, though, if it's not out of your way. And how about dinner tonight, Sam? I'd love to treat you and your husband. I've had a craving for New Mexican food ever since we left for Texas."

Sam ushered him toward the bakery van, thankful there had been other arrangements for the crew, since the back seats were folded away.

"I'm not sure what Beau's schedule is right now," she told Bookman as she stowed his bag in the back, hoping there weren't greasy bits of buttercream icing lurking in its path. "He's working on a big case right now, but I'll check with him and get back to you, if that's okay?"

"But you'll join me for dinner? What was the place we went last time? That's the food that's calling out to me right now."

Sam thought it was The Taoseño, but it might have been Orlando's. As they drove toward his hotel, she described each of the restaurants and he confirmed the former. Wheeling under the portico at El Monte Sagrado, the poshest of Taos's accommodations, Sam told her client she would be back to pick him up at six o'clock.

Beau or no Beau, she needed to spend time with Bookman, to get a better fix on his plans. She pulled away from the hotel and decided to drive the five minutes to the sheriff's department rather than call. Parking on the street was always at a premium here, and the public lot was two blocks away, so Sam scanned the employee parking area where there was nearly always a spot not filled with someone's cruiser.

Beau's felt Stetson caught her attention as she slowed to make the turn into the lot. He stood beside his department SUV and reached a hand toward someone who was emerging from the back seat. Sam took the first empty parking slot and watched. A female suspect with curly blonde hair, wearing a lightweight jacket and jeans, with hands cuffed behind her back, stepped out. Sam froze. She knew the woman. It was Missy Malone.

Sam leaped out of her van. A deputy arrived with another suspect in his cruiser, a teenage girl who looked familiar to Sam as a bakery customer. Beau said something to Walters then tapped on the rear door that led directly to the booking area. He hadn't spotted Sam yet, and something made her hang back, even though she was dying to know what Missy had done to bring the sheriff around.

The two men and their suspects went inside, where Sam knew they would be put into interrogation rooms or the holding cell, eventually fingerprinted and booked. She went to the other door, the one to the squad room and knocked. Rico opened it.

"Sam? What are you doing here? Beau went out on a call and isn't back yet."

"He is. I just saw him take a suspect inside. I need to know what she's here for."

"Uh, sure." The deputy paused, trying to make the mental switch to what Sam was saying. "Well, you know where the interrogation rooms are. Go on back if you want."

She was already on her way. Beau was coming out of one of the rooms, pulling the door closed behind him, when he saw her.

"Hey—nice surprise seeing you here," he said, giving his winning smile.

"Hey. I ... um, I stopped by to see if you were free for dinner with my client, but I saw you bringing in someone I know."

He froze in place. "What? You know her?"

"Yeah. Well, she's not exactly a friend. She's been coming in the bakery the past week or two, chumming it up with Jen."

"What's her name?"

"Missy Malone. Well, that's what she told us. She's told Jen that she's married and they own homes here and in Albuquerque. Well, you've met her." She reminded him of the mix-up with money the first time Missy came in the shop, then the little gifts that began showing up. "My suspicions rose about the gifts when I was in Clarice's shop and learned several of those items had been shoplifted. I don't know, Beau, it could all be coincidence."

They had walked back toward the squad room as they talked, and Beau turned now to Deputy Travis.

"New background check," he said. "Find an address, priors, anything we can get on a Missy Malone. New Mexico driver's license."

Sam watched her husband in sheriff mode. She'd grown so accustomed to seeing him at home, working with the ranch animals, helping in the kitchen, she'd forgotten how authoritative and respected he was on the job.

"Rico," Beau said, "back to the Lukinger case, see if you can get fingerprints from these brochures. If there's anything readable here, run the prints through the databases."

He handed Rico a Ziploc bag that appeared to contain religious tracts, then turned toward his office, his hand on Sam's back.

"What time is the dinner with your client?" he asked.

"Six. Look, I can tell things here are pretty busy. I can meet with Mr. Bookman by myself, it's just that he always enjoys chatting with you too."

He glanced at his watch. "It'll be close, but I'll try. I've got two suspects to question and I never know how long it will take."

"What's Missy being arrested for?"

"Looks like she was trying to pull a con on a pawnshop owner, dragged a teen girl into it, tried to snatch an emerald ring from the jewelry case in the shop. At this point, we've got attempted robbery and property damage, at best, so she may be out before you know it. I need to talk to the teenager and get her side of it."

Sam was torn between her curiosity about the arrest of Jen's new friend and her need to organize her notes and dress presentably for her dinner meeting with Stan Bookman. Duty won out. She squeezed Beau's hand as they said goodbye in the squad room. He would tell her all about Missy Malone later.

Chapter 26

Beau felt badly, telling Sam not to count on him for her client dinner tonight. The more he thought about the variety of things going on in the Lukinger case and now this pawnshop incident, the more he realized he wouldn't be good dinner company anyway. He turned back to the interrogation room where young Daisy Ruiz had been shaking and in tears the last time he saw her.

As for Missy Malone, he doubted much of anything brought that woman to tears. She'd gone from fighting wild-woman in the pawnshop to mildly flirtatious when he got in the cruiser and she'd suggested rather than arresting her they could 'work something out' if he would only join her in the back seat. As if she were the only female suspect in history to suggest such a thing.

He peered through the narrow window in Room 2 before opening the door. Daisy sat at the metal table, wiping the back of one hand across her nose. Beau grabbed a box of tissues and carried them in with him. He set them on the table before he sat down.

"Okay, Daisy. Want to tell me what happened with you and your friend before I got to the pawnshop?"

The girl mopped smeared mascara from her lower lids, doing a bad job of it; the black mess made her look as if she'd come from the set of a zombie movie. She blew her nose twice and sniffed loudly.

"I don't know that lady—she's not my friend. I stopped by Applebee's to use the bathroom 'cause I was walking to Walmart but I needed to go pretty bad. So, I'm washing my hands at one of the sinks and this woman comes to another sink near me. All at once she kind of breathes like"—a sharp inhale—"and she's all like 'Whoa, look at this ring!' and she asks if it's mine. Well, *no*, I tell her."

"Describe the ring," Beau said.

"A diamond, like an engagement ring."

"Go ahead."

"So she's holding the ring and is really looking at it. And I tell her we should turn it in at the desk because somebody will come back looking for it. She says, 'nobody's been in this restroom for more than an hour. I was sitting nearby. No one's coming back for it, and if we turn it in, the hostess will just have herself a really nice ring for free.' And I'm thinking, well, isn't that what you'll have if you take it? But I didn't say that."

"And then?"

"Well, she starts with the idea of the pawnshop, that she knows a guy who would give us a good deal on the ring and we'd split the money. Sheriff, I know it wasn't honest but I really, really needed some money to get a ticket for the Adele concert. All my friends are going."

"So you went to the pawnshop where she knew the guy?"

"Yeah, except the guy she knew wasn't there and Mr. Nieto was real nice and wanted to wait on us. I could tell she really didn't want to deal with him, but she handed over the ring and he started to look at it with that little eyepiece thingy. The lady got all edgy and the next thing I knew she'd reached toward this display of rings and swiped one. He was quick—he grabbed for her wrist but she threw the display box and ran for the door. He caught up with her, then he twisted her arm behind her back and marched her off to that cage in the back. I was screaming for them to stop it. I tried to get out the door ... all I could think of was to run home. But he'd somehow locked the doors and I got all panicky."

Beau was taking notes of all this.

"Once he had her locked up, he told me to sit down and be quiet and then he called 911."

"Did he threaten you or do anything to you?"

"No. He guessed my name, though. Said he remembered that I was Carina's friend, said she's his niece. He said something about Christmas Eve and I remembered a bunch of Carina's relatives being at her house after church that night. So then I wasn't quite so scared of him."

"What was the other lady doing all this time?"

"Mostly yelling and screaming. She told him I had stolen the ring from her, but he obviously didn't believe it. So then she changed her story and said I'd found the ring and convinced her to come to this pawnshop because I knew him and I'd told her he would give us a good price for the ring. It made me mad 'cause she was turning everything around from what really happened."

"It's okay. I'll talk to her next, and it's good that I have your story. Are your parents at home right now?"

Daisy nodded. "My mom will be there."

She didn't look any too happy about what was going to happen, but Beau got the phone number and called. Once he knew Daisy's mother was on the way, he released her from the interrogation room and told Dixie to entertain the girl until her mother arrived.

"Sheriff?" the desk officer called out. "There's a gentleman here to see you."

It was Robert Nieto from the pawnshop. Beau invited him into the room just vacated by Daisy Ruiz. He debated making the shop owner wait while he questioned Missy Malone, but the man wasn't a suspect and was only doing his duty as a citizen. The woman could wait.

"Quite a day, Mr. Nieto," Beau said as they took seats.

"No kidding. Well, anyway, you wanted me to make a statement about the robbery and my brother came in to watch the shop for me, so this was a good time."

Beau thanked him and took notes. Nieto's details matched Daisy's story, and Beau felt relieved that the young girl had been telling the truth.

"Did she actually get away with any items from your shop?" Beau asked.

Nieto shook his head. "My glass display case has a big crack in it where she lunged with all her weight. A velveteen ring display went flying, with rings all over the place, but I crawled around and found them all, including the emerald in the guitar. Even the diamond she brought in to show me, which turned out not to be a diamond at all. It's a decent cubic zirconia, but not worth more than fifty bucks or so. The setting's cheap silver plate is all."

"Since she didn't actually take anything, all we can call this is attempted robbery and she'll probably come up with a story about how she tripped and fell into the jewelry case. It'll amount to your word against hers, although you do have a teenage witness on your side. You can press charges for the property damage and a judge might award you enough to replace the broken display case."

"Truthfully, I'd just as soon be done with all this, Sheriff. My insurance will cover the broken glass and my brother's a decent enough cabinet maker to replace it in the case for me."

He thanked Nieto for coming by and they shook hands at the door.

Beau repressed a sigh. He didn't blame the guy a bit, and he had no charge serious enough to get Missy Malone locked away. If what Sam said proved true, the woman was a habitual thief and liar, but there was simply not enough evidence—nothing she wouldn't deny every which way—to arrest her. He had no choice but to release her. However, she didn't need to know that, not quite yet.

Through the one-way glass in the room where Missy sat, Beau observed her for a couple minutes. She sat in the chair with her back to the mirror, a sign she knew he would be watching. Walters had evidently offered her a soda—the can sat on the otherwise empty table. Well, he couldn't arrest her for the diamond ring incident, but he might be able to shake her up enough she would take his warning seriously when he advised her to leave town and conduct her activities elsewhere.

Chapter 27

Stan Bookman reveled in his breakfast burrito, exclaiming over the green chile sauce, which the Taoseño tended to make on the hot side.

"You know, one of the things about traveling a lot is sometimes it becomes confusing which meal you're supposed to be eating. The thing I find about breakfast is that it grounds me, makes me feel like I'm home, no matter what time of day I eat it," he said, digging into another bite of the egg, bacon, potato and cheese combination in its tortilla covering. "That's why I love local restaurants, where I can order breakfast anytime."

Sam smiled over her own *carne adovada* burrito. She couldn't disagree.

"So, tell me, on this new world tour you'll be doing,

which is your favorite destination?"

He paused for only a moment. "Machu Picchu, in Peru. No doubt. It's not quick to get there, but when you're standing among those ruins you feel such a sense of peace, and the silence is ... sublime. I guess that's the only way to describe it. Especially when the clouds are misty over the surrounding mountains. I can imagine myself as one of the ancient people who lived there."

"I get that feeling when I step out our back door at the ranch," Sam said. "I love to look up at the stars and realize the sky goes on infinitely."

He nodded and she felt as if he had gone back to that faraway place for a minute. They'd certainly left the realm of burritos.

"Tell me, what's the flavor of the place?" she asked.

"Hmm ..." His sharp eyes focused back on Sam again. "I know what you're asking. What flavor will remind our passengers of their trip, right?"

"Yes, something like that."

"Can green be captured as a flavor? It's dewy and moist ... mossy. What about that—moss? Is it a flavor?"

Sam laughed. "I don't think so. But you've given me some ideas to think about."

Stan scraped the last of his chile sauce from his plate, pushed it back, and excused himself to go to the restroom. He asked Sam to order him a cup of coffee when the waitress came around.

Moss. How will I capture something so ordinary yet so exotic and make it a chocolate flavor? And what about the many other locations on his travel itinerary? She opened the folder she'd brought with her and jotted notes about the clouds and mist.

Down in her pocket, her phone buzzed. She pulled it

out and looked, hoping Beau was thinking of joining them. No such luck—it was Delbert Crow.

Her old supervisor was never in a good mood at the end of the day. Face it, she thought, he's never *really* in a good mood. He'd be nagging about the status of that house she'd offered to help Sadie Holmes with, and she didn't have any news for Delbert. The plumber wasn't due to fix the broken pipe for another week, although Sam had to admit, in the old days when this was her job she would have at least checked on the place a time or two more, making sure no additional damage had occurred. When she spotted Stan Bookman headed back to the table, she let Delbert's call go to voicemail.

They feasted on sopapillas drenched in honey for dessert while they talked about ideas for the new line of chocolates.

"Our world travel itinerary initially won't have a lot of passengers," Bookman said over coffee, "but we want the chocolate designs and flavors—even the boxes themselves—specific for each country. We've configured two of our larger jets so eighty passengers will ride in spacious comfort. Eighty pax, that's forty couples. Each couple will receive a box of candy when the flight departs for the next destination, an introduction to the tastes and themes of the upcoming country on the itinerary."

"How many chocolate pieces would you like per box?"

"Not an overabundance, since it's the flavor and shape that will really speak to them. Maybe a dozen pieces. What do you think?"

Sam looked at the schedule he had emailed. Nine countries. Quick math told her she would be making more than four thousand pieces of chocolate each time one of his worldwide tours kicked off. Not to mention finding boxes to represent each of the nine countries. Forty of each wouldn't be enough to commission mass production of each theme box, but stumbling across enough of them in a standard retail store would be impossible. Challenges abounded.

"We haven't talked price yet," Stan said, signaling the waitress for their check. "Can you do it for two hundred a box?"

Two hundred *dollars—each*? Sam felt her eyes widen. "I want to be fair with you ..."

"Sam, you've always been fair. This isn't about the money. The amenities are built into the price we charge the client, and these people can afford anything. With them, quality is everything, Sam, and I know you won't let me down."

He picked up the check and headed for the cash register while Sam gathered her papers.

It was a two-edged sword—with such generous money came extremely high expectations. Would she be able to prove herself this time?

She arrived home, after dropping Mr. Bookman at his hotel, to find Beau taking a carton of ice cream from the freezer.

"Want some?" he asked, holding up Caramel Ribbon Delight.

"No thanks, I'm stuffed."

"Good meeting?"

"Challenging. How was your day?"

"The same. Didn't have firm enough charges to hold your Missy Malone, but I let her know we were aware of the shoplifting and would be keeping an eye on her."

"I wonder if she'll be popping in at my shop again."

"Let me know if she does." He eyed the heap of ice

cream he had scooped into his bowl and put one of the mounds back into the carton.

Sam carried her folder to the living room and tried to come up with ideas for Bookman's project, but it had been a long day and her mind refused to do any more work. A glance showed Beau dozing in his recliner in a haze of ice-cream overload, so she suggested they go to bed.

Her dreams were filled with images of foreign cities with market tables laden with unfamiliar foods and spices. By five in the morning, she'd been at the kitchen table for an hour, making lists, and thirty minutes later she was at Sweet's Sweets, where she spent some time online looking at images of the world-tour destinations.

Out of curiosity, she went to Book It Travel's website and found the description of the trip. A person could feed a third-world village for a year for the amount of money these rich folks would spend on their month-long trip. They must truly have unlimited funds. Maybe they were all lottery winners. She shook off the notion when she heard Jen's voice out front. Lost in the online world, she'd barely registered the arrival of her employees.

"Sam, could we talk a minute?" Jen was standing beside her, fidgeting.

"Sure." They walked to the sales room, where the nighttime lighting was still on and the coffee hadn't been started yet.

"Was Missy arrested yesterday?" Jen asked. "Mrs. Chaves came by to pick up her cake and said she'd just driven down Gallegos Road and recognized one of our customers being put into a Sheriff's Department vehicle. The description sounded a lot like Missy, especially when Mrs. C said it was the lady who always bought a truffle."

"Yeah, it was Missy." Sam told the little she knew about the situation, ending with the fact Beau had not been able to hold her. "Just be careful, if she comes around again. We don't *know* that she stole the little gifts she brought us, but it kind of fits with the rest of what happened."

"Ohmygod, I can't believe it. I was completely taken in by her." Jen reached behind her neck and unhooked her pendant chain. "I want to take this back to the shop. And the jade unicorn, too."

Sam thought of the carved cupcake Missy had given her. "Good idea. I know the place. I'll take these and show them to the owner. If they're the pieces she was missing, I'll let her know she can contact Beau."

"I feel so stupid, Sam. She completely fooled me, with all that talk about how rich she was, how she and her husband know so many important people, that they own two homes and have traveled all over the world. She must have seen me as a dumb little small-town girl." Jen's voice became husky and her nose turned pink.

Sam handed her a tissue. "Don't cry over it, sweetie. She's not worth the effort. People like that ... well, I guess they have a way of spotting those of us who would trust them."

"But you didn't trust her, Sam. You saw what she was like."

"I noticed a few little clues, that's all. I had no idea she was anything beyond a shoplifter, and I had no proof of that." Sam had moved to the beverage bar where she measured coffee, started the machine, and put water on to boil for the tea.

"Well, if she comes here again, I won't let her in the door."

Sam was stacking cups and paused. "Actually, it might be interesting to see how it would play out if she did come in. I'm curious whether she would act as if nothing's happened."

Missy knew Beau was connected with the shop, though—odds were she'd never show up again.

Chapter 28

I feel like we're spinning our wheels. We've made no progress at all toward solving Percy Lukinger's murder," Beau said. "All this effort to locate his wife—and why? We need to be reconstructing his last few days. See who he was in contact with, who might have had motive to go after him."

Rico sighed. "Doing the best I can, boss, but watching these videos is a drag."

"I know. Didn't mean to point fingers. Ninety percent of police work is a drag."

Travis spoke up. "I've got something over here. The prints on those brochures match Ramona Lukinger, for what it's worth."

"Well, it proves she was in on the home repair scams

with her husband. So we now have reason to go after her. At least one of their victims can place the pair together, and she would be willing to sign a statement and press charges." His mood plummeted almost as quickly as it had risen. They still had no address or vehicle description for Ramona.

"Whoa! Wait, wait, wait … Look what just came up." Travis was practically bouncing in his chair.

Beau crossed the room and looked over the deputy's shoulder. On the computer screen was a line of data about Ramona Lukinger.

"What—?"

"Woo—I *knew* that hunch would pay off," Travis said. "I just had *no* idea—"

"What hunch are we talking about?"

"When it turned out we couldn't hold Missy Malone last night, I just couldn't let her get away without so much as a photo or a fingerprint. So, I took the can from the Coke she drank, dusted it, and ran the prints. This is what came back," Travis said, triumphantly pointing at his screen. "Missy Malone *is* Ramona Lukinger."

"No—" Beau was about to say 'no way' but something held him back.

Crap. He had not only let her go but had as much as ordered her to leave town.

How had he not recognized her, after carrying Ramona's license photo around with him for days? He dashed to his desk and retrieved Ramona's picture. The dark hair, fuller face, eye color … nothing about the photo would have immediately told him this was petite, blonde Missy Malone. He took the picture to the squad room and asked Rico, Travis, and two other deputies to look at it.

Tell me I'm not crazy, he thought.

Travis was the first to speak. "You're saying this is the same woman we had in custody yesterday? I don't see it."

"We've had witnesses who've described Ramona Lukinger with black hair, with blonde hair, and now I'm beginning to think the redhead in the casino video—the one who approaches Percy while keeping her face hidden from the camera—I'm thinking that could be her as well."

Rico took the picture and studied it. "The height and weight don't seem right. Missy Malone was no 150 pounds. I'd guess her at 110, max."

Beau smiled at the image of his young deputy as a weight-guesser.

Rico squared his shoulders. "Hey—it's a well-known fact that men will lie about their height, women lie about their weight."

"Never saw one who lied with a higher number—they always want to be thinner than they are," Travis observed.

"Unless they have a reason not to have their license photo actually look like them." Beau studied the picture again.

In Ramona's California photo, she wore almost no makeup, had her dark hair hanging in front of her face a bit, and must have been wearing dark brown contact lenses. No smile, and a little air puffed into her cheeks—yeah, she could have passed for heavier. Missy, on the other hand, had a very animated face—both when she was screaming in the pawn shop, and later when she'd turned friendly in the car.

Shit. The car. Her flirty manner and offer to 'work something out' had come right after he had ushered her into the back seat on the right-hand side. She must have spotted the religious pamphlets in their plastic bag on the front seat. She *knew* he was close to identifying Ramona.

Again, he kicked himself for having sent her packing.

Travis was back at his computer screen. "Boss, I've got something more. Electric company has a service address for a Missy Malone."

Beau could almost bet money on how this would turn out, but he had to check it out.

"Walters, come with me. Travis, keep up the background check in California where Ramona got her driver's license. Rico, sorry to say this, but keep watching those videos and this time be extra vigilant for Missy Malone sighted anywhere near Percy."

Beau worked at piecing it together as he drove toward the address Travis provided. He wished it was Sam riding along in the seat beside him. She was observant and sharp, and a hell of a lot more fun as a deputy than Walters. He'd never had the chance to ask more about her big chocolate contract. It seemed business and work were keeping them apart more and more these days. Would they ever again have spare time to spend together?

The apartment was located in a tan-stuccoed two-story building with dark brown trim, ten apartments on the ground level, ten above. The place was so ordinary it could be any of a dozen around town. Which might have been exactly the reason the Lukingers chose it. Few cars were parked out front, and he didn't hold very high hopes for actually running into Missy, er, Ramona. He pulled up to the on-site office and rapped at the manager's door.

"I'm not sure I can let you inside if the tenant isn't there," the timid twenty-ish woman told him. Her television set blared with the cast of some talk show where all five hosts talked at once. A baby screamed in the background.

"I can come back with a warrant," he said. This was where Sam would have an idea that would get him much quicker answers.

The young woman sent an annoyed glance toward the middle of the room and told Beau to hang on a moment. She came back with a key to apartment eight.

"Are these places rented furnished or unfurnished?" he asked.

"Some of each."

He raised his eyebrows and held up the key.

"Number eight was rented with the furniture." The baby in the background was really wailing away now, and the woman said she needed to go.

Beau and Walters walked nearly to the end of the little strip. Each apartment had a brown door and two windows, most curtained. Beau rapped at the one with the cheap brass 8 on the door and wasn't the least bit surprised when no one answered. Using the key, they entered.

Despite the furniture, the apartment had an empty feel. The layout consisted of a living room with extension to a tiny galley kitchen and enough dining space for a small round table and two chairs; a bedroom with double bed and a bathroom smaller than those in most hotel rooms completed the picture. Brown carpet, tan sofa and chair. An empty TV stand. Double bed and an upright chest of drawers in the bedroom. The closet held women's clothing in a size six, and on the floor was a large black suitcase.

When they investigated, they discovered it held three men's suits, six dress shirts, four casual button-down shirts, a new package of black socks, a pair of good quality black shoes (male, size 9) and a paper sack full of cash.

The latter was neatly bundled in stacks and banded in paper wrappers, although the bills were not new.

"Looks like we may be able to make refunds to some of those folks who were fleeced," Walters commented.

"I'll need to log it in as evidence, and we need to take statements from the victims. I sure hate to see this thing get tangled up in court though, especially if Ramona shows up and insists this is money Percy legitimately won at the casino." Before any of that happened, Beau knew he would need a warrant. Right now they were here unofficially, trying to learn more about their murder victim.

Walters grumbled a bit about how law enforcement used to be a lot simpler. He was a man who liked the old-school methods.

"Meanwhile, I'll make the calls to get the paperwork started," Beau said, "and I want somebody out here in a plain car to watch the place to be sure Missy or Ramona or whoever she really is doesn't come back and clean the place out."

He pulled out his phone and made a call to the judge most reasonable about search warrants. Walters continued to poke around in drawers. He came up with several lottery tickets and a business card.

"Isn't this the same guy you already talked to?" he said, holding the card out to Beau as soon as he'd finished leaving a message for the judge.

Grant Mangle Enterprises. "Yes, indeed. More evidence that blows a hole in the guy's story about a one-time meeting."

Beau remembered the way Mangle had sweated over his questions. A little more background on the property manager could give Beau firmer footing for their next round.

"Look at this." Walters held up a small paper envelope. It looked remarkably like the one Beau remembered seeing Percy receive at the casino. The tape hadn't caught a lot of detail. Beau took the envelope and looked inside.

A diamond ring. It could be a twin sister to the one Missy had used as bait for Daisy Ruiz at the pawnshop.

Chapter 29

Judge Albright called back while Beau was debating about leaving the diamond ring, the cash, and the other evidence behind.

"Sheriff," the judge said. "Your message said this warrant request was urgent?"

"We've got a suspect who's tied to a number of con games, and she has already skipped from California and ended up here in Taos." He didn't want to mention that he'd basically ordered Ramona to leave town. "We'd like to search her apartment for evidence that would tie her to several of the victims who have lost their money. And since the woman's husband died a few days ago under suspicious circumstances, we need to see whether his death can be explained by anything in the home, as well."

"Two cases for the price of one warrant, it seems," Albright said with a chuckle.

"Basically, yeah."

The judge agreed to issue the warrant and reminded Beau he needed to have the document in hand when he entered the premises. Beau sensed the wink in Albright's demeanor—here was a man who'd been known to look the other way a time or two—but knew he'd better play by the rules when dealing with someone as slippery as Ramona Lukinger.

He immediately called Rico and told him he could abandon the video footage long enough to run by the courthouse and bring the paperwork to the apartment, where he and Walters would meet him out front. Meanwhile, Beau remembered he'd been on the way to visit Grant Mangle again when the pawnshop call had come in yesterday.

Thirty long minutes passed while they stayed warm in the cruiser, keeping an eye on the apartment door in case Ramona should be so foolish as to pull into the lot with a department vehicle sitting there. Rico seemed happy to be out from behind his video monitor. He didn't squawk a bit about presenting the warrant to the apartment manager and staying behind to help Walters bag evidence and finish searching the hidden crannies of the suspect's residence.

Beau left the two deputies to handle the search while he drove back to the office of Grant Mangle Enterprises, toting with him the small envelope Walters had just discovered. He parked in the lot of a fast-food restaurant next to Mangle's building and walked over. The man looked up from his computer screen when Beau pushed open the glass door, surprise registering on his face.

"Hey, Grant," Beau said as he strolled toward the desk.

"Well, Sheriff, you're back." Mangle made no move to stand or shake hands.

"Yeah. Seems there was a little more to your encounter with Percy Lukinger that you forgot to mention." He pulled out the bagged envelope from Missy Malone's apartment.

Mangle's eyes widened for a fraction of a second before he got his reaction under control.

"I'm not sure what you mean."

"Taos casino. December fifteenth."

"Sheriff, I still don't know what you're talking about." His eyes couldn't quite look straight at Beau.

"It's on the casino's video surveillance tape. You walked up to Percy Lukinger—you called him John Lukinger, if you'll recall—and handed him this envelope. It contains a diamond ring. A man doesn't usually give another man a diamond ring, unless it's some kind of a business deal."

Mangle took a deep breath and repeated his insistence that he didn't know anything about the incident or the ring.

Beau knew when to back off. The guy clearly wasn't about to blurt out an explanation that might prove to be his undoing, and this type was more likely to shut up and call his lawyer if pushed too hard.

"Okay, then. Thanks. If I think of anything else, we'll be back in touch."

"Fine." Mangle picked up his coffee mug, trying to look nonchalant, but the liquid sloshed and he set it down again.

Beau suppressed a smile and walked out. Halfway across the parking lot, he turned and caught Mangle standing at his office window, staring. Beau got in his cruiser and pulled onto the street. Half a block later, he circled and found a spot where he could see the property manager's vehicle parked behind his office.

Less than five minutes later Mangle emerged, got into the Cadillac, and drove northward out of the alley. Beau followed, staying two blocks behind. When they got into the congested area around the plaza, Mangle pulled into the public parking lot on Calle de la Placita, and Beau knew he would be spotted if he followed. He stopped on the street and watched the man drop coins in one of the meters and pull his coat tighter around himself as he set off walking toward the plaza shops. He was debating whether to follow on foot when a voice came over his radio.

"Sheriff, Travis here. You copy?"

Beau watched Mangle disappear around a corner as he answered. "Yeah, Travis."

"Interesting stuff has come up about our suspect."

Grant Mangle's face popped into Beau's mind, until he realized Travis had to be talking about Ramona Lukinger.

"I'm only a block away. I'll be right there," Beau told his deputy, with a final glance toward the place where Mangle had last been seen.

He knew the man was hiding something, and it had to do with the diamond ring in the small envelope they'd found, but darned if he could figure out how it all fit together. He started the cruiser once again and was walking in the door of the squad room five minutes later.

"Look at this, boss," Travis said, pointing at his computer monitor, before Beau had even removed his jacket.

Beau hooked the coat on the rack near the door and stepped to the deputy's desk.

"Ramona and Percy Lukinger were living in San Diego until a few months ago. There's a string of cases where they were questioned."

"What about?"

"Well, let's see … There's a few street cons—three-card monte and the like—a few that happened in bars, one involving a lottery ticket …"

"Busy people," Beau observed. "You said they were questioned—no arrests?"

"Looks like last October someone filed a complaint and the Lukingers *were* actually arrested. It's about a missing diamond ring."

Beau's coincidence-alarm went into overdrive and he could practically feel the evidence bag in his shirt pocket.

"We got a contact number in San Diego?"

"A Detective Rodriguez. Here's the number."

Beau jotted the information from the screen onto a yellow note and carried it to his desk. The call was answered on the second ring.

"Bunco. Jorge Rodriguez speaking."

Beau introduced himself. "Your department records showed up when we ran a background trace on a suspect we have here in Taos County, New Mexico. Her name's Ramona Lukinger."

"You have her in custody?"

"Unfortunately, no. She's been operating here in town, but we only learned about your warrant on her after we had to release her."

"She and her husband are a wily pair, I'll tell you. We thought we had them on a string of Priceless Pooch cons on several local bartenders."

Beau's silence encouraged him to go on.

"The couple splits up and one of them enters a bar with a valuable item. Sometimes it's actually a dog, which is how the con gets its name, but other times it's a piece of jewelry or even a supposedly Stradivarius violin. Ramona would ask the bartender to keep an eye on the item because she has to run an errand in a sketchy part of town and doesn't want to carry it with her. She leaves and almost immediately her accomplice walks in, spots the thing, comments how he's been looking for one of those for a long time, and asks if the bartender wants to sell it. Usually names some outlandish price. Bartender has to admit it isn't his, but can give the guy's phone number to the owner when she returns. The guy—in this case Ramona's husband—leaves his number and goes away. When Ramona gets back, the bartender offers to buy the item for half the amount the other guy said he'd pay, knowing all he has to do is make a phone call and double his money. Ramona reluctantly parts with the item because she needs the cash right now. When the bartender calls the number he was given, it's a fake and the couple has made off with the bartender's money."

"I'm surprised the bartenders report the crime."

"Usually, they don't. We caught onto the Lukingers because one of our guys happened to be sitting in the bar one afternoon and witnessed the whole thing. We put the word out and a few came forward to admit what had happened. Timing is everything on that con—the husband and wife have to appear as strangers who have just barely missed each other each step of the way. Otherwise, the bartender has time to think about it or make a call to someone. Doesn't always have to be a bartender. Once the Lukingers figured out we were watching them, they switched over to shop clerks. It can work on anyone in a relatively low-paying job, where there are not a lot of other customers around to witness what's happening."

"The lure of easy money, right?"

"Gets 'em every time." Rodriguez cleared his throat. "The lottery ticket is a real favorite. Guy approaches someone and says he has the winning lottery ticket from last night's drawing, but he can't appear in person to claim it because his ex is after all his money. A lot of people are suspicious, but the mark who sees an opportunity will offer to buy the ticket for a fraction of its value. He thinks he can cash it in himself for big bucks. If he decides to verify that these are the winning numbers, he calls the lottery office and, yep, those are the right numbers. Only problem is, the ticket in his hand was purchased this morning and is for next week's drawing. By the time he figures that out, the con man and the money have disappeared."

Beau had to wonder whether the very same scams had been going on here in Taos, right under his nose.

"You mentioned questioning Ramona Lukinger. What about the husband, Percy Lukinger?" Rodriguez asked.

"He was here in town, too. Unfortunately, now deceased." Beau covered the basics. He could hear Rodriguez tapping computer keys in the background.

"Any chance you could pick up Ramona Lukinger again?" the San Diego bunco detective asked.

"We'll try. The pair of them had two residences and we've just now discovered Ramona's place, rented under an assumed name. My deputies are searching it for evidence right now. So far, the most shiny clue has been a diamond ring. I'm heading out to have a jeweler verify whether it's real."

"There's probably a real and a fake. It's a variation on the pigeon drop. Con places the ring in an envelope after proving to the victim's satisfaction it's real. Places the envelope in his pocket, when it comes out again, it's an identical-looking envelope but the ring inside is the fake. Or they hand it over to the victim's custody—maybe the glovebox of their car—but make the switch as the envelope goes inside, so the vic only ends up with the fake. Watch out for those—it's another favorite con of the Lukingers."

Beau made a note to revisit the pawn shop and chat with Robert Nieto about the ring Missy Malone had tried to pass there.

"Will do. Thanks for the info. Of course, the bigger crime I have to solve here is the murder of Percy Lukinger. Do you think any of his victims from your area were angry enough to track him all the way to New Mexico?"

"Somebody with some medical knowledge and the means to get hold of enough benzos to kill a guy? Right off hand, I can't think of any but I'll review the cases and see if anything jumps out at me. I'll give you a call if it does."

Beau thanked the detective and hung up. A new thought hit him. What if Percy had somehow double-crossed his wife and *Ramona* was the one who killed him?

Chapter 30

Sam grumbled about Delbert Crow's phone call from the moment he interrupted her research on exotic flavors, right up to the point when she pulled into the driveway at the abandoned house he wanted her to check. Her assurances that the plumber was still planning to come in a few days to fix the broken pipes didn't suffice. Delbert wanted her to be sure the house was in shape for the real estate agent who would be showing up today to take pictures and write up the listing.

She got out of her van and gave the yard a quick perusal as she walked toward the front-porch flowerpot which concealed the key to the door. Everything looked as one would expect a place to look in January—bare and frosty.

The shaded half of the front yard held onto its six inches of snow from the storm that had passed through. Where the sun hit the ground, the grass showed, dry and winter-brown. Deciduous trees waved their bare sticks in the air, while the evergreens hunkered down, ready for the next onslaught. They somehow knew spring was still a good four months away. The wise ones knew there would be a fake-out in late February, when the temperatures would rise just enough to catch the unwary before the next winter blast hit them. Those who sprouted fresh greenery would be goners. The old ones would stay wary and live to see summer.

Raised voices caught Sam's attention as she was unlocking the front door. Instinctively, she glanced toward the house next door, the only one on the block where she'd noticed activity. Arnold Zuckerman seemed to be demanding that someone in the house follow him toward his car, but the voice of the unseen female was adamantly not going along.

Sam wondered if the old man's daughter was visiting again. Dolores had told her the two of them clashed a lot. But if the subject was that of nursing homes, it seemed more likely Arnold would be the one sticking close to home. Besides, it wasn't the daughter's blue minivan parked in the driveway. She started to wave toward the neighbor, but his attention never strayed from the front door of his own home; Sam decided to attend to her duties and get back to work before she could be pulled into some other family's spat. She ducked inside before Zuckerman could turn his attention to her.

The interior of the place felt colder than her walk-in fridge at the bakery, but Sam didn't see any sign of further water damage. She spent a few minutes sweeping up bits of debris she'd missed the last time and left a note for the Realtor about the situation with the pipes, suggesting a later date would work better to get optimal photos inside the house. Delbert Crow's insistence that the place be spotless and the real estate listing be finalized right this minute still made no sense to Sam.

She called Beau and was pleased to hear he hadn't eaten lunch yet. They agreed to meet at the deli on the plaza, where the soup was guaranteed to take the chill off any winter day. She rechecked all the windows and door locks, then stooped to re-hide the key on the front porch. A man's voice caught her attention and she saw Arnold Zuckerman. It appeared he was casting some ice-melt granules over the frozen parts of his driveway.

Well, there was no avoiding him. She had to get to her van if she hoped to meet Beau on time.

"You still here?" Zuckerman said when he spotted Sam.

She waved and pretended she hadn't heard his words.

He stomped snow off his boots and walked toward the low wall that separated the two properties. "Not finished with this place *yet*?" he asked with a nod toward the house she'd just left.

"A few more trips, I'm afraid. We're waiting on a plumber to fix the broken pipes."

"Well, I'm doing fine—thanks for asking," he groused. "Except the damn girl wants me drugged."

Sounded as if the argument from earlier hadn't quite ended yet. Dolores must be pushing harder than ever to get her dad into an assisted living arrangement. Sam wanted to tell him she was sure his daughter had his best interests in mind. But who knew, really? Maybe she didn't.

"Yeah, and my wife has basically banned Dolores from the house. So that's just a barrel of fun. She used to travel a lot on business, but now she informs me she won't be doing that for a while. Can't even watch my basketball channels now without catching hell."

Was he talking about the wife, or the daughter? Curiosity tugged at Sam but she had too many other things on her mind to get pulled into this. Strange dynamics existed in families, for sure.

"Well, I'm sure you'll work out something," she said, smiling as she opened her door. "I'll catch you another time."

Whew! A glance at the dashboard clock told her she had two minutes to be on time for lunch. She longed for one of those days when she and Beau used to take long lunches together and actually make plans for the evening, but right now things were simply too crazy for both of them. Zuckerman had approached her passenger side window but she pretended not to notice until she'd begun to back out of the drive.

I'm sorry for being rude, she thought as she backed out and waved to him. Whatever he had to say would have to wait. No doubt it was some other complaint about the house next to his and a suggestion for what she ought to do to fix it.

The deli felt toasty compared to the chilly outdoors. Sam immediately shed her jacket as she walked toward the corner table where she had spotted Beau.

"Hey beautiful," he said, greeting her with a kiss. "You've got roses in your cheeks. Were you working outside?"

"Not much. Just hustling a bit to break away from the neighbor so I could get here on time." She draped her coat over the back of her chair and sat, taking a glance at the menu even though she knew she wanted the vegetable beef. "How's your case going?"

"I feel like I'm dealing with a herd of runaway steers. Every new string of evidence leads me off in twelve directions. I started out wanting to reconstruct the accident victim's last few days, but couldn't find much to go on. And you know how our efforts to locate the next of kin went. Now I'm off with all these new tangents—is the woman really Ramona Lukinger or is she Missy Malone?"

"Jen was shocked at the way Missy wormed her way into a friendship. She immediately gathered up the little gifts Missy brought, and I took them by the gift shop where the woman had told me some items were stolen."

"Did the shop owner identify them?"

"Two things—little carved fetishes of stone—came from her shop. There was a zodiac necklace, too, but that wasn't one of her items. So, good old Missy must have had her sticky little fingers busy all over town."

"Would the shop owner press charges if I went by and talked to her?"

"Probably. But how much of a sentence would Missy get for shoplifting fifty dollars' worth of merchandise?"

"Not enough to get her off the street for long, that's for sure. I'll stop by and talk with the lady though. Part of the problem with these con artists is that no single incident involves a lot of money, and too many of the victims just let it go."

Their soup arrived, and Sam busied herself for a minute by buttering the warm bread that came with it.

"I spoke with a bunco detective in San Diego this morning. You wouldn't believe the variety of con games Percy and Ramona pulled out there. And yet this cop, Jorge

Rodriguez, said even when they had witnesses, he was hard-pressed to get any of them to file a formal complaint. He estimated the pair of them earned an easy two to three thousand a month, and they did it a couple hundred dollars at a time."

It explained why the Lukingers had no employment records and none of the usual paper trail.

"Rodriguez had one case where the stolen amount would have put the punishment into the felony category, but the prosecutor didn't want to bother with it. Told the cops his office was pushed to the limit with 'important' cases and he didn't have the resources to follow up on this petty stuff. Rodriguez sounded ready to boil, but admitted it's the same everywhere. Too many criminals, too few people to track them down, too few facilities to lock them up."

Sam looked up from her soup. She could tell the morning's conversation had hit a hot button with Beau.

"I'm not going to be one of those," he said. "We found cash in Ramona's apartment, and I'll at least try to get it back to the victims if I can figure out who lost what."

"It'll work out, sweetheart. You're a great lawman, and you'll get the answers. Somehow, I have the feeling you'll be the one who finally stops the Lukingers."

He almost chuckled. "Well, since Percy Lukinger already got stopped, half the job's done."

Sam paused. "Sorry. I guess I'd forgotten that what you're really trying to solve is a murder case. How's that part of it coming along?"

"While I was talking to Rodriguez, it struck me that Ramona could be the one who killed her husband. She sure showed up quickly to claim his body and have him cremated—thinking, maybe, she could have the toxin destroyed before it was discovered."

"So, catching her might wrap up the whole case?"

"Or not. Rodriguez talked about all the scams the couple pulled where they worked as a team. I have to ask myself whether Ramona was dumb enough to get rid of the partner whose help was critical in earning their living."

"I don't know ... you see cases all the time where good marriages go horribly wrong. People don't always act rationally. Heat of the moment, and all that."

"Yeah. I know."

Sam thought back to her few encounters with Missy Malone—she was still having a hard time thinking of the flighty blonde as Ramona Lukinger. Sam could picture her fast talking and wide-eyed innocence as the means of getting herself out of shoplifting and petty theft, but murder? The woman must be a hell of an actor.

They talked of other things while they finished their soup, until Sam checked the time and realized she was about to be late for Stan Bookman's visit to the chocolate factory. She told Beau to take his time over lunch, but he set down his spoon and put money on the table.

"I need to get back to work, too," he said when they reached the sidewalk outside. "Sure wish you had the time these days to come back to your deputy duties. You have a good eye for discrepancies, and I think you could go through those casino videos a lot quicker than Rico is."

"Uh-uh, sorry. Spending days watching videotapes of people at slot machines just isn't my idea of a good time."

He laughed and the sparkle came back into his eyes. Sam hoped he would solve his case soon—she had missed that sparkle.

Chapter 31

Sam took a deep breath and stared at the drawings she'd made for Mr. Bookman's chocolates. The sketches covered her desktop but nothing about them satisfied her. This was a dumb idea, trying to draw concepts for chocolate candy. She needed to get into the kitchen and simply create. The chocolate would take shape and inspiration would come.

A scene flashed through her mind—Bobul, the chocolatier who seemed to show up in her life when he was most needed, working the chocolate with his fingers, creating miraculous delicacies with ease. She sighed. If only he were here now.

Sounds from downstairs told her Stan Bookman and his pilot had arrived. Since their last meeting, her client had flown to Houston, New York, London, and back—while Sam had produced very little in the way of tangible results. For the first time, she felt an energy-lag regarding her business. Somehow, it wasn't as much fun as it used to be.

"Cut that out!" she told herself. "Put your faith in the fact that things do work out well in the long run."

This morning she had blended some new flavors for sampling and, although the form and design were lacking, she wanted Stan's opinion on the tastes. She'd actually come up with a blend of exotic flavors she hoped would come close to his vision of what the Peruvian Andes tasted like. With a glance at the drawings on the desk, she selected two and left the others behind as she went downstairs to greet her most important client.

"Sam! Good to see you again," he said, as if it hadn't been less than a week since he'd been here. "I hope you don't mind that I brought Rollie along. My newest pilot, it turns out, has a great palate for chocolate."

Sam sent the man a smile, all the while hoping that a new opinion wouldn't send her back to square one with the plans for the international line.

"I've got some new things for you," she said. "I hope you don't mind tasting them in the corner up front. As you can see, my crew has the rest of the floor space pretty well occupied."

She hoped Bookman wouldn't take this to mean Sweet's Chocolates didn't have room to handle the additional work. *What's with all the negative thinking today?* She stifled all thoughts of proving inadequate to the task and concentrated on the winning aspects of her new creations.

She showed the men to a quiet corner of the cupola area where she had set up a small table with three chairs. A carafe of warm lemon water and three cups would provide the means to cleanse their palates between tastes.

"Make yourselves comfortable and I'll be right back."

In the kitchen, a tray with nine squares of chocolate sat at the end of the long counter. Sam picked it up and dodged Benjie as he turned from the stove with a large bowl of melted chocolate that appeared ready for tempering. When she returned to the alcove, the men were admiring the view of open, snowy fields.

"Sam, I have to say that I really love your location. It must be a joy to work from such a quiet place," Stan Bookman said. "I'll bet this old house has some real history."

"I have to admit I know very little of it, other than the last resident was an eccentric writer named Eliza Nalespar."

There had been hints of darker doings in times past, and for a time Sam had begun to wonder if the place was haunted. But most of the weirdness turned out to have perfectly logical, human motivated explanations. Kelly's fiancé, Scott, had promised to look more deeply into the history of the house, but Sam had forgotten to ask during the holidays and the professor was back in his classroom now.

She set the tray with the chocolate samples in the center of the table.

"We'll move from the subtler flavors to the stronger one. First, I'd like you to try this lightest colored one. The cacao percentage is higher than in milk chocolate, but it's still a mild one. The flavor is a floral—see if you can tell me which."

Each of them took one of the chocolate squares and bit a corner from it. Sam let the chocolate melt on her tongue and felt the subtle infusion fill her mouth.

"Hibiscus?" Bookman guessed.

"No, it seems a little stronger," said Rollie. "Jasmine."

Sam smiled. "A little more unusual than that. It's passion flower. I chose it as a tropical flower that would be found on Samoa, and it will be featured in the sampler your passengers receive on that leg of their world tour."

Both men nodded approval and finished their samples. Sam mentally added hibiscus to her list of essences to experiment with. She already had jasmine in mind for India.

With their second samples, both men correctly guessed that the country it fit was India. "Not curry, but something reminiscent of it," Bookman said.

"You're right." She gave an enigmatic smile, which told them she wouldn't divulge *all* her secrets.

"Sam, I love it. So, what's this final one?"

"Well, I aimed for what you described in Machu Picchu. It's a deep South American cacao, but you tell me what you think the flavor combination is."

Bookman took a small nibble, a thoughtful look on his face. Rollie almost grimaced. Uh-oh, Sam thought.

"It's very unusual," Stan said. "I'm not sure if I like it."

Sam resisted the urge to say anything.

"But I can't say that I dislike it either."

Rollie nodded at the boss's assessment. "The bitter chocolate is nice. I just can't pinpoint the other thing. It's earthy."

"Stan told me when he was there he thought of moss. That's what it is, an edible moss."

"Use it." Stan rubbed his hands together. "It's the kind of taste that grows on you, and I think it'll be a big hit with those folks who pride themselves on having tried everything. You know, the ones who brag about eating rattlesnake and such."

Sam refrained from saying that rattlesnake wasn't such

an unusual dish, especially here in the Southwest. As long as Stan okayed her choices for the chocolates she could proceed.

"These are fantastic, Sam. Don't change a thing. Can you have sample boxes made up for the whole itinerary in another week or so?" he asked as the men stood to leave.

None of the designs had been finalized and she still had no ideas for three of the locations, but somehow the words that popped out of her mouth were, "Sure. A week will be fine."

Chapter 32

Beau looked at his watch. Nearly an hour had passed since he'd followed Grant Mangle to the parking lot near the plaza. It was worth driving by there to see if the man was still around. If not, he would surely show up at his office. Armed with the information from Rodriguez, Beau could come a lot closer to rattling the property manager with a good guess at what had happened between him and Percy Lukinger.

He snagged his coat and walked out to his SUV. The afternoon sun was already behind the trees surrounding Civic Plaza Drive, and he could feel the temperature dropping. Another storm was due tonight.

The parking lot was only half full and Mangle's Cadillac sat where he'd last seen it. Beau parked his cruiser between two other vehicles, two rows away from the Caddy, and watched the three sidewalks where a person would have to come from the shops to the lot. Most folks were rushing to their cars with their heads down as the frigid wind picked up. Grant Mangle was no exception. He was aiming his key fob at his vehicle when Beau stepped into his field of view.

"It's okay to admit that Percy Lukinger tried to scam you," Beau said.

"Sheriff, I told you, I don't know anything about this guy you're talking about."

"You really want to stick with that story, even though we have the two of you together on camera? He was a crook and a con artist, and you can't bring yourself to tell me what happened?"

Grant shivered in his jeans and light jacket.

"There's a warmer place we can talk about this," Beau said, "and I'm getting sick of the runaround. If I have to cuff you and take you in for questioning, I will."

"I don't want to press charges. I got fleeced, okay? Can't we just drop it?"

"It's not that simple. Let's get inside, warm up with some coffee, and we'll talk about it." Beau took the man's elbow and steered him in the direction of the cruiser.

Inside the station, Beau led his guest to an interrogation room, hoping the official surroundings would encourage cooperation. Mangle played the cool customer while he was left alone. Beau noticed through the mirrored glass that the man sat back in his chair, legs sprawled, arms relaxed—a guy without a care in the world—although he did glance toward the mirror regularly.

Someone had brewed fresh coffee. Beau poured two cups and carried them to the interrogation room, along with a folder he'd tucked under his arm. Mangle straightened in his chair when Beau tossed his yellow pad of notes onto the table.

"Okay, a few more questions today, Mr. Mangle. We're just tying up some loose ends here."

Mangle nodded, took a sip of the coffee, made a slight face, took another sip. His eyes were on the yellow pad, but Beau always left a blank sheet on top of any he'd written on.

Beau reached into his shirt pocket and pulled out the small envelope with the fake diamond in it. "Recognize this?"

He didn't need to ask. Mangle's reaction told him a lot more than the man's verbal denial.

"Funny, because we've got you on footage from the casino, along with Percy Lukinger. John Lukinger, as you called him. This envelope seems to be in the exchange between you two."

Mangle's fingers gripped the coffee cup a little tighter.

"I've been on the phone with a detective in San Diego, where the Lukingers apparently worked this scam a lot. You're not the only one who thought he'd found a treasure, only to find out it was worthless."

"It wasn't like that," Grant said. By now his shoulders had slumped.

"Then tell me how it was."

"My wife's engagement ring. She loved the setting but always wanted a larger stone, and for our tenth anniversary I'd promised to get one. A jeweler could remake the prongs to hold a two-carat diamond instead of the half-carat I'd originally been able to afford when we got engaged. I'd already talked to one jeweler and planned to take the ring to have the work done."

Beau sat back and let the man talk.

"So, okay, I admit I talked too much, was bragging a little to some friends at the casino one evening. My wife was wearing her old ring and she was so proud that she'd be able to get a flashier version of it soon." He fidgeted with the rim of the Styrofoam cup a little more. "This guy, John, was at the same blackjack table and he took me aside and asked which jeweler I was going to. Told me that place was a rip-off, that his brother was in the wholesale diamond business in South Africa, and he could get me any stone I wanted. He described some knockout diamonds at fantastic prices, and, well, I could imagine the way my wife's eyes would light up. I mean, I have my little business, but we're not exactly high rollers. I wanted to do something really nice for her. We could get a five-carat stone for what I'd been about to spend on two carats. Which wasn't cheap, by the way."

Beau nodded. He was getting the idea where this was going. "Did you hand over your wife's ring to the man?"

"Well, no. I mean, we'd just met him."

"Where does the little envelope come into it?"

"We met a few more times. He even came by the office and brought some stones to show me. I chose one and agreed on a price, which included him taking Sally's diamond in trade. He even knew a jeweler in New York who could mount the new stone. He said we didn't have to pay for the new stone until we saw the finished ring."

"And here's where it got tricky?"

"Well, yeah. I thought I was being so careful. I talked to the jeweler on the phone and he said John knew how to package the ring and send it registered mail. They would handle the whole thing. All this time, my wife thought I'd just taken her ring to our normal jeweler on the plaza. You probably know the place—it used to be owned by an old guy who retired, and a younger gemologist is there now."

"And the envelope?"

"A couple weeks later, I saw John in the casino and asked how the ring was coming along, told him I thought it would be done already. He's all happy to see me, and he tells me he's got it right there. Reaches into his pocket and hands me this little envelope. It sure looks like Sally's ring, and it has a huge stone now. I wrote him a check and thanked him."

"That's it? Everything was fine?" Beau had to admit he was surprised the story had turned out this way.

"Uh, no. Sally takes one look at the ring and says it's not hers. The inscription inside the band got our wedding date wrong."

"Oops."

"Yeah, huge oops. Not only did I look like a fool in front of my wife, but I began to panic about the five-grand I'd given John Lukinger. I called the number he'd given me, but no answer. I called the jeweler in New York. It was a real store, all right, but they'd never heard of me or anything about the ring I was describing."

"But you got the larger diamond."

"Except it was a fake. When I took it to Randolph's, they took great pity on me but said the stone was just a zirconia. As were all the smaller stones, and the gold in the band was plating over a cheaper base metal. John Lukinger got five thousand dollars from me, plus a ring worth another couple thousand."

"What did you do next?"

"Well, I knew he hung out at the casino a lot, so I went

there. I gave him the fake ring and demanded Sally's real ring back."

Beau had been writing notes on the pad. So far, this gelled with what they'd seen on the tape.

"Did you ever catch up with him again?"

Grant Mangle got quiet. "I wanted to, Sheriff. Boy, did I want to."

"Maybe your paths crossed again. Say, about a week ago?" Beau had stopped writing and made direct eye contact with his suspect. "If you met up at the casino again, we'll know. We are currently going through the footage from every one of Lukinger's visits."

Mangle got quiet. "What happened a week ago?"

"Let me ask the questions. Where were you on the thirteenth?"

The suspect gave an impatient sigh. "I don't know. Where were you? Do people actually remember where they were all the time?"

"They do if something important was happening. Like, maybe, if a guy was retrieving a valuable item he thought he'd lost."

A variety of emotions crossed Mangle's face, and Beau couldn't tell with a certainty what any of them signified. "Mr. Mangle, I should let you know that Percy Lukinger, a.k.a. John Lukinger, is dead."

"Whoa! Hey, you should have told me that earlier."

"I'm telling you now. You know anything about that?"

"Couldn't happen to a nicer guy." But when Mangle noticed Beau's expression, he backtracked. "Sorry. I don't mean that. But if it's true about all the people he gypped, someone must have had it in for the guy."

"I didn't say he was murdered. Maybe you know

something about *that*."

Another flicker of emotional turmoil "I'm not saying that at all. And if we're having this conversation, I want a lawyer."

Chapter 33

Beau had told Grant Mangle he wasn't under arrest for anything; they were merely trying to locate people who had dealings with Percy Lukinger and establish alibis for them. But the man was insistent upon calling his attorney. The two of them were conferring at the moment, and Beau was using the time to phone Rico to see if anything new had turned up during the search of the apartment.

"Nothing with this suspect's name on it," Rico told him. "We're still here, poking around in corners."

When Beau walked back into the interrogation room, the attorney sat up a little straighter in his chair.

"My client is ready to cooperate," he said.

Beau felt as if he was starting at the beginning. "Okay, Mr. Mangle. Have you remembered where you were from noon onward on the thirteenth?"

"I was working alone in my office."

"Did anyone call or stop by, anyone who can verify you were there?"

"The phone rings a lot. I'd have to look at my records to see who called that particular day."

"How do you handle calls when you're away from your desk? Do they go to an answering device, get forwarded to your cell phone?"

"Some of each. When we're especially busy, like at the first of the month, I have a part-time girl who comes in."

"What did you do on that particular day?"

A flicker of irritation. "As I *said* … I would have to check my records."

"Anyone come by?"

"No."

"You didn't see another person all day?"

Grant fidgeted in his chair and glanced at his attorney, who gave a small nod.

"I had a late lunch with my wife, met with a client for a few minutes, then I was back at my desk by about three-thirty or so."

Pulling teeth. Seriously. Beau had to work to keep his annoyance from showing. "And this client's name?"

More fidgeting. "It was John. Lukinger."

"He was a client of your business, too?"

"Well, okay, maybe 'client' is the wrong word."

"You saw John Lukinger—Percy—within hours of when he died, and you couldn't have simply told me this?"

The attorney spoke up. "Sheriff, there's no need to harass my client."

"And there's no need for your client to make me play

twenty-questions to get the simple information I asked for an hour ago, before you ever got here. He's wasting both your time and mine."

Clearly, the attorney didn't care how much time was wasted at his hourly rates.

Beau took a breath and resumed. "Mr. Mangle, what transpired between you and Mr. Lukinger at that meeting?"

The attorney nodded toward his client, giving the go-ahead to answer.

"Well, it wasn't actually a formal meeting. As Sally and I were leaving the restaurant, she got into her car and I was walking over to mine when I saw Lukinger across the parking lot. I caught up with him and asked about my wife's ring, the real one."

"What did he say?"

"He laughed. Actually laughed. Said he didn't know what I was talking about."

"And your reaction to that comment?"

"I was stunned. To claim he didn't know what I was talking about—after being so chummy at our previous encounters."

"Did you want to retaliate? Punch him?"

The attorney gave Mangle a nudge with his elbow.

"Lukinger hopped into his car and zoomed out of that parking lot so fast, I didn't have time to say or do anything. I don't know what I would have done if he'd stayed around. I ran over to my car and got in, but by the time I was able to cross the traffic, he was long gone."

Beau made notes, trying to formulate his next question, when the attorney spoke up.

"Sheriff, my client has given the information you asked for. He's being cooperative. He's a man of good standing in the community, with a business, and his wife's employment keeps her here. They won't be going anywhere, so unless you have evidence and are ready to make an arrest, I'm asking that you release him."

As much as Beau would have liked to have a suspect for the murder locked away in his cell, he had to admit there was nothing but circumstantial evidence against Mangle at this point.

"Advise him, counselor, to stick around town and to be ready to answer any clarifying questions we might have later. Meanwhile, I want a list of your appointments and phone calls, Mr. Mangle."

The attorney nodded toward his client to acknowledge all of it, and the two men pushed their chairs back. Beau watched them leave, hoping his number one suspect would heed his own attorney's advice and not try to run.

Back at his desk, he fiddled with the bags of evidence they had so far. The fake diamond glinted at him from its plastic bag. He thought of Mangle's story about how Lukinger had switched the rings. If Beau hadn't personally taken this stone to a jeweler, he might have thought this stone could be Sally Mangle's. Unfortunately, it wasn't. The real ring and real stone were probably long gone. The situation was sad, but it could also be a reason for Grant to have gone off the deep end. The man had not exactly given an iron-clad alibi.

He picked up the paper envelope Walters had found in Missy/Ramona's apartment. The ring inside must be the fake Mangle had described, the one his wife recognized immediately because the inscription had got their wedding date wrong. He dumped the ring into the palm of his hand and held it up to catch the light. It seemed lightweight for its size; otherwise, he wouldn't have had any idea it wasn't made of real gold and real diamonds.

He thought back to his conversation with Detective Rodriguez. When a con man was pulling a pigeon drop scam on someone he had to have a way to know which packet contained the real item. Beau set the ring aside and looked carefully at the envelope. On the back bottom corner he spotted a dot of black ink, inconspicuous, the kind of spot most anyone wouldn't notice. Anyone but the con man. This had to be his way of telling two otherwise identical envelopes apart.

He picked up the phone and dialed Rico's cell.

"Have you guys left the apartment yet?" he asked.

"Just about ready to. Why?"

"Did you find another envelope like the one Walters found with the ring in it?"

Some shuffling in the background, Rico asking Walters the question.

"Nope, doesn't look like it."

"Could you do another quick check? Pockets of clothing, purses or wallets … anywhere a person could carry it. The other one may or may not have anything inside. Probably won't."

"We pretty much—"

"It's important," Beau said.

A long sigh, but Rico agreed to go through the place one more time. Beau felt badly, asking them to stay. Searches could become mind-numbing after several hours. But coming up with two identical envelopes in the con couple's apartment would go a long way toward proving the fraud once the district attorney took the case to court. Visual evidence always worked better in front of a jury than theoretical explanations.

He'd placed the fake ring and the paper envelope

back inside its plastic evidence bag when another thought hit him. Even if Grant Mangle had walked away from Lukinger, there was still the possibility Ramona had turned on her husband. Maybe he'd planned to double-cross her by taking the cash and the real ring.

Chasing down two different suspects with two entirely different motives … yeah, this would definitely complicate things.

Chapter 34

Sam sat at her desk upstairs at the chocolate factory, head in her hands. The harder she pushed her brain to come up with new ideas, the more blocked she felt. Stan Bookman and his pilot had left two hours ago, saying they must rush to get airborne before the storm closed in.

She'd been pleased with their initial reaction to the three samples she presented, but the problem remained. She needed to come up with boxes for nine destinations, a dozen chocolates per box. More than a hundred pieces of candy for each couple, and Bookman expressly said he wanted them unique and destination-specific. He'd hinted that it could be intriguing for each couple aboard the flight to get something slightly different in their boxes; it would spark interesting conversations.

Sam hoped she had quelled that idea by suggesting it could spark claims of favoritism or worse. You never knew what wealthy people would find to nitpick.

"Surely, no one would want a refund of their travel fee based on something so minuscule as a fellow passenger getting preferential chocolate?" she had asked. That was the moment Bookman had agreed all the boxes should be identical.

Still, it didn't exactly solve her current creativity crisis as she struggled to come up with ideas for shapes and flavors. A dark cloud of despair settled over her—until she looked out the window and realized the storm was quickly moving in.

Okay, Sam, get your mind on something else for a while. Sometimes it helped when she was stuck for a cake idea just to take a walk or scrub something. She left her sketchbook behind and went down to the kitchen.

Benjie took her aside. "Weather station says snow will start accumulating within the next hour," he said. "Do you think we should let everyone go home a little early?"

Sam looked out the kitchen window and saw the light flurries had become large flakes, which had already given the ground a light coating of white.

"Mr. Bookman took seven cartons with him for his charters," Benjie said. "That's all we had ready at the time, except the box I was going to send with you for the bakery. Tomorrow's orders for Book It are already underway. The chocolate has been tempered and molded. I can stay a while and decorate."

"You should probably leave too," Sam said. Benjie drove a little rattletrap car that she wouldn't trust when the roads became tricky. "Have you said anything to the others yet?"

Her attention flicked around the kitchen, where everything seemed well organized. Together, they walked to the packing room. Lisa and the new girl, Dottie, were working on the last two racks of chocolates, placing them carefully in boxes. In the shipping room, three cartons labelled BOOK IT stood near the door. Ronnie and Lucinda were filling a fourth with the decorative beribboned boxes Bookman's charter passengers received.

Twelve more cartons were ready to be shipped by UPS to the three boutique hotels where Stan Bookman had secured contracts for his charter passengers to stay; chocolates were part of the deal there, as well. Sam wasn't quite sure how her little company would keep up with demand if his grand plans for a cruise line were to develop.

"These will be ready whenever the customer comes to get them," Ronnie told Sam, indicating the boxes he and Lucinda were working on. "They took seven already."

"Thanks. That should be enough to keep them stocked for a few days, in case this storm keeps their planes from getting to town right away," Sam told him. "Meanwhile, Benjie suggested we all go home a little early today. I agree. We want everyone safe. Tomorrow morning, as usual, we'll go by whatever the schools do. If they're open, we are. If they call for an abbreviated day, that's what we'll do."

Smiles appeared, although Lisa tried to tamp hers down and even offered to stay late if needed. "I have all-wheel drive," she told Sam.

Sam patted her arm. "It's okay. It's already after four. Everything's in good shape here, so go home, everyone, be safe. See you tomorrow." She would call Sweet's Sweets and pass the same message along to the crew there. Unless a customer was scheduled for a late cake pickup, they could close up shop.

Frankly, after the crazy morning pace and the meeting with Bookman, she was looking forward to a little time alone. Constant hustle-bustle wasn't exactly conducive to the creativity she needed right now. Sam had brought her pickup truck today; the beefy four-wheel drive machine could get her through fairly deep snow, if it came to that.

She watched the others get into their vehicles and drive away, making distinct tracks on the now-white driveway. She breathed a sigh and allowed herself five minutes to take in the beauty of the open fields. Black branches on the surrounding trees spiked upward against the pale grey sky, the larger ones already becoming topped with a gentle sugaring of white.

Walking through the rooms, she saw her workers had covered the racks of candy with light cloths, and the gift boxes and ribbons were neatly organized, ready for work to resume on a moment's notice. Kitchen vessels had been put away clean, and the chocolates that had been unmolded stood ready for Benjie's talented hand at decorating them. For an instant, Sam saw Bobul standing at the worktable at Sweet's Sweets when he'd shown up to help with her first Christmas season. His large hands were able to work the most delicate designs, a fact that constantly amazed her whenever she watched him work. She blinked and the hazy picture vanished.

"Inspire me," she whispered to the empty kitchen. "I need your ideas."

Aside from ideas, it occurred to her she'd better check her stash of the special powders she used, the mysterious ingredient the Romanian chocolatier had supplied, the unexplained magic that made her chocolates completely irresistible.

Right now was one of the rare occasions she was alone

in the old Victorian building. Might as well take advantage. She reached for the shelf above the stove where she kept a tin canister with three cloth bags inside. Benjie was under strict orders to personally add a pinch from each—the blue, the green, and the red pouches—and never to discuss them with his coworkers. Somehow he knew not to question where the powders came from.

Sam pulled the lid from the tin. As always the small bags were nearly weightless, but she gave a small squeeze to each to judge the volume of the contents. Satisfactory, for now. She once kept an extra supply of each on the wire shelf in the supply room, but the addition of so many new employees required that she take extra care. The safe in her upstairs office was now the repository for the rest of the precious magic. She returned the tin to its place above the stove and checked the lock on the back door.

Outside, the late afternoon sky had grown darker. She pulled shades over the downstairs windows, turned on the nighttime lighting, and made certain the front door was also locked before heading upstairs.

Her sketchpad lay on the desk, the feeble attempts at chocolate designs mocking her. She turned away and opened the closet where Beau and Rico had installed a small safe to hold important financial papers, a bit of cash, checkbook. But Sam's most valued possessions weren't money. She entered the combination and opened the heavy steel door.

On the bottom shelf sat the three bags Bobul had left for her last fall—cloth pouches, larger versions of the three small ones down in the kitchen tin. She took them out. They felt lighter in weight than she remembered. Sitting cross-legged on the floor, she opened the red one and reached inside.

More than halfway down, her fingers encountered the powdered substance. She took a pinch and brought it out to the light. The red flakes reminded her of the tiniest of snowflakes with their crystalline surfaces that sparkled in the lamplight. She let them fall back into the bag.

The blue bag and the green one were also less than half full. She dipped her fingers into them, just to be sure. Would there be enough to meet the demand of these new orders? There was no way to know for certain, and she would simply have to trust.

She flicked bits of green sparkle from her fingers, which tingled slightly. A rush of energy traveled up her arm. All at once, images began to appear in her mind, images of places and sights. The scent of chocolate came to her, along with smells that were at once exotic, tropical, moist, dry ... foreign.

Sam dropped the cloth pouches on the floor and raced downstairs to the kitchen.

Don't overthink this, she told herself. *Just go with it.*

She reached for her favorite copper pot and the double boiler insert, a bar of her richest cacao, butter, cream. As the mixture warmed to the melting point, she added pinches of the ingredients from the tin. On the cold tabletop she watched the chocolate temper, and with her fingertips it began to take shape.

The images from her mind took over. One by one, small details emerged in the chocolate as Sam formed and shaped, placing a tiny decorative touch here and there. Alone under the glow of the overhead light, she lost herself in the work as the sky blurred into night and the earth became coated in a thick mantle of white.

Chapter 35

With Travis at work to unearth Grant Mangle's phone records, deputies Rico and Walters at the apartment of Ramona Lukinger, Beau decided his best bet was to take up where Rico had left off with the casino video footage. Boring, yes. Fruitless, possibly. Necessary—an inescapable yes.

The afternoon shift change had happened already. With snow accumulating on the roads, he needed every deputy out there ready to respond to the inevitable calls, so Beau took the seat in front of the video monitor.

Rico had kept precise notes about his progress, having made it about halfway through the list of Lukinger's recorded casino visits. The deputy had noted the times when Percy interacted with anyone, a list that was fairly extensive because it included casino employees. Beau discovered he already knew about the most important encounters, but it was good for him to review them now that he'd interviewed Grant Mangle and had interacted with Ramona. He looked over the notes to get the time sequence firmly in mind, then started the tape and fast-forwarded it to the next date and time on the list.

For the most part, Percy Lukinger had gambled alone and his visits consisted of sitting at one machine for twenty or thirty minutes, moving to another, ordering a drink from one of the roaming cocktail waitresses. On Friday and Saturday nights, he became more social, strolling the casino floor and chatting with other patrons. Rico had noticed the pattern—harder to catch because Lukinger often didn't swipe his club card and therefore didn't show up on the printout the security man had given them. Rico had made a note in his small, precise printing: Elderly—victims?

Once Beau began looking for the pattern, it was fairly obvious. Lukinger did his serious gambling in the early morning hours when he sat alone and concentrated on his machine. On the weekends, he played the slots a bit, but it was obvious he was really playing the other customers as he chatted them up. Beau found it hard to watch the old people, many of whom probably didn't have any spare money, as they became animated in conversation with the con man.

There were a few instances where small envelopes changed hands, quite a number of times where Percy would drop what appeared to be a five-hundred-dollar casino chip on the floor, then tap an old lady on the shoulder and apparently ask if it was hers. When she shook her head, Lukinger would engage her in conversation.

Beau chafed at the fact the video had no sound. He could imagine, based on what Rodriguez had told him about con games, that when the pair on film moved out of camera range, the old lady's money was probably ending up in Percy's pockets. He added to Rico's notes, wondering if there would be any point to reviewing the tape with casino security personnel and attempting to locate the victims and manage to get restitution for them. It would be a huge, daunting task and probably impossible in the long run.

He flexed his hands and stood, needing to stretch, when a new image came onto the screen. He recognized the woman who moved to the slot machine next to Lukinger. It was Ramona. With her natural blonde curls and upscale clothing, she was in her Missy Malone persona, the one Sam had identified as trying to pull a fast one at the bakery and shoplifting small valuables from Clarice's gift shop. Beau's attention sparked. This was no coincidence. The two con artists were up to something.

Ramona's lips moved, although she kept her eyes on the machine in front of her. To the casual observer, she wasn't having a conversation with Percy—she was probably talking to the machine. But Percy's subtle reactions and responses told Beau the two were conversing. When an elderly man stepped into the picture, Beau slowed the tape to see which of the con artists would drop the chip or envelope.

To his surprise, the old man walked right up to Ramona, put his left arm around her shoulders, and handed her a drink. She smiled up at him and batted her long lashes. She touched his arm, then proceeded to introduce him to Percy. From all appearances, it looked as if the older man was her date for the evening and she was introducing him to a fellow gambler she'd just met. Beau backed up the tape and watched the sequence again.

A gust of cold air caught Beau's attention and he spun his chair to see Rico and Walters coming in the back door, stomping snow from their shoes.

"Whew, it's getting a little crazy out there," Walters said, shaking flakes from his jacket as he hung it on the rack near the door.

Rico carried a cardboard box filled with small evidence envelopes, which he set on his desk before removing his own coat.

"Traffic moving okay?" Beau asked, noticing with a start that it was already dark outside. How long had he been sitting at the video monitor?

"A few snarls," Walters said. "Town police and our guys seem to be responding to everything all right."

"Rico, come here a second," Beau said. "Take a look at this segment. It's only a few minutes of footage, but it seems to tell a story."

The deputy rubbed his hands together and tucked them close to his sides as he walked over to the table where Beau sat.

"Okay, I backed up the tape. Tell me what you see."

Rico stared at the screen. "That's Lukinger. The woman ... wait. She's the one we hauled in here. His wife?"

Beau nodded.

"So who's the other man? She appears to be there with him."

"Exactly what I was thinking. My guess is that he's just another mark."

They watched for a few more minutes, but Ramona and the older man did nothing more than put a few more coins into their machine, then they walked away. Beau couldn't help feeling there was something significant to the encounter. But he was damned if he could figure out what.

"Want me to take over?" Rico asked, with a nod toward the monitor.

"Nah, your shift was over a long time ago. This can wait. You ought to get home." Beau glanced toward the dark windows, where the lighted glare from the room reflected back. "Hell, *I* ought to get home. Surprised Sam hasn't been calling to see why I'm not there for dinner."

He looked at his watch, startled to see it was after eight o'clock. A ripple of apprehension sliced up his spine. Why *hadn't* Sam called to check on him? He picked up the box of evidence from the Lukinger apartment and carried it to his office where he could lock it away for the night. Setting it on the desk, he picked up his phone and tapped in Sam's mobile number.

No answer. The ripple grew stronger.

Okay, he told himself. I'll feel pretty silly when I get home and she's sitting there in front of *Dancing With the Stars*. She just doesn't have the phone nearby.

He grabbed his coat and Stetson, checked out with the night dispatcher, and went outside to his cruiser. It took five minutes to clear the snow from his windows. More than six inches had accumulated since those first few flurries, and the white stuff was quickly freezing to the surface. It looked as if this might turn into the major winter storm the weather guys had predicted. With his heater blasting, he backed out of his spot and turned onto Civic Plaza Drive.

The county snowplows had already made passes along Paseo del Pueblo, making it reasonably clear for the few cars that were still out. Taos wasn't much of a nighttime town, especially not in inclement weather. The residents liked to be at home to keep their woodstoves stoked.

Beau made a left turn onto the main drag and headed

north. His mind kept returning to the Lukinger case, but he made himself put it aside. Oftentimes, he found it helpful to give himself a break, put a little distance from a problem, and an answer would come to him. His stomach growled and he realized it had been hours since he'd thought about food. Too late now for a big dinner, if he hoped to get a decent night's sleep, but a cup of soup or a little snack would be welcomed.

The cruiser's automated four-wheel-drive kicked in when he came to the part of the highway where the plow had only cleared one blade-width down the center. Only one other set of tracks stretched out in front of him, a passenger car, he guessed from the width and tread pattern. In the distance, two small red taillights glowed. All was calm.

He made the turns for their road, then the driveway. One glance told him things were not right. The house was dark and the dogs paced the front porch. Sam's truck wasn't in its usual place. His headlights alerted the dogs and they rushed out to greet him, streaks of black against the white snow. He got out of the cruiser and studied the ground. Not even the slightest indentations to show Sam might have come home and left again.

He signaled the dogs to come inside, where he switched on lights and called out to Sam, although he knew she wasn't here. He gave the pets food and water, then pulled his cell phone from his belt and went through the numbers. The bakery's automated after-hours message came on. Same at the chocolate factory. Sam's cell didn't bring a response either.

All his emergency worst-scenarios went through his head, mainly the possibility of a mishap on the roads. He flashed back to the afternoon Percy Lukinger had died after going off the snowy highway.

"Okay," he said out loud. "We're not going there. Sam wouldn't have any reason to be on any highway except the one I just traveled. She's gone somewhere and left her phone behind, or it's in her bag, or ..."

The border collie was staring up at him.

"... or something. I just have to track her down." He realized how obsessive that sounded. On a pleasant night, if she'd told him she would be working late, he wouldn't worry a bit. Sam was extremely capable. She also checked in with him several times a day so they could coordinate plans. This felt different.

He called the department and asked the night dispatcher if there'd been any call that involved a red Chevy Silverado or a white minivan painted with a fancy bakery logo. Sam might have found herself caught out in the van, having left the truck at the shop while she made deliveries or something. But none of his possible scenarios felt right—she would have called him.

When the dispatcher replied in the negative—no problems with either of Sam's vehicles—Beau knew he couldn't just sit around the house and wait. He scribbled a note and left it where she always set her bag down, on the chance she would somehow get back here without his seeing her along the way. At least she would know he was out there looking for her. He gave each dog a treat; they had already settled on their padded beds near the furnace.

Then it was back out into the storm. Lawman logic kicked in as he decided what to do. If this was an official call, the first thing he'd do was ask the missing person's family about their habits and the places they frequented. That was pretty easy with Sam. Closest of her normal haunts was the old Victorian house, location of her chocolate factory. He headed in that direction.

The highway bore a few intrepid tire tracks, but when he turned off the main road, the side streets hadn't been plowed and by now there had to be close to eight inches of the fluffy white stuff. His SUV remained in four-wheel mode the whole way. With visibility near zero, he nearly missed the turnoff to Tyler Road. The cruiser kept good traction, though, and his quick swerve didn't faze it.

Ahead on the left he spotted the fuzzy glow of the lamp Sam left as a nightlight in one of the lower windows. It wasn't until he pulled even with the driveway, that he saw another light in the kitchen toward the back of the building. Her red pickup truck was parked under the portico. No tracks—she'd been here all along.

For half a second, his ire flared. She couldn't have called?

He checked the emotion. He didn't know for certain she was okay. He pulled in close behind her truck and went to the back door. Unlocked. His hand instinctively went to his holster. But when he walked in, there was Sam at the worktable. Her hands were coated in chocolate and smears of it traced across her forehead and one cheek. She apparently hadn't heard him come in.

"Sam! What the hell?"

Her head came up, her expression looking something like a mole emerging into daylight.

"Beau—look at these!" She smiled with complete joy.

She was pointing to the trays of chocolate candy on the table, an array of designs that fairly sparkled in the light. "I've done it," she said with awe. "I've come up with the perfect chocolates."

His earlier tension evaporated and he crossed the room in two steps and pulled her into a gigantic hug.

"Honey, what's the matter?" she asked.

He couldn't be angry. She seemed truly bewildered. He held her so tightly she began to squirm.

"What?"

With one arm around her shoulders, he led her to the window and pulled back the curtain. Snow rimmed the frame, almost obliterating the view. In the distance, the sky was nothing but a black space filled with a million flying scraps of white.

"Oh my god, it's dark out. And the snow!" She stared for a full minute before turning back to him. "What time is it?"

When he told her, she was astounded. "It's been six hours since I sent the employees home. I can't believe it."

A blob of white icing on the tip of her nose caused him to laugh. "Oh, you creative types."

She picked up a damp towel and began to wipe the chocolate from her hands.

"So, do you plan on coming home?" he asked. "Or do you just want to camp out here for a few days?"

He thought of what she had told him about that silly wooden box and its effects on her energy. She must have been at it again.

Chapter 36

Sam woke up and snuggled next to Beau's warm back. She felt badly about worrying him last night. It still felt amazing that she'd concentrated so intently on her chocolates that she'd been completely unaware of the storm, the darkness, and the passage of time. She'd seen the look cross his face, his wondering whether she'd been under the influence of the magic box. She hadn't, and that was another thing that surprised her.

She breathed a contented sigh. It felt good to be back in her creative zone. At some subtle level, she realized she'd been worrying over whether she had lost her knack for coming up with new ideas.

Beau rolled over and ran his hand up her arm to her bare shoulder. "Um, this has been out from under the covers—it needs warming up."

He proceeded to plant kisses where his hand had been, trailing them up her neck, nuzzling her hair, which still smelled of sugar and chocolate. They'd fallen into bed immediately after they got home last night. Her breath caught when the hand went under her gown. The room had grown decidedly warmer—then their phones rang. At the very same time.

"That's going to be the dispatcher," he said. "I have to—"

He reached for his nightstand and Sam turned toward hers. She didn't immediately recognize the number on her screen, but the name was a familiar one. Isobel St. Clair. Director at The Vongraf Foundation.

"Samantha, I realize it must be early there," said the woman's voice. "I apologize."

"It's okay." Sam couldn't think of any other way to begin the conversation. She certainly didn't want to ask whether anything was wrong.

"I just need to know whether the box is safe. There has been some new … some increased activity."

"It's been with me the past several days," Sam said. Had it? Her mind struggled to switch gears. She remembered taking it with her to the new break-in house, but that had been more than a week ago. It was on the seat of her truck yesterday—or was it the day before?

"If you have it in your hands, that's fine," Isobel said. "But if you need to go out, please be sure you have it locked away. Marcus Fitch seems to have disappeared from the East Coast and we think he may be headed in your direction."

Sam had to work at remembering all the players in the game she had learned about last summer. The box that had come into her possession was one of three. She had only been told of the dangers associated with the various factions who were trying to get their hands on all three boxes only because one group, OSM, had Sam in their sights. Fitch had personally come after Sam with the intention of taking away hers.

She assured Isobel she would keep the box under lock and key, and they ended the call. Once again, Sam felt tempted to package it up and mail it to The Vongraf for safekeeping, taking herself completely out of the picture.

"Darlin'?" Beau asked. He'd finished his own phone call with about three words and now sat on the edge of the bed, pulling on his uniform pants. "Everything okay?"

She nodded. He only knew the barest of details about the situation and she preferred to keep it that way. His lawman instincts would dictate that he become involved and protect her, and this was something that went way beyond the realm of the county sheriff's office.

She walked over to the window and looked out. Their flat pastureland was covered in a fluffy white quilt. Fence posts wore puffy white hats, and the trees in the distance appeared as black arms and fingers coated in sugar. Judging by the accumulation on the edges of their back deck, she guessed the snowfall had ended shortly after they got home. The clouds were still white, but clear patches had begun to reveal stars as the storm moved off toward the mountains to the east.

"Are you opening the bakery today?" Beau asked through a foam of toothpaste.

"I told the chocolate factory staff to go according to the school announcement. I think the bakery crew will do the same—it's what we normally do in the winter."

He rinsed and spat water into the basin. "Just asking in case you want a ride into town. I need to call Roger to come out and shovel the path to the barn, clear our driveway. As soon as I reach him, I'll be leaving for the office."

Sam considered for a second. "Do I have time for a quick shower? I think I still have chocolate in my eyebrows."

He smiled. "Your eyebrows look fine, but you've got time for the shower if you want." He watched her drop the nightgown, a wistful look for the bad timing of the phone calls. "I'll make some coffee, tend to the dogs, and meet you at my cruiser in fifteen minutes."

Sam did the fastest wash-shampoo-rinse she'd done in a long time, aimed the dryer at her hair for two minutes, and pulled on fresh jeans and a soft flannel shirt. Downstairs, she grabbed her keys and went out to her truck, instantly regretting that she'd put on sneakers instead of boots. Oh well. Once the shoes were snow-filled, another few steps didn't matter. She brushed enough snow aside with her bare hands to open the passenger side door. The wooden box wasn't on the seat. A mild current of concern went through her.

Marcus Fitch may be headed in your direction.

"Calm down, Sam," she whispered in the empty truck. "It's going to turn up."

Beau had come out the front door and she turned toward him.

"Ready? Or did you decide to stay home?"

She looked at the white expanse all around. She really should go to the bakery, look around for the box and check her delivery van. She couldn't remember which vehicle she'd been driving the last time she'd seen the box.

"I blew it with these shoes," she admitted, holding up

her foot. "Give me a minute to get dry socks and change into my boots."

He tapped his watch face, although his expression didn't register true irritation. She imagined he was no more eager to start the workday than she, but his job didn't afford the luxury of weather days. She raced into the house and up the stairs. In under two minutes, she'd gathered what she needed and was stuffing her feet into her warmest snow boots.

Road crews had made decent headway during the night. Once Beau had slow-poked his way down their own driveway, he found the roads into town had been cleared. Paseo del Pueblo Norte already had light traffic, as evidenced by the slush thrown to the sides of the street. Beau cruised past the turn to his office.

They circled the plaza, where the streets were clear except for huge mounds of snow piled at the corners of the square. The adobe buildings still wore their picturesque winter lighting and the snow added a Norman Rockwell charm to the whole scene. At the stop sign leading to Camino de la Placita, Beau waited while an orange county truck with flashing yellow beacon roared past, its plow to the pavement.

Across the way, Sam could see a smaller, private truck with a plow working on the parking lot of her building. Old man Tafoya, surprisingly, hadn't skimped on this very basic service for his tenants. He wasn't exactly known for providing anything without pulling some teeth to get it.

"So, to the bakery or my office?" Beau asked.

Sam thought of the box. "I'd better spend some time here," she said, indicating the bakery with a tilt of her head.

He obliged by pulling right up to the front door. "You

can always come help out at the office if things get too boring here," he said.

Sam reached for her keys and sent him on his way with a kiss. Normally, Sweet's Sweets would be opening about now but seeing as how there had been virtually no private vehicles on the streets yet, Sam guessed she had a little time to spare. The sky was only now beginning to show pearl gray in the east.

She surveyed the bakery cases and saw that, due to their early closing yesterday, there was adequate stock of cookies and cupcakes to get started. Half remained of an amaretto cheesecake and there were a dozen cinnamon rolls, which should satisfy the mid-morning crowd if it materialized. She switched on the lights and started the coffee maker— remembered she had meant to go out back and search for the box in her van, so she switched the lights off again and locked the front door.

In the alley the van sat under a mound of white. Sam went back indoors for a broom, then cleared enough to let her crawl inside. The box wasn't in plain sight on the seat or floor and trying to see beyond that in the dark was ridiculous.

The man who'd been plowing the parking lot now came around to the back alley. This was most likely the real reason Tafoya paid him to be here. The city wouldn't pick up garbage unless access to the dumpsters was clear, and if it remained blocked for more than a day or so, there would be a fine. Sam got out of the van, swept the remaining snow off it quickly, and waited until the truck had made one clear strip before she started and moved the van around to the front parking lot.

The light was better here, as the eastern sky now

glowed. She intensified her search for the carved box and found it stuffed under the driver's seat. As she pulled it out she felt it scrape the seat-adjustment mechanism. A new scratch now showed on the bottom. She rubbed the wood tenderly, as if she'd just scraped her own hand.

"What new drama are you about to bring to me?" she asked quietly, thinking of Isobel's phone call. The box responded by gleaming faintly. "I suppose I won't know until it happens."

She carried the box into the bakery, where the aroma of coffee filled the room. The box, by now, had warmed her cold hands. She switched the salesroom lights back on and took the box to the kitchen, where she stuffed it into her backpack purse.

Bag and coat safely hung on the hooks at the back wall, Sam turned the large bake oven to preheat before going back to fetch herself a mug so she could brew a cup of good English Breakfast tea. She stood at the front windows, staring out at the predawn morning. It would be a few hours until traffic really began moving. For the first time in a month, she felt an easy calm about the way the day was beginning.

The mellow feeling didn't last long. She looked closely at the two cakes in her window display and saw one of them had suffered a mishap. Most likely a customer's child who wanted a closer look—two of the large frosting roses were missing.

Since the cakes themselves were plastic forms, they never spoiled, but it was good to change the windows regularly and give people something new to look at. The current design went along the Winter Wonderland theme—very appropriate at the moment—but she should be revamping them soon for the Valentine season. She studied the space and began to get some ideas. Meanwhile, she could quickly whip out a couple of replacement flowers to fix the obvious boo-boo.

She started for the kitchen when the flash of headlights across the back wall alerted her. A vehicle had pulled up to the front of the shop. The small car didn't seem like the type to be out on a snowy morning with icy roads filled with slush and the mixture of sand and cinders spread by the road crews. Sam caught herself staring. But the bakery lights were on and the front door unlocked, so it looked as though she had her first customer of the day.

She set down her tea mug and gave a quick glance to be sure the tables were clean and the beverage bar was neat. When she looked up again, the driver had emerged. It was Missy Malone.

Chapter 37

Sam's mind reeled. Missy was the suspect in Beau's case, the woman he'd called Ramona ... something .... At the moment, Sam couldn't think. Beau had questioned and released Missy, but then hadn't he learned something new?

Missy pulled a stylish fur hood over her head as she emerged from the car. Her boots—more fashionable than functional—slipped a little on the icy pavement, but she balanced herself well and came to the door. Sam itched to reach for the phone and call Beau, but Missy was inside before she could make a move.

"Oh—I was hoping Jen was here already this morning," Missy said.

If she remembered that Sam had been at the station

when the sheriff questioned her, she was pretending it never happened.

"Well, anyway. All I need today is something for breakfast. My husband's sweet tooth is on the prowl, and well, I just don't bake." Her eyes scanned the items in the display case. "Four of the cinnamon rolls, please."

Sam waited for the flicker of recognition, the subtle acknowledgement of what had gone on. And husband? Beau was investigating the death of this woman's husband. Apparently, she was sticking to the charade she'd been playing in front of Jen, that she was married to some rich guy.

Sam took her time removing the four rolls from the tray and placing them into a paper bag. How could she report Missy's appearance here without alerting the woman that she was calling the sheriff? She wanted to ask a dozen questions, but didn't know enough about his progress with the case to risk messing it up by saying the wrong thing. She took the ten dollar bill Missy held out, but when she opened the register to make change, the woman simply grabbed her bag of cinnamon rolls and walked out. In a few seconds, she was in the car and backing out.

Sam rushed to the window. She needed to see the back of that car, to get the plate number for Beau. She barely made it before the car reached the end of the parking lot near Puppy Chic. Repeating the numbers in her head, she jotted them on the back of an order form then dialed Beau's cell phone.

"Missy Mal—no, Ramona whatshername," she blurted. "Red Mercedes SLC Roadster. All I got of the license was SPV 4. I missed the last two digits. Sorry, I couldn't keep her here."

"Darlin' take a breath," Beau said. "I only got part of that."

Sam went through it again, slowly, starting with her surprise at seeing the woman in her shop again.

"Why do you suppose she would take the chance on coming here?" she asked. "She must know you're looking for Ramona, even though Missy is off the hook."

"I'm thinking that myself," he said.

"You know ... when she was hanging around before, she kept asking Jen little things about your investigation, hinting around. Remember how she first said she might go into forensic work, then it was because she planned to write a crime novel. Maybe she thought she would catch Jen here and keep up that pretense."

"It makes sort of roundabout sense, but this is an accomplished con artist. They usually cut and run as soon as suspicion turns toward them. I'm surprised she's even in town."

"Well, she wouldn't have gotten anything from Jen. She's royally pissed at Missy for trying to buy her friendship with stolen gifts."

"At least with the information about her car, we can try to catch up with her and bring her in for more questioning. Thanks for being quick on your feet with that, Sam."

Sam stared at the phone for a minute after they'd hung up, wondering if there was anything she could do to help. She couldn't think what it would be. Beau's deputies would be out patrolling the streets anyway; maybe one of them would spot Missy—or, Ramona. Her tea had gone lukewarm; she added hot water and headed to the kitchen. At least she could bake some muffins, in hopes that once the sky cleared people would be eager to get out.

With Julio normally at the oven in the early mornings,

it had been awhile since Sam had mixed and baked much. She had to consult the recipe, muttering to herself that she'd better not be losing her skills. It all came back though, and within minutes she had batches of apple-cinnamon, blueberry, and honey-bran muffins in the big oven. While they baked, she looked through the order forms on her desk. Nothing seemed urgent. If Becky made it in today, she could easily handle everything.

Sam felt her attention wandering to the chocolate factory. She'd evidently been in such a trance-like state last night, she'd created dozens of pieces for Mr. Bookman's approval and this morning she couldn't remember what they were. She itched to get back there and see how they'd turned out, whether she would want to add finishing touches. But she kept reminding herself that the road out to her place was too remote to have been cleared by county crews—too remote to take her bakery van through deep snow and risk sliding off. The chocolates could wait, she decided.

She picked up one of the cake order forms. According to the checklist, the layers had been baked. Pulling them from the fridge, she gathered buttercream frosting and color paste. The design was a simple one for a baby shower, and the time sped by as she formed tiny booties and pastel ribbons. She'd just set down her piping bags when she heard a noise at the back door. A second later, Julio stepped in.

"Oh, I wasn't sure if you were really here," he said. "Saw the van out front."

"How did you get here?" She thought of his prized Harley.

"A buddy with a big Dodge Ram." He sniffed the air.

"I made some muffins. Not sure how many customers

we'll have, so I hadn't planned to bake a lot."

"Sky's clear in the west already," he said. "We could do the afternoon stuff."

"Good idea."

The bells on the front door tinkled and Sam started toward the sales room.

"It's just me," Jen called out. She came through the curtain into the kitchen. "I got a ride and decided to come in."

"Is the sun coming out?"

"Bright and clear," Jen said. "The main roads aren't bad at all. I thought you'd be at the chocolate factory today. How's it going with Mr. Bookman's order?"

"I'm not really sure." Sam realized, the moment the words popped out, how true it was.

With the passage of a few hours, last night's frenzy of creation had begun to feel a bit surreal. Had she actually come up with designs and flavors for all those exotic destinations? Would they look and taste as fantastic as she'd imagined them to be?

Jen was giving her a puzzled look.

"I mean, I think everything's coming along fine."

"I doubt Becky will be in," Jen offered. "I talked to her this morning, and the fact they closed school has her in a little tizzy with those two rowdy boys at home."

"It'll work out. None of the factory crew is coming in today either. I imagine half the town will just snuggle in at home or spend the morning outside, building snowmen in their front yards."

For a moment, a vision passed through her mind, a picture of Kelly as a kid. Had those school days really been more than twenty years ago? She stared at the finished baby shower cake. It wouldn't be long before she was baking one of these to celebrate her own grandchild. Or not. Young couples these days didn't always opt for the traditional family patterns. Kelly and Scott might spend their lives exploring the historic haunts of some far off country, for all Sam knew.

While she had her piping bag handy, she carried it to the front window display and patched the damage on the wedding cake. Jen was right, the sun was beginning to glow through the clouds now, although the air still held the bite of frost. The shrubs out front were thick with snow that didn't appear to be going anywhere. She stared up the street to the north.

When she turned around, Jen was arranging the display trays, making room for the new muffins.

"Your ex-buddy stopped by this morning," Sam said. "Missy or Ramona or whatever her name really is."

Jen dropped a warm muffin but managed to catch it left-handed. "What did she want?"

"She asked if you were here, but didn't say why. Bought four cinnamon rolls and left super quick."

"Nervy."

"Extremely. Especially since Beau wants to question her again. I got part of her license plate and told him about it."

"Well, if she comes back, you can be sure I won't talk to her. I am *so* done with that fake friendship. If she shows up again, I'll figure out a way to tie her down and then I'll call Beau."

Sam laughed at the image of Jen lassoing the woman and tying her up, but she felt a rush of gratitude. A tiny part of her had wondered whether Jen would succumb again to the con woman's charm. Then she wondered whether any of the deputies had spotted the red car yet.

"You know, I think I'll walk over to Beau's office and see how things are coming along," she said, remembering Beau's suggestion that she spend the morning with him. "Aside from Missy, we haven't seen anyone here all morning and there's barely any traffic out on the streets. You guys can call me if anything comes in that I need to handle."

Sam put away the pastry bag and cleaned up the worktable, stowing the baby shower cake in the fridge to await pickup. A few minutes later, she bundled into her coat and stepped outside into a crystalline world.

Despite the sunshine, the air held no warmth. Her breath came out in a frosty plume. She pulled her scarf tighter around her neck, hiked her bag onto her shoulder, and began walking as quickly as the snowy sidewalk allowed.

Chapter 38

The station seemed warm when Sam stepped into the squad room after her five minute walk from the bakery. The morning briefing must have already taken place; things seemed quiet. She spotted Rico at a table at the far end of the room, where he appeared to be watching TV, except it wasn't the lively banter of any morning show she'd ever seen. The younger deputy, Travis, seemed intent on his computer monitor. She didn't see any sign of Beau. Maybe she should have called first.

She was about to interrupt one of the other men when she heard Beau's voice. He came around the corner from the niche where the coffee machine sat and spotted her immediately.

"Well, my number one tipster," he said, waving her toward his office.

"Did you guys stop Missy's car? Sorry, I mean Ramona."

"Not yet, but I've got a BOLO out for it. She may have dashed straight home after the bakery—I mean, who wouldn't, for one of your cinnamon rolls—but she has to come out sometime. I sent one officer over to the apartment we searched yesterday, but that doesn't seem to be her current hiding place."

"I wonder ... 'Missy' told Jen she was married to some rich guy, and she talked about a big, nice house they own. Maybe in addition to her own place, and Percy also having a house, she really does have somebody else on the side."

One of his shoulders gave a half shrug. "Could be. I know the landlord where Percy lived has already cleaned the place out and may even have a new renter in there by now. I cruised by yesterday, and the few personal items belonging to Mr. Lukinger were stacked at the curb for the garbage men to take. So, she wouldn't go there."

Sam pondered that. "You said there wasn't much. And Ramona's apartment didn't hold a whole lot of her personal things either, right?"

"Yeah, they live a fairly portable lifestyle, it seems." Beau picked up his mug, apologized that he hadn't offered Sam anything, but she declined. "It'll be interesting to see what, if any, information I can get from her when we bring her back in. Now that I know her history with Percy and all the con games they pulled, I want to see if I get a positive ID from that witness, Helen Flagler. Several of the other neighbors were also swindled. We might be able to put together a decent case. San Diego PD is also looking for her, and maybe they can put her away."

His phone rang and the desk officer's voice came over the intercom, announcing a Jorge Rodriguez on line one.

"Well, well, speak of the devil." Beau picked up the phone. "Detective—what's up?"

Sam heard a male voice at the other end. Beau said "Really?" a couple of times then told the man he wanted one of his deputies to listen in. He hit the speaker button.

"... went back to one of the Lukinger's victims—a Mr. Hiram Efram—from our files. I'd told you we were primarily on the trail of Percy, but this one was perpetrated by both of them with Ramona served up as the main dish."

"What do you mean?" Beau asked.

"A classic sweetheart con. Attractive woman takes up with an older man, always a rich one, and proceeds to bilk him of his life savings. Or as much of it as she can get her hands on before he catches on. They start out with gifts of expensive clothes and jewelry. Then the guy starts giving her 'spending money' and eventually, in the cases where she gains his full trust, he'll add her as a signatory on his bank accounts. That's when the big money really vanishes fast. I've seen them clear out a person's whole estate in under a month. They grab all they can and get out before the next bank statement reveals what's going on."

"Even in this day of electronic banking?" Sam asked. "I check my bank balance every few days, and my daughter's on hers all the time."

"Remember, we're dealing with an older generation who are more trusting and not tech savvy. These are the guys who wait around for the bank statement in the mail. One month he's got all his cash, the next month he's broke—and always completely stunned."

"But if she married this Mr. Efram, isn't that bigamy? We know she was married to Percy," Beau said.

"Or we think we do. Most likely, Ramona and Percy

really were married and she went through some kind of sham ceremony with Efram."

Sam looked at Beau, questioning.

"That's the real reason for my call," Rodriguez said. "Efram is after the Lukingers and he's headed your way."

"You'd better fill us in," Beau said.

"Okay. From the start—or close to it—here's the nutshell version. Ramona met Hiram Efram, age eighty-three, on a cruise out of San Diego. The Mexican Riviera, they call it. All the party ports south of the border. Lots of margaritas, Viagra's cheap at those Mexican pharmacies, old guy thinks he's the luckiest man on earth that he can please this young hottie. Says he bought her some gorgeous silver jewelry in the boutiques, she swore she'd never met anyone like him, batted those long lashes a lot, and he fell hard.

"She was on the cruise with her 'brother'—we later figured out it was Percy—and the brother gives his full blessing. Over late-night drinks with Mr. Efram, Percy tells him he's never seen Ramona this much in love. He hopes Hiram won't dump her the minute the cruise is over because it would break her heart. Hiram swears that won't happen. Obviously he's getting the best sex of his life, although he doesn't tell the brother that. He's had a few scotches and says 'Call for the captain. I want him to marry us right now.' Well, that won't do because it would actually be legal, so Percy says he'll talk to Ramona. She'll want to get a nice dress and everything. Next port, they're on the beach saying vows. I have no idea who officiated this ceremony, but my guess it was some well-dressed Mexican who would say what he was told to say for a few hundred pesos."

Sam tried to wrap her head around the idea of such a

quickie marriage.

"Fast forward to home. They settle into Hiram Efram's home. His kids have an absolute fit but there's nothing they can do. Dad is a stubborn old guy and won't listen to a thing they say. He's got a marriage certificate and the sex is still pretty good, although he has to admit having a few nights off a week is all right. He can use the rest.

"Being old-school in his ways, he immediately puts the new wife on his bank accounts, gives her a checkbook and three credit cards. She tells him she'd love to redecorate the house, and he basically tells her to spend away."

"Oh boy," Beau said.

"Yeah. While the kids are trying to figure out what they can do legally, Ramona isn't bound by such constraints. She does a few test withdrawals of a few hundred, then a few thousand dollars. Hiram doesn't care. He thinks the new furniture will be delivered any day now. She must have prowled through all his business papers. She had his social security number and practiced his signature. Within three months, she managed to divert his retirement savings, drain a great big 401k account, and cash in all the CDs he'd ever purchased. We're still trying to track where the money went, but Percy's name shows up on some of the accounts that received it. Meanwhile, on the day—the very same day—the last withdrawal happened, Ramona said she was going shopping and she never came back. The car he'd given her turned up at a used car lot in Bakersfield, but the lot owner swears he never took it in trade and has no idea how it got there. Most likely she just parked it there and caught a ride with Percy to wherever."

"You said Mr. Efram is heading to New Mexico?" Beau asked.

"That's what his daughter told me this morning. Her

brother, Danny, age fifty-seven, is the one who's been pushing us to catch this pair. Apparently, when they got wind of the Lukingers being in your area, Danny and Hiram decided to take matters into their own hands. They left California and Danny's parting words to his sister were, 'I'm going to kill Ramona.' Now you're telling me Percy's dead under suspicious circumstances ... Well, I have to wonder if the Eframs didn't catch up with them."

"Okay, then." Beau was rubbing both temples as he stared at the speaker box. "I'll see if we can get a lead on where these Eframs might be."

"Good luck with it. I'd offer our department's assistance, but we're short staffed and underfunded. Nothing outside our immediate jurisdiction gets any notice. I personally can't spare enough for a plane ticket out there."

"That's okay. Not your problem. If we uncover anything that'll help your case, we'll pass it along."

The line went dead and Beau blew out a long breath as he looked up at Sam.

"Holy crap," she said. "This is *way* more complicated than I imagined."

"No kidding. Last week I thought we had a simple traffic accident." He stood and paced to the door and back.

"I'll grab a refill for your coffee," Sam said.

"Better not. I'm wired six ways to Sunday already." He sat and flipped through the pages of notes he'd taken on the case. "So, Percy's dead. I suspected a double-cross by Ramona, and it still could be that. There's also Grant Mangle, the guy who lost a diamond ring and a bunch of cash to Percy. And now we've got this father-son team from California, who could have easily been here in Taos when it happened."

"I think you said Percy died from some kind of drug,

right?"

He nodded.

"So, let's think who would have access to that substance. Someone in a medical profession, a pharmacist, anesthesiologist ..."

"Most likely," he agreed. "I'll call back and see if that applies to any of the Eframs, and Travis is doing some background on Mangle. I'll see what he's got. Mangle was furious with Percy, and I really thought he was our best bet."

"If furious-with-Percy is the criteria, it sounds like people will have to line up to join it."

"You're so right." He chuckled and picked up the phone to punch the two digits for Travis's desk. "Update me on what you've found on Grant Mangle."

A minute later, Travis appeared at the doorway to Beau's office, notebook in hand. "He's got no criminal record, so there isn't much. Basic credit and background check shows him self-employed in property rentals, his wife is a nurse with a steady job at the hospital, average-sized mortgage, no kids. Looks like they went on a seven-day cruise for their tenth anniversary last fall."

"The wife was the one most upset about the loss of her diamond ring, and she works at the hospital." Beau glanced toward Sam but spoke to Travis. "Pay a visit to Sally Mangle and see if she'll come by and answer some questions."

"Can we *make* her come in? I mean, if she resists the idea, is it okay to give the impression her ring may have been found? We did find that loose fake diamond among Percy's things," Travis said.

"Use your imagination. Hopefully, she'll come willingly since she's eager to know about her ring." Beau let Travis go, asking him to send Rico in.

The other deputy seemed relieved to be off video monitor duty. He stretched when he stood up, and rubbed his eyes as he crossed the squad room.

"Got you a new task," Beau told him after he'd greeted Sam cordially. "Pretty routine, but better than staring at those tapes."

Rico grinned. "Most *anything* would be a nice break from staring at those tapes."

"We need to find out if a Hiram Efram or Danny Efram have been in town within the last two weeks. Hotel records, credit card charges, the usual. I'm looking especially at any visit around the time of Percy Lukinger's auto accident."

Rico wiggled his fingers. "Back to the keyboard and phone," he said.

"Okay, while all that's going on, I'm starved and would like to take my prettiest deputy to lunch."

"You'd better rephrase and say you're taking your wife to lunch. The other guys will be jealous." Sam picked up her bag. The weight of it reminded her the carved box was still inside.

Over burgers at Five Star, Beau reiterated the facts in the case. Sam knew it was his way to process, to mull things over until it began to coalesce. She decided to help him along with questions.

"So, aside from this Grant Mangle and the man from California, do you have any other suspects for the murder?"

"I had considered Mangle as number one—the guy was furious. His wife most likely has a way to get the drug, and they're both pretty cranked. But the loss of a diamond ring doesn't hold a candle to what the Eframs went through."

"Yeah, can you imagine your entire life savings gone in a couple months like that?"

"So they're all viable candidates. And, of course, there's Ramona herself. Who's to say she didn't get Efram's money and decide to strike out on her own. She had to consider, why bother to share it with Percy."

"And yet they were such a team. I have to wonder if she could carry off another of those big cons without him," Sam said, dipping a French fry in ketchup.

Beau's hand was halfway to his mouth with his soft drink cup when he stopped abruptly. "I think she may already be working on one."

Before she had the chance to think about what he'd said, Beau's shoulder mike squawked. Whatever the code meant, clearly he didn't think it was a good idea for Sam to go along. He told her to wrap up her burger; he'd be dropping her off at the bakery.

Chapter 39

Sweet's Sweets felt like a little patch of quiet after the excitement of the sheriff's office and the new discoveries in Beau's case. Sam worked automatically as she rolled fondant to create the vase for a spring bouquet cake. Obviously, another customer was tired of winter. Julio had asked if he could leave early because he'd already baked more than they could possibly sell to the trickle of customers and because his ride was leaving. Jen had cleaned and refreshed the display cases, the counters gleamed, and she'd added a few new touches to the window presentation.

By three o'clock it was obvious business was fairly well done for the day. No school kids, few after-lunch desserts, and the afternoon tea-and-scone crowd never materialized. It would be dusk soon and the lowering temperature guaranteed the slush on the roads would soon become icy.

"We might as well close up," Sam told Jen as she put bright, finishing touches on the flowers in the vase. "I'll give you a ride if you'd like."

Her van gave a bit of argument about starting in the cold, but once running, it warmed quickly and purred along. Jen thanked her for the ride and Sam made her way carefully back to the clearer roads, and home. Pulling in beside her snow-covered truck, she made a mental note to take the bigger vehicle with its four-wheel drive tomorrow morning. She grabbed her pack from the space behind her seat and headed for the warmth of the house.

First order of business was to pull out the carved box and stow it safely away. Isobel St. Clair had already sent one reminder text during the day. Sam had bit back a flash of irritation over the woman's persistence, although she knew Isobel only meant to keep her safely out of the clutches of those who wished to steal the valued object. She entered the combination for Beau's gun safe, hidden away at the back of the coat closet, moved a couple of fat envelopes aside and stashed the box. With the door securely locked once more, she gave a sigh of relief. *Okay, Isobel, no worries now.*

She was browsing the freezer for dinner ideas when Beau called.

"Hey you. Sorry I had to bail so quickly on lunch." In the background, she could hear the familiar sounds of the squad room—voices, radio calls, an occasional laugh. "We had a house fire. Faulty gas stove, whole family incinerated. Nasty stuff."

Sam felt a flash of empathy. "Oh, Beau, how awful. I can't imagine." Unfortunately, having just handled the box, she *could* imagine. A ghostly image of a burned structure appeared to her.

"I'm lucky the fire department investigators handle the really gruesome parts, but I had to get the names of the deceased, locate next of kin, and notify them. Not fun."

She closed the freezer door, unable to think about food after that news.

"Anyway, just calling to see that you got home okay and let you know I'm on my way. Do we need anything from the store?"

She told him of her indecision about dinner plans and suggested he bring whatever his appetite would handle. He'd had the more disturbing afternoon. When he showed up an hour later with a bucket of chicken and full selection of side dishes, she knew he'd be just fine.

"I guess it's a little early to have more information on any of your suspects," Sam said as she got plates from the cupboard.

"Travis came back with Grant Mangle's phone records, and the calls he claims between himself and Percy seem to check out. It looked as if Grant tried multiple times to reach Percy after the episode in the restaurant parking lot, but the calls were so short he could have only left messages."

"It would be a clever way to cover for himself, right?" Sam helped herself to a chicken leg and a biscuit from the bucket.

Beau had loaded his plate with mashed potatoes, coleslaw, and three pieces of chicken. "Yeah, and he's still adamant that he had nothing to do with what happened to Percy."

"You believe him?"

"Not sure. My impression is that he can be hot-headed, but he doesn't seem devious. Although … he had a hard time looking me in the eye during questioning, at several points. Maybe he was just struggling with appearing foolish over being scammed." He was picking up his second piece of chicken when his phone rang.

"Yeah, Travis," he said, after checking the screen. "What's up?"

He listened for a minute. "That's pretty late. Rico's on tonight. Have him handle it. Tell him he can call me if he's got reason to hold her or if things take a weird turn during the questioning. In fact, put him on the phone."

"Is it Missy—or, I should say, Ramona?" Sam asked while Beau was on hold.

He shook his head. "Sally Mangle, Grant's wife. Travis says he reached her at the hospital. She gets off at eleven and agreed to come by and answer some questions. I got the feeling she wasn't thrilled, but most people would rather talk in the privacy of our interview room than have the sheriff show up at their place of work."

"Hey, Rico. Sally Mangle is coming in later and I'd like you to conduct the interview. Travis told her we may have located her stolen diamond ring, so use that as a lead-in. Show her the one we found, she'll say it's not hers, then lead her around to questions about her work. What we really want to know is whether she would have access to benzodiazepines in the course of her work." He paused to spell the word, and gave Rico the brand-name equivalents.

"Go soft, for now. I don't want to spook her. We'll check other hospital sources to verify anything she tells you. Depending on what she says, we can see what measures they have in place for accountability before we drill any harder." He repeated what he'd said about calling, no matter what hour, if Sally Mangle should actually break down and confess.

"That would make it easy, wouldn't it?" Sam said, when he set his phone down.

"If only it really worked that way. Seems like everybody reads too many crime stories in the paper—they all think a good lawyer will get them off, no matter what they did." He polished off the wing in three bites and put the other piece back in the bucket. "We got any ice cream?"

Sam laughed and gathered their plates. "There's more of that caramel if you haven't already got into it. If that's gone, there are brownies from the bakery."

"Ah! A brownie sundae is just what I need."

How did the man keep his waistline? She stored the leftovers and put the plates in the dishwasher. She fought the calorie battle all the time. He bundled back into his warmest coat and went out to the barn to be sure all was well with the two horses, even though his ranch hand, Roger, had been around early in the day to feed and water them. When he returned, he concocted his own sundae and retired to the living room, where the sounds of a football game came from the TV.

By the time Sam finished tidying the kitchen, his chair was fully reclined, the empty dessert bowl sitting on an end table, and his eyelids were drooping.

"Unless you're only planning on a catnap, you might as well go to bed," she told him gently. "It was an early morning."

He roused enough to be attentive to the game on television for another thirty minutes, but when he began nodding off again, he kissed her goodnight and headed up the stairs. Sam took the dogs outside, where the thermometer on the deck read a cozy fourteen degrees. Once all were back inside, she too succumbed to the lure of an early bedtime.

By morning Sam was feeling antsy about getting back to her creations at the chocolate factory. She couldn't believe it had been thirty-six whole hours since she'd pulled her late-night creative blitz to come up with the concepts for the pieces to fill the sample boxes for Stan Bookman. She also couldn't believe the presentation deadline was now only two days away.

A little wave of nerves went through her as she started her truck and headed toward the Victorian in the gray light of pre-dawn. The roads held a treacherous coating of frozen slush, and she had to concentrate on her driving, although her mind wanted to go back to her chocolate creations.

The big four-wheel-drive vehicle handled the turn onto Tyler Road easily enough, and cut through the crust on top of the unbroken snow on the driveway. Wind had obviously whipped across the open fields surrounding the chocolate factory; her tire tracks from two nights ago had been obliterated. She steered up to the portico, then decided to make a path for the employees. In addition to the deadline for the Travel the World program, they would soon be falling behind on their regular orders if they weren't open for business very soon.

She backed out again, turned, made two more runs down the road to pack the snow. The employee parking area was a bit too much of a challenge for her pickup. She pulled again into her slot near the door and phoned Roger to see if he was available to come out and clear the space for her people. He assured her he could be out within a half hour, so she called Benjie and asked him to notify everyone else that the workday would begin on time.

She unlocked the back door, a little nervous about whether the new designs were as great as she'd remembered.

A creativity frenzy was one thing … examining the results with the same critical eye as her customer was another.

But there on the worktable lay the light cloth she had draped to protect the racks of candy. When she lifted it, the truffles, creams, and nut clusters gleamed up at her. Her breath caught a little at the sight of the glistening decorative touches. She circled the table, seeing the pieces from all sides. They were perfect.

She felt a surge of pride. All this had happened without the magic of the wooden box or the creative genius of her mentor chocolatier, Bobul. This was her work alone.

Peru, Chile, Australia, India … She had come up with innovative flavors for each country and several designs to represent the cultures and sights Mr. Bookman's wealthy clientele would experience in each location. Despite the fact that she'd practically been in a trance when she actually worked the chocolate, each design so clearly depicted its location, she had no trouble picking them out now. She hoped Bookman would see them the same way.

Now, she must consider presentation. How Book It Travel's clients viewed their gift at the moment it came into their hands would be nearly as important as what they discovered inside each box, so the containers were nearly as important as the contents. She needed to come up with a unique way to make the chocolate represent the journey to each destination.

For the past week, she had reviewed every style of gift box already in her collection, and decided they were far too generic for this purpose. None of her suppliers carried anything substantially different. Sam gazed at the beautiful chocolates once again. She walked to the storeroom where—no surprise—no solution had magically appeared.

"Come on, Sam, *think!* You've got two days before he comes to see what you've come up with." She paced the circular route from storeroom to kitchen, to packing room, to shipping area, up the stairs to her office, down again to the storeroom, and yet nothing came to her.

Okay, she thought. What the heck am I going to do now?

Chapter 40

Rico spent the morning with Beau, despite having been at work half the night, and they went over the video of Sally Mangle's interview. Beau took in the obvious details first: attractive slender woman in her late thirties, blonde hair in a short style they used to call a pixie, makeup faded after a long shift at work, wearing dark blue medical scrubs and a thick down coat when she walked into the interrogation room. She draped the coat over the back of a chair and sat down with the tired air of someone who'd been on her feet all day, yet there was an appearance of anticipation about her.

"We'd told her we found a ring that might be hers," Rico said.

Beau watched as his deputy began the interview with

the offer of coffee, water, or a soda. Sally declined. She asked about the ring.

"I've got someone retrieving it," Rico said. "Before we get to that, I just need to verify a couple things your husband told us."

He had his small notebook in hand and pretended to consult it as he flipped through a few pages.

"Grant says you and he had lunch together on the thirteenth. Can you verify that for me?"

Sally actually rolled her eyes. "Probably. We meet for lunch once or twice a week."

"It's important that we verify the thirteenth was the day."

She reached for a pocket of the coat and pulled out a phone. Thumbing across icons and screens, she stared at it. "It's on my calendar, so I'm sure of it."

"You're good at details," he told her. "I suppose that's part of your work, keeping good records."

"Of course."

"Tell me how that works with the drugs at the hospital. You must administer some pretty potent stuff. I assume everything has to be tracked pretty closely."

"What?" She seemed startled at the abrupt change of subject.

"C'mon, hospital employees must 'borrow' medications from time to time, a little something for a headache, a remedy for a family member … There must be a system in place to be sure no one's running a little sideline business. Drugs are pretty expensive."

"I suppose they are. I'm not connected with the billing department." She busied herself putting her phone away and pulling a tube of lip balm from her pocket.

"And you've never taken a little something from the drug cabinet for yourself?"

"No, deputy, I haven't. How does this relate to my stolen diamond ring?"

"I'll go check on that," Rico said, rising. "You can just wait here."

While he was out of the room, Sally started to apply her lip balm, but her hand shook so badly she ended up rubbing most of it on with a fingertip before putting the tube back in her pocket. Her gaze darted around the room, she drummed her fingers on the tabletop, sat forward in the chair and intertwined her fingers to keep them still.

"Seems a little edgy," Beau commented.

"Yeah, I thought so. I watched from here until it seemed the right time to go back. I had the ring with me the whole time." Rico patted the button-down pocket on his uniform shirt.

On the video, he was walking back into the interrogation room with the evidence bag in hand. He told Sally she couldn't break the seal, but should look at the ring through the plastic. "Sorry, but at this point it's still evidence in our case."

She examined the ring in the bag and shook her head. "No. This is the same one Grant brought home. I knew the minute I saw it, this wasn't my ring. I can't believe he let himself get tricked like that."

Anger flashed across her face, but Rico didn't question further. Beau wondered if Sally was more angry with the con man or with her husband.

Rico thanked Sally for coming in and said they would be back in touch if they had further questions. She didn't exactly seem pleased with the idea.

"I went home after she left," Rico told Beau, "but on

my way back this morning, I stopped in at the hospital and talked with the administrator. Wanted to find out what the official procedures are for handling and tracking the various medications. They literally have a book on it, a procedures manual."

"I'll take the condensed version, if you can give it to me," Beau said.

Rico picked up the publication, which must have run fifty pages or more. "Basically, every pill and injection in that place is tracked from the moment it's ordered through the pharmaceutical company, through receipt at the hospital, inventoried into the hospital pharmacy, and dispensed to the patients. They've got a form for everything, requisition books that are numbered and tracked, and kept under lock and key. The only personnel who are allowed to sign for the drug's movement from one area to another are doctors, registered nurses, or pharmacists. Two signatures are required for controlled substances."

"Sounds pretty thorough. It takes that whole book to lay it out?"

Rico rolled his eyes. "I've barely started reading it. What I told you is what the administrator said to me. He insisted I take the manual, I suppose to prove to us how diligent they are."

"Well, the last thing a hospital wants is for the law to believe they've got a leak anywhere in their system." Beau adjusted the lights in the room and flipped the manual open. "Based on what you've read about the procedures, what would you say the weak points are? We all know that in a perfect world an instruction book would keep everything on the up-and-up, but it's not a perfect world."

"Okay, playing a little game of what-if, let's say it's time for a patient's meds to be given. A lower-ranking nurse can do it, but has to get the nurse supervisor or a doctor to sign off. Doctor has already made rounds, he or she is gone now. Nurse supervisor has an emergency situation, so the bedside nurse approaches and asks him or her to sign the authorization form. The supervisor signs it but maybe doesn't notice the quantity written in the little space for that. Or she doesn't know that patient's history … maybe a higher dosage is called for in that particular case. The lower-ranking nurse takes the form to the dispensary and has it filled, pharmacist signs off. She gives the patient his proper dose, pockets the rest to take home. Repeats it often enough that she soon has a big fat lethal dose saved up."

"Why, Rico, I'd say you've been hanging around those with criminal minds," Beau teased.

Rico looked at the floor and blushed a little. "Hearing about the way these con men operate has got me looking at all the angles."

"Hey, I'm not saying that isn't a good thing. Plus, you've saved me having to read this entire procedures manual." Beau glanced back toward the screen where they'd been watching the interview video. "The knowledge sure doesn't get Grant Mangle off the hook, does it?"

"Neither him nor the wife. Both of them had pretty good reasons to be furious with Percy Lukinger, didn't they?"

Beau nodded. There had been that flash of anger from Sally, along with some nerves. Grant had been both angry and embarrassed, and Beau had to admit he didn't know either of them well enough to know how likely they might be to act upon their anger. If Sally had been stealing drugs from the hospital, how much would she need to accumulate for a lethal dose, he wondered. If questioned, she could always come up with the excuse that someone in the family had insomnia or some other ailment requiring heftier drugs than you could buy in a bottle over the counter.

Beau sent Rico to type up his notes from the interview while he went to his own office with more questions on his mind. He got out his own case notes and came up with the phone number for Dr. Ralph Plante, the pathologist who had alerted him to the fact that Percy's death came from a toxin rather than the auto accident.

Plante came on the line almost immediately.

"Thanks for taking my call. I hope I didn't catch you at a bad time."

"It's never a *bad* time, just almost always a *busy* time."

"I have a couple of follow-up questions on the Percy Lukinger autopsy," Beau said, "and I'll try to be quick with them."

"Let me pull up the record," Plante said. Clicks from a computer keyboard sounded in the background.

"I wonder if the tissue samples from the victim revealed the quantity of benzodiazepine he had in his system."

"Um, yeah. Let's see … Looks like it calculated out to about a 100-milligram dose. That's quite high, no matter which of the brand name versions was administered."

"And Lukinger had all this in his bloodstream at once?"

"Yes, definitely. Of course, mixed with the alcohol, it was a very lethal combination. Remember, Mr. Lukinger probably had two or three drinks in his system at the time. Slamming him with a hundred mils of benzos all at once … well, everything in his central nervous system would have just shut down."

Beau flipped the page in the case file and saw the medical investigator's notes. "Sounds like it's a nasty way to go. I can't imagine the sensation he would have felt."

"Yeah. Bad. Whoever wanted to be rid of him, really

did it thoroughly. There was also the head injury."

Beau had nearly forgotten about that. He thanked Dr. Plante for his time and hung up, considering the new information. At this point, either Grant or Susan Mangle seemed to have easiest access to the murder drug. Grant admitted seeing Percy after lunch that day, but hadn't said anything about the man having a head injury. Still, it didn't necessarily rule out Ramona Lukinger or the Eframs. He buzzed Travis and asked for an update on the California pair.

"I found 'em, boss. Didn't you see the note I put in your mail slot?"

Beau had to admit he'd not checked.

Travis showed up at his office door a minute later, note in hand. "Anyway, Hiram and Danny Efram did come to Taos," he said. "Stayed at the Adobe Inn the nights of the twelfth and thirteenth. They must have gone very early— left their key in the room and no one remembers seeing them drive away. A credit card charge shows they bought gas in Gallup at 9:37 a.m. on the fourteenth."

Beau pondered the information. The Eframs arrived the day before Percy's death. They would have been looking for Ramona and Percy as a pair, once they discovered her 'brother' was actually her real husband. If they'd tracked down the couple and killed Percy, it would have given Ramona the heads-up she needed to claim his body and skip out quickly.

So, why hadn't she left town? She must have known the Eframs had figured out the con and were after her, so why had she hung around the bakery, calling herself Missy Malone?

Chapter 41

Jorge Rodriguez wasn't in when Beau called, and it took a few hours before he was able to speak to the bunco detective in San Diego. He began with Travis's findings and ended by explaining that he'd never had the chance to question the Eframs.

"Can your department pay a quick call to be sure they went back home?" he asked.

"How's the hunt for Ramona Lukinger coming along?" Rodriguez countered. "I still want the woman extradited back here so we can press charges on behalf of Mr. Efram."

"I'm as frustrated as you are," Beau assured the other cop. "I've got an officer watching her apartment, but we've seen no movement there since the day we searched the place. There's a BOLO out for her car, but since buying cinnamon rolls early yesterday morning—which provided the lead on the vehicle's plate number—it hasn't been seen. She's either hiding out somewhere or she's switched vehicles. I'll trade my icy roads and eight inches of snow for your sunny California day, any time."

"Okay. Didn't mean to get testy," Rodriguez said. "We're all doing our best. I'll see if I can find out what the Eframs' story is."

Beau spent the next hour checking with his deputies to see if there had been any sightings of the red Mercedes, although with his entire department and the town police on alert, surely he would have heard about it. He topped up his coffee mug and got a bag of cookies from the vending machine—knowing what a disappointment they would be after Sam's bakery delights—arriving back at his desk at the exact moment the duty officer informed him he had a call from a detective Rodriguez.

"That was quick," Beau said. By the amount of background noise, he guessed the detective was on a hands-free mobile phone.

"I'm leaving the elder Efram's house now. Hiram admits he and his son went to Taos. He says they hadn't made much progress in tracking down Ramona or Percy Lukinger, but they saw a news story about a man who was killed in a car accident and knew police were looking to identify him. The picture on the TV matched the man they remembered as Ramona's brother. Danny Efram mistakenly understood the story to say a woman was also killed, and they believed their chance at getting their money back was now gone. When I told Hiram Ramona had not been involved in the accident, he got pretty excited, although I doubt they'll turn around and come back after her. He's expecting me to bring her back."

"I wish I had an instant answer for you on that, Jorge. We're working on it."

"That's what I told him."

"One other question. At any time during your investigation, would you have reason to believe anyone in the Efram family has access to prescription drugs—specifically benzodiazepines?"

"Like, are they dealing or something?"

"Well, I was thinking of someone in the healthcare field—a doctor, nurse, pharmacist—anyone like that?"

"No one's mentioned it to me. Hiram was retired from real estate, back when big fortunes were being made out here. Danny tried his hand at it but, frankly, he doesn't quite have the charm of a natural salesman. I get the feeling he and his wife are sort of professional country-clubbers. Golf, lunches and dinners out, hanging around the pool seem to be their style. Why?"

"We've discovered a link between the cause of death and some anti-anxiety drugs called benzodiazepines."

"Those have to be pretty common, and it sounds weird to me as a murder weapon, but I'll keep my ears open. You can always get that sunny California day if you want to come out here and question these guys."

Beau laughed. "Keep that option open for me. A month from now, I'll be more than ready to get out of the mountains."

He hung up the phone and reached for the cookie packet, only to realize he'd already consumed them all. He wadded the cellophane and tossed it toward his wastebasket. Missed. A heaviness hung over his mood. Lots of clues, lots of suspects—but none of it was coming together.

Chapter 42

The snowplow had no sooner finished clearing her employee parking lot than Sam saw the first of their cars arrive. Benjie, bless him, was the most diligent of her people. It was a pleasure working with a guy who genuinely loved his work. She watched from her second-story window as he parked and walked to the back door. She had moved the chocolates for Bookman's presentation, placing them on the desk in her office so they didn't get damaged or accidently packed up and shipped out.

She'd spent the two hours since she arrived this morning stewing over what type of gift boxes she could come up with. Each had to be special, and it should represent the country the charter tour would visit that day. Although this was an exclusive trip to be taken by very wealthy people, the boxes couldn't be so artistic as to be prohibitively expensive or so one-of-a-kind that she couldn't come up with hundreds of them.

As Stan Bookman had explained it, the planes would carry eighty passengers—forty couples, although on some trips there would be singles. She had to plan on fifty copies of the gift box for each flight. Book It Travel hoped to fill a tour each week, so four hundred boxes a month during the travel season.

From experience, Sam knew her client tended to dream big; if he could fill a plane every day, year round, he wouldn't hesitate to call upon her to meet the demand. And she was due to show him the nine gift boxes, filled with each unique assortment, tomorrow afternoon. Yikes.

She had stared at the chocolates until her mind went completely blank. Granted, it didn't help that she'd become sidetracked this week by the weather, by Beau's case, and the appearance of Missy Malone again yesterday. At the moment, she could see only one solution—handle the carved box and see what visions came to her. Only problem was that she hadn't thought of it soon enough, so she would need to make a trip home to get it.

She walked downstairs, feeling a little overwhelmed.

"Hey, Sam," Benjie said when she reached the kitchen. "Wait 'til you taste the new flavor combination I'm going to try. I think having the day off yesterday was good for my creative juices. I came up with a few new ideas."

Sam's smile felt weak as she reached for her coat on the rack at the door. Day off—she wished she could remember what that was like.

"Everything okay?" he asked, his smile wide and his eyes bright.

She stopped in her tracks and really looked at him. The

entire burden of creation didn't have to fall to her.

"Benjie … I have to admit I'm stumped for ideas right now. How would you like to help?"

Lisa and Dottie walked in the back door just as she said it. Both had rosy, winter brightened cheeks and smiles. "Help with what?" Lisa asked.

Sam let her coat drop back to the hook. "Let's get everyone here. I've got a question for you all."

By the time Ronnie, Lucinda, and the other two chocolatiers had arrived, Sam felt her enthusiasm meter rise a touch. She had them pull chairs into the kitchen, where the smells of chocolate and flavorings, along with the sight of the decorative molds and icing tools often inspired her.

"Okay, I need ideas," she said, her notepad and pen handy. "Toss me whatever comes to mind."

It lifted her mood just to see the anticipation on their faces. She randomly picked a country from the list on Bookman's itinerary.

"Okay, everyone. If you were in India and were given a very special present, how would it be packaged? Describe the box for me."

"Does it have to be a box?" Lucinda asked.

As one of the shippers who only packed and labeled shipping cartons, Lucinda didn't get much creativity in her job, Sam realized. She needed to listen to these kids and their ideas and literally think outside the box.

"I'll be a little more specific," Sam told them. "If it can hold a dozen of our chocolates without damaging them, that's the goal."

Lucinda fairly wiggled in her chair. "I'd make it be the Taj Mahal, only the front would open like a dollhouse, and inside would be little compartments—like rooms, maybe—

and each compartment would hold a piece of candy."

Sam felt her pulse quicken. "I love it! Anyone else?"

Suddenly, they seemed shy. Lucinda's idea had been such a good one they were afraid to compete.

"Any and all ideas," Sam said. "Toss them at me."

"A Hindu shrine? Or, like, a reclining Buddha?"

Sort of a mix of cultures, but Sam could sort all that out later.

"Okay, what if you were in Australia and you're visiting the Great Barrier Reef. How would that gift be delivered?"

"A big seashell," Ronnie indicated the way a giant clamshell would fit together and open.

"How about Morocco?" Sam began tossing out the destinations and writing ideas as fast as she could.

"Aladdin's lamp," Lisa said. "I can picture the genie saying 'open the top of the lamp for your surprise' and I would be really blown away with that."

"A treasure chest would be so cool for Samoa," Benjie said. "Picture something that washed up on the beach and you were just walking along and found it."

After thirty minutes, the torrent of ideas had slowed and the team had discarded a few of the less-workable ones, leaving Sam with some terrific ideas—and the daunting job of locating the containers that would be prototypes. Bookman's budget was generous, but she had to be realistic and keep in mind the bottom line—she couldn't lose money on this deal. And the packaging had to be replicable. As much fun as it could be to have every box one-of-a-kind, that simply wasn't feasible.

She started with the internet. Her normal packaging suppliers offered nothing along these lines. She'd already chosen their most unusual boxes for her everyday chocolates. On to a few of the art and craft sites, where she was able to find a crafter who made clamshell jewelry boxes. She called the woman, who instantly picked up Sam's excitement and said she had originally designed her boxes larger than the ones she was currently offering on her website. She would be happy to overnight ship a couple of her early efforts for Sam to use as prototypes, and, yes, she could gear up for greater production if the client approved the design. She had two nieces who were eager to come into the business with her.

Sam ticked the seashell box off her checklist. One down, eight to go.

By noon, she'd only come up with three more and was feeling a little panicky. She still had to make enough of the candy to fill the unique containers, and she had to be ready for the meeting with Stan Bookman in less than thirty hours. When one of the shipping clerks offered to go out and bring back sandwiches for lunch, Sam had a brainstorm.

"Let's shut down for two hours and go on a treasure hunt," she said when the whole crew assembled in the kitchen. She ripped a sheet of paper into five strips and wrote a word or two on each. "Divide up into teams. We need five items. Your mission is to scour this town until you find the item on your paper. Get creative. If you buy the item in a shop, ask the owner if we can get more of the thing at a discount. Make notes on your paper if there are options or variations."

As the employees moved into groups, she handed each team fifty dollars. "This is a pretty generous amount," she warned them. "We can't spend this much for every box. Ideally, I'd keep the cost around twenty, if possible. But for prototypes, we can justify a little extra. We'll call it R&D."

Smiles all around the room. Sam could see their brains clicking away with ideas as they read the descriptions on their assignment.

"First team back gets a little bonus," she said. "And there will be a prize for the most amazing rendition."

The smiles turned to whoops of excitement and they all rushed for their coats. Sam looked around the empty kitchen and realized she'd just brought chocolate production to a complete halt. She set Benjie's racks to one end of the worktable and brought out the exquisite pieces she'd created during her frenzied night. She loved the way the light caught glints of gold atop glossy chocolate ovals. An egg shape with white-chocolate finish and alternating chevrons of dark chocolate, topped by miniaturized loops of chocolate ribbon was a show-stopper. But she had to admit that the mirror-finished truffle with its swirl of fuchsia glaze and a fresh raspberry on top was probably her favorite.

A chocolate Incan pyramid with a sun-god mask, cones with molten lava centers dusted outside with cocoa powder to give a matte finish, delicately thin chocolate cups filled with caramel … all of them made her heartbeat quicken. Now, if she could only remember the recipes and flavor combinations.

Chapter 43

It felt as if she had barely started on the new chocolate pieces when the teams began to return with their finds. Ronnie and Lucinda returned first, having only spent ten dollars of the fifty Sam had given them; she allowed them to split the remaining forty as their bonus. They had found a charming basket woven of grasses, and the animal design on top easily fit the theme and feel of the Serengeti Plain in Tanzania. Sam had to admit she was impressed at the ability to pick such an unusual piece from the offerings here in Taos.

They all got a laugh over the colossal colored egg Dottie had thought would represent Easter Island, but when she pulled out the real item, a stone box with fitted lid, carved to look as if it had been created by the Rapa Nui themselves, Sam and the rest found themselves staring in wonder.

"I couldn't imagine how you would find a stone box that didn't weigh a ton," she told Lisa and Dottie, "but this is beautiful and actually fairly lightweight."

"The woman at the shop said it was carved of a special stone. It fools everyone. We all expected it to be really heavy."

"Can we get more?" Sam asked.

Lisa had written a note with the name and phone number of the factory in the Philippines.

"The shop owner gave you this information?"

"At first, she was hoping to get the order herself, but when I told her how many we would need, she backed away. She said her profit on them is very small. It's a tiny shop, and I don't think she wanted to take the chance."

Sam looked at the box again, and the note. "Okay, then. I love the box. If Mr. Bookman does, too, I'll send the lady a finder's fee for her generosity."

One by one, the other items came out. The trickiest had proven to be Lucinda's idea for a dollhouse-like Taj Mahal. But Benjie and his two chocolatiers had come close. They'd found an artist who'd created papier *mâché* replicas of the famed St. Francis Church with its bell towers and crosses. The little churches opened on hinges to show the altar and pews inside.

The woman artist had been in a chatty mood in her gallery this afternoon. She had actually visited the real Taj Mahal once, and said she would love to try to create a more Eastern version of a building with minarets and other details. She had set to work on it right away, but asked for a week to complete the piece. It wouldn't make Bookman's deadline for tomorrow's meeting, but Sam had a feeling this would be such a special piece he would be thrilled to see it on his next trip through town.

Everyone voted for the Easter Island stone box as the most innovative piece, although if the hinged church building had actually been of the Taj Mahal, all agreed it would have won. Sam decided if the finished piece actually turned out as beautifully as it had been described, both the team who had located it and the artist should be rewarded with something of an after-prize.

Of course, the challenge would be to create dividers to hold the individual pieces of chocolate without destroying the beauty of the artistic piece. Sam glanced toward the rack of chocolates she had made and narrowed her eyes in concentration. Ideas began to form.

"Do you mind if I completely take over one of the worktables?" she asked Benjie.

Without another word, he began moving all the standard production gear to one table, clearing the other for the newly found containers and Sam's unique chocolates. She opened each of the containers, eyed the candy, and began to choose pieces for each of the tour locales. Trial and error, frustration with the fit and configuration of certain pieces; she was dimly aware of the employees leaving and the sun setting as she fitted small fluted paper cups into the spaces and added the candy.

Standing back, she was pleased with the results, as far as they went. Unfortunately, everything she had made so far came nowhere near filling the nine containers she needed for the presentation—now only twenty hours away. She'd resisted, but it was now apparent the magic box would be her only way to meet this deadline.

With no other choice, she dashed out to her truck and

raced home. A quick note to Beau, explaining it would be another late night, and she grabbed the carved box from the safe. She'd forgotten lunch and it was nearing their normal dinner time, but leftover chicken from the fridge would have to do.

Five minutes later, she was headed back to the chocolate factory, resting the palm of her left hand on the box on her lap. Before she reached the turnoff to the Victorian, her body had begun to warm from contact with the box, and she glanced down to see the dull wood now glowed with a golden light, and the colored stones were sparkling. She set it aside, not wanting to be awake *all* night long.

In the kitchen she surveyed the work she'd done so far while she polished off two pieces of chicken and an apple. She was pleased with the creativity of the new designs—Bookman would notice she had included exclusive chocolates and a few techniques she'd not used before. She began to think of the containers she'd ordered online. They would arrive by overnight delivery tomorrow morning. With no time to come up with new designs after their arrival, she should have the contents ready for each package ahead of time.

She trotted up the stairs and collected the pictures of each item she'd printed from its sales page. The giant clamshell would be a challenge, she thought as she walked down to the kitchen. The shape didn't exactly lend itself to the conventional display for a box of chocolates. She stared and pondered.

What if I created a reef inside the shell? This leg of the passenger's journey goes to the Great Barrier Reef—they open their shell and inside are all the colorful corals and fishes they will see when they arrive.

Her heart rate quickened. This was the right track.

Back in the kitchen she found modeling chocolate and began tinting batches of it in yellow, orange, red, black—and, of course, shades of aqua and blue for the water. She would need the shell on hand in order to make the water's surface from the blue candy, but she began forming the chocolate into the shapes of tropical fish. Tiny details emerged—scales of transparent glitter, a dark eye, a fluted fin. Each little fish was a perfect piece of candy, to be mounted on the oceanic background with a toothpick, so the guest could pick them up one at a time and nibble away.

Her eye caught sight of the picture of the metal Aladdin's lamp she had ordered. It would be the gift for the Moroccan leg of the trip. What could be more perfect than to open the lamp and find an Arabic-themed feast? While her fingers continued to make fishes, her mind began to envision a table set with bowls of fruit, plates of sweets, lush cushions surrounding it, an elaborately carved screen as a backdrop.

She set the last of the tropical fish aside and immediately started on the Moroccan scene. Time dropped away and she lost herself in the magic of artistic creation.

Chapter 44

Sam straightened, stretching to ease the muscle cramps in her lower back and shoulders. The orange glow of sunrise outside the kitchen window caught her attention. *Oh god ... I didn't* really *mean to work this long.* She stepped to the window and pulled the curtain aside. The energetic high from her contact with the wooden box was wearing off and she felt the inevitable crash starting to settle upon her.

No—not this morning! There was too much to do yet before Stan Bookman came in ... ugh, seven hours.

The chocolate pieces were made, but none of the presentation boxes was assembled. To anyone but Sam, the worktable looked like a tornado zone. She quickly cleared dirty bowls and decorating tools, placing them in the sink to soak in hot water. For each of the tour destinations, she set the candy alongside the box or container where it belonged. The marzipan fruits for the Arabian banquet were set well enough for final highlights to be added, the colorful fish for the clamshell just needed their ocean background before they could be set in place. Everything was nearly done, but so far from ready ... she would need to put in at least another two hours before they were ready to show to the client. Another wave of exhaustion hit her.

She glanced at the clock on the kitchen wall. If she got right home and set alarms, she should be able to grab three or four hours sleep, have a quick shower, and still be back here in time to finalize the presentation pieces.

A groan escaped her. Working up to the moment the client walked through the door was not her usual style. She'd been raised with the ethic that you finished your work first, then you could rest or play.

"Can't do it this time," she said to the room at large. "Gotta get some sleep."

She draped a thin sheet over the precious pieces she had toiled with, then grabbed her coat and pack and headed toward home.

Beau was in the kitchen, fresh from a shower, pouring his first cup of coffee.

"I saw your note, darlin'. I bet you're pooped."

Her smile felt weak as she allowed herself to be pulled into his embrace, melting against him with her eyes closed.

"Hey, no falling asleep on your feet," he said. "You'd better go upstairs."

"I am. I will," she mumbled. "What's on the agenda for your day?"

"I'd bring you up to date, but you'd be asleep five minutes into it. As for this morning, I'm hoping we'll finally get a lead on Ramona Lukinger. I can't believe she's completely vanished. I even extended my lookout order to the rest of the state, in case she headed for Albuquerque or elsewhere. It's as if the woman can make herself invisible."

"Poor sweetheart. I wish I could—" A ping from her pocket interrupted the thought.

She pulled out her phone and saw a text message: Confirming appointment. Jake from ABC Plumbing at your location 8:00

Crap! Less than an hour from now. She showed the message to Beau.

"Would you like me to go?" he asked.

"No, it's okay. You've got a full morning too, and a murder investigation is a little more important than a broken pipe, no matter what Delbert Crow says."

She'd been ignoring her former supervisor's messages for the past few days. Almost as much as she wanted to get the Bookman chocolate order, she really wanted this whole renewed contact with Crow to *go away*.

Beau rinsed his cup at the sink. "If you're sure."

"Yeah, I need to do it."

He kissed her at the door as she was shrugging back into her heavy coat. Together, they walked out to their vehicles.

Okay, I can do this, Sam thought. Go out to the place on Wicket Lane and let the plumber in, get back home for *two* hours sleep ... yada, yada, continue as planned. She started her truck and followed Beau's cruiser down the driveway toward the road. At the intersection, she caught herself nodding off. When her head popped up with a jerk, she realized she shouldn't be driving, not even a few miles.

The box sat on the seat beside her and she reached for it. Trusty friend, it warmed to her touch and she felt soft waves of energy travel up her arms and ease the ache in her tired shoulders. In a couple of minutes, she felt better. She put the truck back in gear and turned south.

She punched the radio dial, bypassing the news and the over-hyped talk radio bunch, until she came to a station playing dance music with a strong beat. Her fingers drummed on the steering wheel.

"Can't keep goin' like this, can't do it, can't do it," she sang, making up words to fit the rhythm of the music.

For a fraction of a second, thoughts of the increased workload of the chocolate factory, especially Bookman's increasingly elaborate plans, pushed into her head. Being privy to Beau's work was interesting and she loved it that he trusted her input. The call from Sadie Holmes, taking on this new break-in house at her request—that had been the final straw, the one she couldn't handle. The realization that something had to go swamped her like a tsunami. Something had to go.

"Okay, Sam." She gave herself an actual slap to the cheek. "Something *will* go. The moment this plumber is done today, I'll never take another call from Delbert Crow, never in my life."

The load lifted a little.

"And for each of Mr. Bookman's new projects, I'll charge him a fortune and hire enough help to handle it."

The sky seemed to brighten.

"As for Beau …" She knew she couldn't say no to him, but then he'd never asked much of her, either. Mostly, she volunteered because she found his work so interesting.

She had passed the plaza, realizing as she turned east onto Kit Carson Road that there were still icy patches where trees and buildings kept the roadways in shade. She slowed, watching for the turn to the house. She was about to make the turn when a red car approached from the right.

Red Mercedes, blonde driver with curly hair. It was Missy—no, Ramona Lukinger!

Ramona looked up and met Sam's eye. When she sped up, apparently trying to zip through the intersection, her Mercedes hit an icy place and began to swerve. Sam didn't give it a second thought—she steered her truck in Ramona's direction.

The vehicles hit with a crunch, Sam's front bumper pushing the Mercedes farther into its spin. With the momentum Ramona had given it, her car smacked the curb hard, jittered a few feet, and nailed a fire hydrant.

Ramona's eyes went wide, her mouth a big O, until she realized Sam had her phone up to her ear. Ramona tried her door handle, but the truck was solidly up against her door and it didn't open more than a couple of inches. Scrambling across the console in a very unladylike move, she tried the same thing with the passenger side door, only to discover it wouldn't open either. The fire hydrant had managed to be in the right place at the right time.

Sam gave the panicked woman an oh-too-bad kind of look at the same moment Beau picked up his phone.

"I've captured your suspect," she said. Adrenaline had completely erased her earlier slumpy mood.

Chapter 45

Beau couldn't help but chuckle as he assisted the squirming, handcuffed Ramona from the back seat of his cruiser and escorted her straight to the interrogation room. Sam had been so cute standing there beside her truck, hands on hips, giving Ramona the evil eye when he arrived. She'd wanted so badly to stay and help with the arrest and interrogation, but the plumbing truck arrived and she had no choice but to follow him. Luckily, damage to her truck was minimal, a dent below the right headlight was all.

He stashed Ramona in Interrogation Room 1, locking her in to stew while he spread the word to Rico and Travis. He asked Travis to call Helen Flagler, the elderly woman who'd been robbed by Ramona while Percy tried to talk religion. If Helen would come in, an ID by a victim would help to get her money back.

By the time he got back to her, fifteen minutes later, Ramona had quieted down. The blonde curls were looking a little frazzled. Apparently, one of her dark brown contact lenses had fallen out because she stared at him with the incongruous combination of one blue eye and one brown one.

"Mrs. Lukinger, we meet again," he said.

She turned her eyes away from him.

"We've received a number of complaints that seem to involve you and your husband. Couple of neighborhoods, in particular, where some older folks were scammed on home repairs and such."

"I know nothing about that. My husband's dead, for God's sake, and you people have hassled me beyond my limits. Poor Percy was so overwrought he couldn't sleep. How can you be so mean? Seriously, you'd better watch out—I'm about to file harassment charges against this department."

Beau ignored the short harangue.

"While we're organizing a lineup, I'd like to show you something else." He pulled out several photos, some of the still shots they'd been able to take from the casino video.

The first shot showed Percy and Ramona at adjacent slot machines, but the two were not looking at each other. At the upper right corner, a older man was entering the picture. Beau laid the print on the table, facing Ramona, and pushed it across to her.

"So?" she said.

"Who's the man walking toward you?"

"How should I know?"

"You honestly believe that's the only picture we have?"

He set out the next sequence. The white-haired man approaching Ramona, her head turned toward him.

Her face remained impassive as she looked at the pictures.

The next one showed the man standing very close to her. In the next, he had his arm around her shoulders.

"You don't seem offended," Beau said. "I mean, if you truly don't know this man."

She breathed very slowly, considering. "Oh, yeah. I remember that night. He was this nice old guy who bought me a drink."

"Somehow, this feels a little more familiar," Beau said. "Do all women let a guy touch them after they've delivered just one drink?"

She gave a get-real stare from beneath her lashes and didn't say anything. None of the other photos rattled her in the least. He gathered them up and wondered whether Helen Flagler had arrived to take a look at the lineup yet.

He left Ramona alone in the interrogation room again and walked to the observation room to see whether she let her guard down. If she breathed a sigh of relief or if her hands shook or if she paced, he never saw it. This was one chilly customer.

Wait until she got sent back to San Diego.

Chapter 46

Sam pulled into the driveway beside the plumber's truck. Next door, the blue minivan indicated another visit by Mr. Zuckerman's daughter. Both yards still had a fair amount of snow in front, the shady side. The plumber's arrival thirty minutes late had a good news/bad news element. She'd been able to detain Ramona long enough for Beau to arrive, but now she was in a time crunch to finish the chocolates before Bookman showed up.

She greeted the plumber, opened the front door, and showed him the place where she'd suspected the leak came from, under the kitchen sink.

"Well, you know water," he joked. "It'll run anywhere. You can't believe what I've seen since that big freeze. Pipes broken inside walls, water gushing down from the second floor to the first … huge messes. Some guy in a first-floor condo had water pouring out of his microwave from a broken pipe in the unit upstairs."

Thanks for the lesson on floods. "Look, I've got an urgent appointment, so I really can't stay. Just do your thing. Here's my number. When you're finished I'll come back by to pay you and lock up the house."

She pointed out the valve for the water main. "If you can't turn it back on, you'll need to call the water department."

"No problem. I can do it."

Outside, she heard voices from the house next door, an argument. Male voice adamant, repeating the word 'no' several times. Female voice raised in anger, although Sam couldn't make out the words. It sounded like another Zuckerman spat. She wondered if the wife was around. According to Mr. Zuckerman, he had all the care he needed right here at home. Maybe Dolores only pushed the issue when she got her father alone.

A glance at her dashboard clock brought her up short. Her two-hour window in which to work on the presentation boxes for Bookman had rapidly dwindled. Her tires lost traction for a moment as she gave the truck a little too much gas.

Okay, take it carefully, Sam.

She itched to stop by the station and see how it was going for Beau with his capture of Ramona Lukinger, but the presentation for Stan Bookman was becoming critical, and the delays had already cost precious time. She headed for the chocolate factory.

Benjie was working at one of the big tables, skillfully forming a tiny swirl atop each truffle on a tray filled with them. His assistants were tempering chocolate and mixing fillings. From the packing room, Sam heard giggles from Lisa and one of the other girls. Her display containers and the associated pieces sat where she had left them.

"What time does Mr. Bookman arrive?" Benjie asked, giving an appreciative perusal as Sam unveiled her work.

"Couple hours. I didn't finish as many pieces as I'd hoped to, but I think these will give the idea of what the product will be."

"You can always fill in with some of these truffles, and I just finished a tray of molded cappuccino squares decorated with coffee bean shavings."

"Ooh, those sound nice. He didn't say *every* piece in the box had to be unique to his tour." Sam pulled a few pieces from the tray Benjie indicated.

She started with the most out-of-the-ordinary parts of her presentation, the giant shell with the Great Barrier Reef pieces. Her idea of molded chocolate tinted blue for the ocean didn't seem as appealing today, so she started something new.

Stirring up a batch of hard candy, which would crystalize when it cooled, she set the gas burner and let the mixture cook on the stove while she created a liner of foiled paper which would protect the shell box as well as provide a reflective background for the translucent blue candy. This would be her ocean.

When the candy mixture reached the hard-crack stage of cooking, she tinted it aqua blue, and quickly drizzled it into the shell's liner. Immediately, it set. Tossing in a handful of ice cubes, she poured more candy. As the ice melted, the small voids left behind would give the illusion of waves and movement. While the blue candy set, she made sure each of the chocolate fishes was ready to be placed on its reef. It would come together with little effort now.

She moved on to the Aladdin's lamp, setting up her little scene of an Arabian feast, then to the treasure chest, which she filled to overflowing with an array of all types of molded and shaped chocolates, giving each a dusting of iridescent gold powder.

From the countertop beside the stove, her phone began to buzz. "Can someone check that for me?" she asked. "I've got gold dust all over my hands."

Benjie wiped his hands on a towel and walked over to take a look. "It's Mr. Bookman."

"Answer it, please. I'll be right there." She didn't take her eyes off the delicate tropical flowers she was piping on the lid of the treasure chest.

Benjie greeted the client and explained Sam's busyness. "Yes, sir. Hold on—she's right here."

His eyes were wide when he handed the phone over to Sam.

"Hey, Sam," Bookman said. "Just wanted to let you know we're on the way over to your place. We had great weather and our plane arrived a little ahead of schedule."

Sam sucked in her breath. *A little?* She'd hoped to have another hour or more.

"I'll be there in five or ten minutes." He hung up.

She stared with dismay at the state of her worktable. Pushing the unfinished items to one side, she placed Aladdin's lamp at the clear end of the table.

"I wish I could rub this thing right now and have a genie show up," she said.

Benjie carried his rack of truffles to her table. "Tell me what to do."

"See that Incan wood box? Fill in the areas I've missed—add truffles and those molded pieces you told me about. Same with the lamp ..." She raised the hinged lid on it. "Same with the basket made of grasses … Yes, that one over there."

The Hindu shrine and Taj Mahal would just have to be explained. She didn't even have the prototypes yet, but with the sketches the artists had provided, she could get the ideas across. The paperboard box with the watercolor of the Lost City of Petra on top was incomplete. It was probably best not to show it yet; in concept, it wasn't as impressive as it would be when finished.

Light glinted through the doorway, and Lisa called out from the packing room to say the customer had arrived. Frantically, Sam began placing the fish around the reef scene. What was missing? The stone box for Easter Island—argh!

In her chocolate-making frenzy, she'd come up with several irregularly egg-shaped chocolates. With their dusting of cocoa powder, they looked the way she would imagine eggs carved from stone and hollowed by wind and weather. Rather than the beauty of unsullied smoothness, they had a rugged feel and the flavors she'd created brought out the saltiness of the ocean surrounding the destination.

"Find that stone box," Sam told Benjie. "I'm not sure where I put it."

He cruised through the kitchen and found it under a tea towel near the sink. Sam had planned to set three of the dusty-cocoa eggs inside the rectangular box, but the first one she reached for slipped and crashed to the floor. No time for broom and dustpan—she kicked the shards under the table. Luckily, she had made spares. At the same moment the back door opened, she set the third egg in place and wiped a sprinkling of cocoa powder off the rim of the box.

Stan Bookman greeted Sam and the chocolatiers with

a smile, but his eyes immediately strayed to the end of the table with the goodies.

"Sam—these are magnificent!" His hand went automatically to the clamshell with the reef inside. "How did you ever think of this?"

Ask any artist how she thinks of her ideas and few can answer. Sam merely smiled and hoped she didn't have too much cocoa powder smeared across her face.

Chapter 47

He loved them!" Sam told Beau, the minute she stepped into his office.

He looked up, puzzled.

"Stan Bookman—he loved what we've done for his worldwide tour package. I kept apologizing because not everything was done, but he really was blown away by what we'd done so far. He'll be back through town in a few days, and I assured him I would have the rest of the samples done by then." She took a deep breath, her eyes sparkling.

Beau stood and walked around the desk to give her a hug. "That's great news, Sam. I'm happy for you."

"Sorry. I didn't actually come in here hoping for praise on chocolate, but the meeting was on my mind. I really stopped by on my way to the bakery to see how the interrogation is going with Miss—er, Ramona."

"No surprises. She won't admit a thing." He waved vaguely toward a scattering of photos on his desk. "She admits nothing about any of the scams she was involved in here, and doesn't even concede that she ever lived in San Diego. Detective Rodriguez gave me a list of questions to ask, and she just clams up. I'm about to start the paperwork to get her extradited back to California so she can become his problem."

Sam picked up the photos, which appeared to be still shots taken from the casino video they had watched the other day. Only this time there was someone else in the pictures, a white-haired man. She gave a closer look.

"Beau, I know this man."

"Really? You hadn't said anything—"

"This is a different part of the casino than what I saw before." She stared again, making certain. "The man with his arm around Ramona's shoulder—his name is Arnold Zuckerman. He lives next door to the caretaking job I took over from Sadie a couple weeks ago. In fact, I really need to get back there and pay the plumber as soon as he's finished fixing the broken pipes."

She pulled out her phone and looked over the list of calls, in case she'd missed him. Nothing yet.

"Come to the observation room a second," Beau said, taking the photos and pulling Sam's hand. "I'll ask her again, and I want you to tell me your impressions about her answers."

Sam hadn't told him that she'd handled the box again this morning after her big energy-lag, but he must have sensed it. She followed along and went into the room situated between the department's two interrogation rooms, where an observer could watch through one-way mirrors on the walls and recording equipment caught video and sound for the official record.

Beau signaled her to remain quiet while he walked into the room where Ramona Lukinger sat at the metal table, her cuffed wrists resting there, her nails tapping an impatient staccato on the surface of it. Her fur coat lay draped over the back of her chair.

Beau took the seat across from the suspect, his back to the mirror. "Just got off the phone with San Diego PD, and we'll have the paperwork ready pretty soon for your all-expense-paid trip to California."

"Ha-ha," Ramona said in a flat tone. "I told you, I know nothing about anything in California."

"Well, you can address that with them. You'll have lots of time to think during your ride in the bus with the bars on the windows. Meanwhile, another question about a local matter so I can wrap up a few loose ends."

Sam saw a wave of energy come off Ramona's body, although to outward appearances she remained calm.

"Arnold Zuckerman—you know the name?"

The energy wave turned brilliant red, although Ramona's face only registered a momentary flicker of recognition.

"I'm going to throw out a wild guess here," Beau said. "I'm thinking he may be the latest of your sweetheart con victims."

The red wave pulsed, then quieted as Ramona took slow breaths.

"Nothing to say?" Beau asked. "It doesn't really matter. I've already got a deputy headed to Mr. Zuckerman's home. It'll be interesting to see if your clothes are in the closets."

At the mention of the deputy, Ramona obviously realized the lawmen knew where she'd been living. Her aura became more jittery. Sam thought of the several times she had been to the house next door to Zuckerman's. She must have missed spotting Ramona by mere seconds. Since, as Missy, Ramona would realize that Sam could recognize her, she'd probably been the one peering out through the curtains, the one who quickly closed the garage door so Sam wouldn't spot the red Mercedes inside.

Sam thought of Beau's description of the sweetheart con—how a younger woman often targeted a wealthy elderly man, how the entire point of the relationship was to steal as much of his money as she could, as quickly as possible.

"Nothing to say about that?" Beau asked, pulling Sam's attention back to the interrogation.

"Doesn't mean anything," Ramona said with a sneer. "You gotta look toward his daughter—she's the real bitch here. Arnold is just a sweet old guy no one would ever want to hurt."

Sam thought of the loud argument she'd heard this morning. Arnold had hardly sounded like a docile puppy, and the fact his daughter hadn't been able to talk him into moving into a retirement home proved he wasn't exactly a pushover.

Beau stepped out of the interrogation room, and Sam met him in the hall.

"Well, her saying Arnold's name at least gives us reason to go talk to him. I guess I'd better actually get someone out there. Meanwhile, we'll stick Ramona in the holding cell until we get her extradition paperwork done. Rodriguez is ready to move with his case. Ours, if she's actually made off with any of Zuckerman's fortune, is just beginning."

Deputy Walters had come in the back door nearest the cell and Beau flagged his attention.

"Soon as you've got your jacket off, take the suspect from Interrogation 1 and put her in the cell."

Walters was rubbing his hands together against the cold and looked as if he'd rather have a cup of cocoa, but he agreed.

Sam walked with Beau back to his office. She was about to suggest they meet up for dinner somewhere—her treat—when her phone rang. Jake the plumber had finished his work.

"Gotta go pay this guy and finish with this house, but it shouldn't take long," she told Beau.

They agreed to touch base later about dinner, but she could see he'd already turned his attention to the computer screen where he would begin filling out forms. The squad room was quiet when she walked through, but before she reached the back door she heard a shout from the corridor behind her.

"Hey!" It was Walters' voice. "Hey—Sheriff!"

A door slammed hard, and Sam heard the pounding of feet. Beau ran out of his office, heading toward the sound. Sam turned and ran after him. Walters was hobbling on an obviously painful leg, facing the other end of the hall.

"What happened?" Beau sounded a little breathless.

"She rushed me when I opened the door. Kicked me in the shin hard enough to knock me down, ran for the back door."

A layer of cold air filled the hall, but there was no sign of Ramona.

"How'd she get the combination?" Beau demanded, running toward the back door. "Damn!"

It didn't take a rocket scientist to spot the problem. Apparently, a small stone had become lodged near the doorjamb when Walters came in only a few minutes earlier, and it had prevented the door from closing completely. The combination lock had never engaged.

Beau ran out the door, saying something about how she couldn't get far wearing handcuffs and no coat. But when Sam caught up with him halfway across the parking lot, they spotted the shiny handcuffs on the ground. No sign of Ramona.

Chapter 48

Sam remembered the phone call from the plumber. Much as she would have liked to be in on the excitement, she needed to take care of her own obligations. She got into her truck and headed toward Wicket Lane. Jake assured her he'd found every break and had turned the water back on and tested the system. Sure enough, she couldn't see any wet places. Big relief. As she watched his truck drive away, she wanted nothing more right now than to finish with this place.

No time like the present, she decided. She walked out to her truck to grab the broom she'd left out there and a trash bag to make one final round through the house. A new box of garbage bags sat on the floor in front of the passenger seat. When she reached for it she realized something was wrong. The carved box was no longer on the seat.

Her heart thumped double-time. When had she last seen it?

Her mind raced back through the last few hours. She'd definitely had the box last night as she prepared to work on the chocolates. But she hadn't left it at the Victorian—she had it this morning as she drove to town to meet the plumber. She began to frantically search the truck, but nothing else had been disturbed and there was no sign of the box. When could it have disappeared?

It had to have been recently, as she'd still felt the effects of it a short while ago, watching Ramona through the mirror in the interrogation room. But her truck had been parked most of the morning at the Victorian ... and she felt sure she'd locked the doors while she was at Beau's office. She tried to remember specifically hearing the double beep as doors unlocked—there had been such excitement, she couldn't recall.

Oh god, Sam, what have you done?

We think Fitch may be headed in your direction ... Isobel St. Clair's words of warning.

"No—it can't be that," Sam said to the empty truck.

What about at the sheriff's department? Could Ramona have spotted an opportunity when she escaped out the back door?—she'd certainly helped herself to sparkly objects in the gift shops.

"Why would she? She knows nothing about the box," Sam assured herself. Does she?

But the suspect had certainly done an unbelievably fast disappearing act. Could she have somehow had magical help?

Sam raised her head too fast and bumped it on the door frame.

"Ouch—dammit!" She gripped the hurt spot.

"Is anything wrong?" The female voice behind her startled Sam again. "Are you okay?"

She turned to see Dolores Zuckerman standing beside her minivan, the door open as if she was about to leave.

"Yeah, I'm just—" Sam rubbed the painful spot again and tried to put on a smile. "A little clumsy at the moment."

Dolores seemed preoccupied, staring up the street as if she was waiting for someone.

"Did your father go somewhere?" Sam asked.

"No, it's Missy. She said she'd be right back and I've been waiting around now for hours."

Missy. It took Sam a moment of headachy indecision before she made the Missy/Ramona connection once again. She pictured elderly Mr. Zuckerman.

Beau's right, she thought with a sinking feeling. Ramona was pulling another scam, and it was happening right here next door.

"Uh, maybe she's on her way back," Sam said, staring up the street and mentally scrambling to figure out what to say.

After her dash from the sheriff's office, Ramona could have set out on foot to come back here—the distance wasn't all that far—although it would be foolish of her to think she could continue to hide out at Zuckerman's house now that Beau knew of the connection.

Sam looked back at Dolores, wondering how much she should tell about the father's fake wife and his being the victim of the con artist. The other woman was staring intently. All around her, Sam perceived a dull orange haze.

"I'll be here a few more minutes," Sam said. "I could give her a message, if she comes."

Stupid suggestion, she realized, the moment the dull

orange aura flared to deep red. The woman was like a volcano, about to erupt with deadly fire. Her features had hardened, her eyes narrowed to slits, her mouth pinched in a straight line. Evil intention came off her in waves.

Ramona's words came back to Sam: *Look toward his daughter—she's the real bitch.*

Sam's eyes must have widened as the facts became clear. What she'd taken for a clash of personalities suddenly took on a whole new meaning when Dolores pulled a tire iron from the floor of her car.

This was no time to reason with the woman. The spark of insanity flared and she started across the driveway. Sam dodged to the other side of her pickup, but the woman was fast. She raced to the open front door of the break-in house, no more than three paces ahead of her pursuer.

A nano second over the threshold, Sam slammed the heavy front door, turned and bolted it just in time to hear the tire iron smack into the wood. It wouldn't take another thirty seconds for Dolores to figure out that windows broke more easily and she'd be in the empty house with Sam.

Running toward the back, Sam pulled her phone from her pocket. Beau had said he would be coming out to talk to Arnold Zuckerman, but with Ramona's escape and the excitement at the station, who knew when he might arrive? She paused to catch her breath and tapped his number. Outside, Dolores smacked the door with her weapon two more times. Then it went eerily silent.

Sam tiptoed through the kitchen and passed through the dining room. Drapes at some of the windows offered a little protection from the woman's view, but the living room—where Sam really needed to assess the situation—had a huge picture window fully exposing her to Dolores's evil glare. Sam tucked in close to the dining room wall, peering around a corner toward the front foyer, to see what was going on.

Beau's phone had rung five times with no answer. She should have dialed 911, she realized. Just as she was about to hang up and redial, his voice came on.

"Little busy here," he said. "Is everything okay?"

"No! Get to Zuckerman's house. His daughter is the killer. She's got me pinned inside the house next door."

"Does she have a gun?" His words came out in huffs as he ran. In the background, Sam could hear him giving orders for the dispatcher to get more deputies on the move.

"Haven't seen a gun, only a tire iron."

"Is she in the house with you?"

"At the front door. She's pounding hard enough to break through."

"Get yourself to a safe place—a hidden room, if there is one. Somewhere you can converse with her but she can't get to you. I'll have someone there within a couple minutes."

Chapter 49

Sam hung onto the words 'a couple minutes.' How on earth was she supposed to hide while conversing with Dolores? A quick peek toward the front window didn't reveal anything about her adversary's position. She crept back through the kitchen, and into the den. A glance out each window didn't show that Dolores had circled the house. From twenty feet away—the distance between the den fireplace to the front door—it appeared the door was still intact.

Dolores could have simply left, have gone back to her father's house or to her vehicle. No doubt, that was Beau's concern, the reason for his request for Sam to keep the woman talking.

A shadow moved behind one of the amber-colored sidelight windows.

"Dolores!" Sam called out. "Are you still out there?"

The shadow jerked, moved behind the solid door.

"Dolores! Just tell me what you want. I'm not a threat to you."

The woman's voice said something, but it was too muffled for Sam to make out the words. Sam glanced at the time on her phone. Had it been two minutes yet?

She approached the door, eyeing it for signs of weakness. It still appeared solid.

"Sorry, Dolores, I couldn't hear you. What did you say?"

"... Missy and her brother. Thieves! Swindlers!"

The first words hadn't come through, but Sam thought it sounded like 'I know they did it—'

"What did they do?" Sam asked.

Through the archway to the living room, light flashed off the wall. A car? A department cruiser, she prayed.

"Dolores? What did Missy and her brother do?"

"They were—" The sentence broke off and the tire iron clattered to the porch.

"You!" The venomous shout came to Sam, loud and clear.

From a distance, Sam heard Beau's voice, calm but deadly. "Move away from the door."

Although he probably meant the order for Dolores, Sam complied. If he had to take a shot at the suspect, she didn't want to be on the other side. She dashed to the living room window and watched the scene unfold as two more vehicles arrived.

Completely outnumbered, Dolores walked down the steps at Beau's command, her hands spread open at her sides. Beau kept her covered while Rico snapped cuffs on her wrists. Sam walked out to join them, noticing that the aura around Dolores had faded to a docile gray.

"Search her before you put her in the cruiser," Beau said to Rico. When Sam pointed out the blue minivan next door as the suspect's vehicle, he ordered Walters to search it as well.

When the deputy patted Dolores's coat pockets, he came out with a large, capped syringe of clear liquid.

"Well, well. What's this?" Beau mused.

Dolores sputtered something about her work.

"She told me she's an accountant in Santa Fe," Sam said. "What does an accountant do with some kind of drug?"

"Unless she has a bad habit," Rico said.

"We'll have it tested."

Walters walked over with a glass vial of liquid and handed it to the sheriff.

"Benzodiazepine," he read from the label. "Well, that's interesting." Beau looked at Dolores. "Looks like you've got way more there than it would take to relax you. We'd better talk about this at the station."

He gave a nod to Rico, who escorted Dolores to his cruiser and situated her in the back seat.

Movement to the south caught Sam's attention. Arnold Zuckerman, wearing a heavy sheepskin coat over his clothes, with bedroom slippers over his bare feet, came striding toward the gathering at the neighboring house.

"What's the meaning of this?" he demanded. "Where are you taking my daughter?"

Beau kept his tone respectful. "We've got some questions to ask her, sir."

Sam joined them. "Hello, Mr. Zuckerman. Dolores told me she was waiting for Missy to come home." She gave Beau a glance. "Has she come back, by any chance?"

"Not yet," Zuckerman said. "She had book club this afternoon and then I think she was going to get her hair done."

This wasn't the time to let him know who sweet little Missy really was, and that she'd been arrested today and had escaped.

"We've got some questions for her, too," Beau said. "Mind if one of my deputies waits here with you?"

Zuckerman shrugged, and Beau took Sam aside.

"You know as much as any of us about the con the Lukingers were probably running here. See if Mr. Zuckerman will admit whether money is missing from any of his accounts. I suspect Dolores was onto the con way earlier."

"I know they argued about his having control over his finances. Maybe she saw right through the Lukingers."

"See what you can learn. He won't want to believe his 'Missy' would harm him, so don't even try to convince him. Right now, we just need facts if we ever hope to press charges against her."

Sam watched Rico's cruiser drive away with Dolores in the back seat. A murder and a whole bunch of con games— the simple traffic accident had turned into a real quagmire. She made soothing sounds to Arnold and walked with him into his house, knowing she was in for a long afternoon.

Chapter 50

Darkness came early in January, and Sam finally left the Zuckerman house. Her afternoon with Arnold Zuckerman didn't net much information, and there had been no sign of his young wife. He'd produced a lovely wedding photograph of the two of them standing on the courthouse steps, but he seemed short on details about the marriage certificate or the judge's name.

As for his financial information, Zuckerman fidgeted a little but remained adamant that he alone controlled his money. He'd given Missy some nice gifts, he said, but he never had given his wife, his daughter, or anyone else control of his bank and investment accounts. Sam passed all this along to Beau when she stopped by the station and suggested they take a dinner break.

"Do you believe him?" Beau asked, as they shared a pizza at his desk.

"I think so. But he was uncomfortable talking about it. I have a feeling he was getting pressured from both sides—the wife who wanted to steal and the daughter who probably did have his best interests in mind. He may have been close to giving in. How about Dolores—is she talking much?"

"I confronted her about the drug in the syringe, trying to get a rise and see if she was planning to get Ramona alone somewhere and do the same thing to her as to Percy. She seemed shocked to learn that we had figured out the drug was the real cause of his death. She'd been convinced the traffic accident would be accepted at face value. Dolores, it seems, was suspicious of little Missy from the day her father met the younger woman. She'd begun driving up to Taos and following Missy around. Missy's prolonged absences from the Zuckerman home and the number of times she witnessed meetings with Percy, made her think Missy was cheating on Arnold. It only took one mention about having Missy take over some of the household banking duties and Dolores truly began to panic. She knew there was a scam going on."

"Murder seems like a pretty drastic solution," Sam said.

"Dolores had apparently contacted the police in Santa Fe and was told that until money had actually been stolen, there was nothing the law could do. So, that's when she started to pursue another angle. She was working to get her father declared incompetent, based on his falling for the illegal marriage and giving such lavish gifts to his bride."

"But the drug—was she lying about being an accountant?" Sam asked.

He pulled a string of melted cheese from the edge

of his pizza slice before he answered. "Oh, she's an accountant all right—we verified it. She works at a medical clinic where they perform day surgeries. They use Valium to calm patients before their procedures, so they keep a lot of it on hand. Supposedly, they have absolutely strict protocols in place for the handling and dispensing of it. Still, we know somehow Dolores got around that. She got enough to kill Percy, and what we found in her pocket was plenty to do away with Ramona."

Sam pushed her paper plate away. "Wow. Well, I understand her anger, but how did Dolores get close enough to Percy to inject him? And then how did he get so far south of town, driving in such a drugged state?"

"We have Rico and our lab tech to thank for putting a lot of it together," Beau said. "Rico went back to our original witness, Brian Reese, who saw the accident happen. Brian remembered seeing two vehicles pull onto the highway ahead of him that afternoon, coming from the overlook at the top of the hill. The first was a blue minivan, he remembered. The other was, of course, Percy Lukinger in the white Mitsubishi. Remember, Brian had told us he watched the Mitsubishi weave wildly and go off the road."

"Blue minivan—Dolores!" Sam said.

"We're fairly certain of it. The brilliant forensics work comes from Lisa and Rico. She gathered mud samples from the tire tread on Percy's car—an exact match for the dirt at the overlook—and she found a small bloodstain on the lid of the trunk. In the trunk was a flat tire, and the spare was on the right rear wheel. As near as we can figure it, Percy had a flat on the way to a meeting with Dolores. His head injury came while he was changing the tire. Once he reached the overlook, Dolores must have got into his car with him and injected the drug at some point when he turned his back on her."

"Does Dolores admit anything about this meeting?"

"Not yet. We still have to piece together how she managed to contact Percy and how she convinced him to meet her. But I'm confident we can find enough evidence to wrap it all up."

"So you've solved your murder case." Sam squeezed his hand. "That's great."

"I'd feel better about it if we'd kept Ramona Lukinger in custody. I won't rest easy until we know she's caught and returned to California. I don't have much hope Mr. Zuckerman will press any charges against her here in New Mexico."

Sam shook her head slowly. "I didn't get the feeling he would. He's going to be stunned to learn that his daughter is going away for murder. Unless he comes to believe that Ramona, um, Missy is the reason behind it, I doubt he'll fully acknowledge how badly the Lukingers messed up his family." She balled up her greasy paper napkin and tossed it into the empty pizza box. "Maybe the other victim, Hiram Efram, would be willing to talk to him, compare notes, get him to realize how tricky that pair was."

"Maybe." Beau sighed. "It's been a long day. I'm going to get Dolores settled for the night in the holding cell. Lots of paperwork."

Sam knew he was still thinking about the ongoing hunt for Ramona Lukinger, how easily she had gotten away, and the complete lack of clues to her whereabouts.

Chapter 51

Two days later, a phone call from Detective Jorge Rodriguez delivered interesting news—Ramona Lukinger had been picked up when she stepped off a Greyhound bus in Lubbock, Texas, and was now in custody in California. Beau put his phone on speaker so Sam could listen in.

"Okay, I have to ask," Beau said to Rodriguez, "how did Ramona get a ticket for the bus? She ran out of here with only the clothes on her back."

"She had a nice fur coat," Sam reminded.

"It *was* a nice coat," Beau said.

Rodriguez had the answer. "Apparently, from a group of ladies in some book club she belonged to. They said she popped in with a story of how her purse had been stolen and could anyone lend her some cash to pay the lock guy to let her into her car."

Beau and Sam exchanged a look—there really was a book club.

"The group took up a collection, and with the cash Ramona flagged down the eastbound bus."

"Well, I have to give her points for resourcefulness," Beau said, looking amazed.

"Yeah, me too. It's too bad she doesn't put the smarts to work for something good. She's no dummy," Rodriguez told them.

"I just can't figure out why she had to come here to Taos and run one more scam on Arnold Zuckerman. Hadn't she just ripped off millions from your Mr. Efram?"

"That's the part that's got her blazing mad. She followed Percy to New Mexico, furious with him for taking off with the Efram money, which she feels she legitimately earned. Once they were back together, though, I guess he managed to cool her down and they stayed with the Zuckerman con to add to the money pile. Arnold Zuckerman, having been in the jewelry business, was good for some fairly pricey gifts, too."

"I saw some of those," Sam said. "She definitely wore expensive jewelry. I don't know why I never clicked to the possibility that she was Mr. Zuckerman's young wife."

"No real reason to, unless you had seen them together."

"She seemed careful about that." Sam remembered the times when she was next door to their home and would spot movement of a curtain, quick closure of a door.

Beau spoke up. "Going on from here ... Even though it amounts to a lot of money, Arnold Zuckerman admits that everything she took from him were given as gifts—the car, clothes, furs, jewelry. The only thing I can really issue a warrant for in New Mexico would be bigamy. She did legally marry Arnold Zuckerman while married to Percy Lukinger. However, there's not likely to be much penalty for it since the second marriage was such a short one and she didn't actually get away with any money other than what he willingly gave her."

"Better news here," Rodriguez said. "We've got grand larceny for the money she took from Efram. No question about that. We've been able to put FBI forensic accountants on the case, and they've tracked movement of it. Originally, the Lukingers transferred money bank-to-bank, then they began drawing out large amounts of cash. There have to be safe deposit boxes or a trusted safe-house or something like that where it's stashed. I got a call late last night, and the special agent in charge is telling me they'd already located some of the cash."

"Good news for the victim," Beau said, "but recovery of the money might make the case sort of squirrely. A jury could look at the outcome and decide the rich guy wasn't really out anything, while the poor woman on the witness stand gets a bunch of sympathy, especially when she breaks down and cries."

"He's right," Sam said. "Don't put anything past Ramona when it comes to theatrics."

"No kidding. She's already tried flirting with our officers, from the moment she got off the plane yesterday. She's a pro when it comes to working the crowd. Our focus will be on building a case to demonstrate her history of con games, making the point to the jury that if she gets away she'll be doing the same thing again, and this time it might be their father or brother she swindles."

Sam felt better when the call ended, but didn't let herself fully believe Ramona would bear the full punishment for her crimes. She remembered how charming the con woman was, with men and women alike.

"So," said Beau. "I've got to attend Dolores Zuckerman's arraignment this morning. That story's turning into a real tragedy. She had first planned to kill Missy, but rage overtook her and she decided to go for them both. Killing a man, planning to kill again, all to save her father from a bad judgment call."

"I saw Arnold Zuckerman when I went by to finish up at the caretaking property. He's pretty broken up. He can't believe his daughter would do such a thing—that's mainly what has him upset—but he's also mortified that dear little 'Missy' pulled one over on him. He's got a point. He was a successful businessman for many years, very sharp, on top of things. It's been a hard pill to swallow, for him to admit he's not making the best decisions any more."

Beau was quiet, remembering how he'd taken his mother into his own home as she got older. Iris had been sweet and willing to let her son care for her. Too bad it hadn't worked out a bit easier between Dolores and her father.

"It's sad," Sam told him. "Just as Arnold is about ready to lean on his daughter for help, she'll be in prison."

Chapter 52

Sam drove to the chocolate factory, the conversation with Detective Rodriguez fresh in her mind. The whole situation was sad, but her part was done and she had other priorities this morning. Stan Bookman was due in town to review, taste, and approve the gift packages for his Travel the World travel package.

Already, Sam had seen the ad campaign on his website and it looked like an amazing adventure. The inaugural trip was sold out (mainly to celebrities and tycoons, Stan had confided to her); second and third itineraries were scheduled and filling fast. It meant a lot of business for her. And, along with Kelly's wedding to Scott, she faced an extremely busy summer. The whereabouts of the carved box, which had helped her through so many seasons when the work became chaotic, still worried her. She'd not had time for a complete rip-apart search of her various premises—a dozen other things had taken priority the past two days.

She pulled onto Tyler Road and drove toward her factory, where a rental car sat in front of the Victorian. *One thing at a time, Sam. Meet with Bookman now, get frantic over the box later.*

Stan Bookman got out of the car when he saw Sam's truck pull into the driveway. He circled and opened the passenger door; he'd told Sam he would bring his wife this time.

Where Stan was a man of enthusiasm and plans, Margie seemed quiet and thoughtful. She shook hands with Sam and said she felt honored to visit the chocolatier who had created the luscious treats for their flights. She patted her stomach when she admitted she'd eaten her fair share of them, many times. Sam liked her at once.

Inside, Benjie and the other chocolatiers had donned clean white chef jackets; the packers and shippers, prompted by Ronnie, had worn white shirts, purple scarves, and black slacks. They stood in the front hall of the old house-turned-business, lined up formally, as one would imagine the staff in a nineteenth-century mansion when the master returned home.

Packing boxes had been moved out of sight and a round table, with a white cloth draped to the floor, occupied center stage under the hall's crystal chandelier. A purple cloth was draped over the irregular shapes of the surprise beneath.

Sam introduced the Bookmans to the employees, giving due credit to all for their hard work on both current and past projects for the travel company.

"Benjie, Lisa? Will you do the honors of the unveiling?" Sam asked.

Dottie had pulled out her camera phone and Sam smiled. Thank goodness someone had thought to capture the moment before the chocolates were history. Dottie snapped a dozen or more pictures as the purple cloth came away and the gift boxes were revealed. Margie Bookman actually gasped.

"Oh, Sam, these are exquisite," Stan said, his voice hushed.

One by one, Sam approached each piece and raised the lid on the container to reveal the works of art inside.

"Every bit of the contents is edible," she told them. "Please—sample."

For a full minute, no one moved. Sam finally reached into the Taj Mahal and pulled out two pieces of chocolate flavored with saffron and turmeric. She handed one to each of the guests. Stan popped his into his mouth and bit down, moaning in pleasure at the blend of flavors. His wife took a bite from one corner, closed her eyes, and let the chocolate melt on her tongue. When she opened her eyes again, there were tears.

"It's … it's … indescribable. So amazingly delicate, yet … I can't think what to say." She turned to her husband. "I don't think I can write an ad that will let our passengers know what to expect. We'll simply have to tell them to expect heaven. Pure heaven."

Her expression conveyed her sincerity. She was genuinely in love with the chocolate. Sam felt her own emotions rise as she watched her clients enjoy another piece, this time a tiny Incan statue from the Machu Picchu box.

"I don't know how you do it, Sam." Bookman turned

to the rest of the crew. "All of you—really, kudos to everyone."

Smiles all around, although the employees would keep their high-fives for later.

"Here—everyone should have some," Bookman offered.

"No, these are for you," Sam told him.

She didn't admit that there had been enough boo-boos along the way for the staff to have already tasted all they wanted. For his money, Stan Bookman would get only the best of the best, the absolutely perfect pieces. She had already decided that the less-than-perfect ones would be donated to local women's and children's shelters where those poor, abused souls would never otherwise have access to such fine chocolate or the magical, positive, mood-altering effects of these particular ones.

The thought reminded her of the special powders she would now need in greater quantity. And the box. A quiver of worry went through her, but she tamped it down. This was not the time.

* * *

Sam raised her head from her desk, looked around and saw the sun was low in the sky already. Once she'd seen to the packing of the gift boxes and sent the Bookmans on their way, she and the crew had pitched in to give the kitchen a thorough cleanup, followed by the rare treat of lunch catered by Orlando's Kitchen. She'd let them all go home early before she walked through her place, admiring the work they'd done, looking forward to the challenges as they all continued to stretch their muscles for inventiveness and creativity.

When weariness overtook her, she settled into her chair and decided to rest her head on the desk for a minute. Obviously, that minute had turned into more than an hour and she woke with a catch in her lower back. She stood slowly and stretched out the kinked muscles. It was time to head home.

She moved through the Victorian building, turning off lights, pulling curtains, leaving only the nighttime lighting on. The quiet old house comforted her, reminded her of when she'd found this place and the work she had put into cleaning and making it ready as a business location. Some months remained on the lease, and now that Bookman's business seemed assured to grow, she would most certainly renew it. Or consider purchasing the old house. She admired its classic lines, the original woodwork on the banisters and stairs. It would be a good purchase.

The appliances gleamed in the kitchen; it had been worth devoting the time today to cleaning and making sure everything was in shape for the work to come. As she reached for the light switch, something caught her eye. On the countertop, in a far corner near the storeroom, stood three cloth sacks, about twelve inches tall, which had not been there earlier.

Sam walked toward them, reaching out. The material was rough, almost like homespun fabric from an earlier time or place. Each sack appeared full of something, with the top gathered and tied with a strip of the same fabric. She lifted one and found it lightweight for its size. Her heart began to race and she tugged at the tie on one bag.

Inside, the rough bag was lined with a fine material. She knew this cloth—it was the same as that which held the magical powders she had so recently wished for. She dipped her fingers and they came out coated with flakes of iridescent blue. Her wish had come true.

Bobul!

She would need to store the powders where she alone controlled their use. Too much in a recipe or spilling a bag would spell catastrophe. She knew what to do.

She thought of the safe upstairs in her office, but a little inner voice said it would be prudent not to put all the valuable powders in one place. She gathered the bags in her arms and headed toward the basement, where a small cupboard near the bottom of the steps could be locked to safeguard these precious ingredients. She unlocked the basement door, descended the stairs. Below the cupboard, a narrow shelf held the bags while Sam retrieved the key from its hidden spot across the room. She unlocked the cupboard and began to place the bags, but one of them hit another object. When she reached inside to move it, her fingers encountered a familiar shape.

The carved box.

She felt her head swim. No way. She knew for a certainty she had not locked it away in this place.

Isobel St. Clair had warned of danger—perhaps Bobul was now looking out for the box, and for Sam.

As in the past, her mentor had somehow known, somehow sensed her needs. She climbed the steps and looked around the kitchen, into the storeroom, but there was no sign of him. She searched the backdoor entry, the portico, the parking area where her truck sat—no evidence of the quirky Romanian there either.

He had come—and gone—while she napped, and she felt a profound sadness that she'd not even had the chance to see him briefly, to thank him for being her benefactor.

She stood beside her truck clutching the box, stared into the deepening dusk, and raised her voice.

"Thank you—thank you for this!"

No sound came back and she knew he was gone.

The frosty air began to chill her. She gathered her coat, locked the door, and got into her truck. It was time to go home.

Thank you for taking the time to read *Sticky Sweet*. If you enjoyed it, please consider telling your friends or posting a short review. Word of mouth is an author's best friend and is much appreciated.

Thank you,
Connie Shelton

* * *

Visit my Pinterest board called Chocolate Heaven to see photos of the elegant chocolates that inspired me for Sam's creations in this story.

* * *

**Sign up for Connie Shelton's free mystery newsletter at www.connieshelton.com
and receive advance information about new books, along with a chance at prizes, discounts and other mystery news!**

**Contact by email: connie@connieshelton.com
Follow Connie Shelton on Twitter, Pinterest and Facebook**

Connie Shelton is the author of the *USA Today* bestselling Charlie Parker and Samantha Sweet mysteries and her newest—The Heist Ladies. She's known for a light touch when it comes to sex and violence in her stories, but is much more lavish with food and chocolate. She and her husband and two dogs live in northern New Mexico.

Made in the USA
Middletown, DE
15 March 2023

26779739R00203